THE COLLECTOR'S DREAM

THE
COLLECTOR'S
DREAM
PIERRE FURLAN

TRANSLATED BY JEAN ANDERSON

VICTORIA UNIVERSITY PRESS

VICTORIA UNIVERSITY PRESS
Victoria University of Wellington
PO Box 600 Wellington
victoria.ac.nz/vup

Originally published in French by Éditions Au vent des îles as
Le Rêve du collectionneur
Copyright © Pierre Furlan 2009

English translation copyright © Jean Anderson 2010
First published 2010

National Library of New Zealand Cataloguing-in-Publication Data

Furlan, Pierre.
Le rêve du collectionneur. English
The collector's dream / Pierre Furlan ; translated by Jean Anderson.
ISBN 978-0-86473-630-7
I. Title.
843.914—dc 22

Published with the assistance of grants from
the New Zealand–France Friendship Fund

Printed by Asta Print, Wellington

My dear brother, when shall we build
a raft and float down from the sky?

INGEBORG BACHMANN

SAILS

This is a story about heroes. A story about sails on the Pacific, sails that swelled like Will Bodmin's heart, when the restless, endless sea called him towards another world. He could sense the immensity of the ocean when he left New Zealand for Europe in 1949. Standing on deck at night, he saw it reflected in the southern skies as he stared up at them, trying to make out the constellation the Greeks called the Argo, that other ship dismantled two centuries earlier by dull-spirited astronomers who broke it down into mere parts: Keel, Sails, Stern. He could see it, he was sure.

Forty years later, on his way back, he flew over that same sea. There were no more great liners linking the South Pacific to Europe. The oceans, now crisscrossed in all directions, sliced through by the steel hulls of enormous oil tankers and other cargo ships, were just dirty puddles struggling to survive. The great adventures of the tall ships were hidden away in books, in his own books especially, in the collection he had built up over many years – the best, the most original collection since the one Rex de C. Nan Kivell had donated to Australia.

This is a story about heroes who are sometimes ridiculous. A father and his son. The encyclopedias tell us the father was a great inventor: in 1900 he designed and patented the crinkled hairpin. Previously these pins were straight and fell out of women's chignons and hats. While this invention didn't have quite the same impact as sliced bread, it was still an ingenious arrangement, nearly as simple as $E=mc^2$, and it earned Franklin Bodmin a fortune. He founded a company in New York, with the writer Mark Twain as deputy director, to market his hairpin world-wide; he would go on to create a great many other devices, including a prototype carburettor fitted to American army trucks in the 1920s. And as for his son, a bookseller who knew him well in England states that Will was a gentle and eccentric man with a prodigious memory who would arrive every year at the Antiquarian Book Fair in York and plant himself in front of the great neo-classical Assembly Rooms, waiting for the doors to open so he could be one of the first inside. He would then work his way round the stalls with the most extraordinary determination and concentration, and might be found kneeling beneath a table or between two piles of books, a torch in his hand to shine on the most out-of-reach volumes, shoulders hunched forward, collar turned up, and wearing workman's earmuffs to block out the background noise, the whole chattering, deluded world that, in Will Bodmin's opinion, was like some nasty soup where only the scum floats to the top. He would peer and poke; he had developed a sixth sense that led him to some astonishing discoveries. But throughout the second half of his life he was obsessed by a pamphlet that had once slipped through his fingers in England: a little tract printed in 1831, denouncing the violent acts of Governor Ralph Darling in Australia.

The pamphlet told the story of two soldiers, Joseph Sudds and Patrick Thompson, who tired of keeping an eye on the convicts in the colony of New South Wales and committed a few minor misdeeds, for which they were to be transported to Tasmania. But Governor Darling, convinced the two of them had deliberately broken the law in order to get out of the army, decided they were getting off far too lightly. So he organised a parade at which the two accused, shackles on their ankles and steel-spiked collars tight around their necks, were drummed out of their regiment and condemned to wear these irons while they worked on the roads. As a result of this treatment Sudds died after just five days, and Thompson went mad. Later, cleared by the Crown of this and several other atrocities, Darling would go on to become Knight Grand Cross of Hanover.

Will Bodmin, the bookseller explained, had taken a strong, almost personal dislike to this relatively unknown governor. He felt the tract was a unique moment in the history of human rights: a step towards ending the slavery that still binds humanity – all the more so, paradoxically, since we claim to be free. And there was another reason for Bodmin's quest: the pamphlet was one of the rarest items relating to the history of colonisation in the South Pacific. If he could have got his hands on it, he might have considered himself the greatest collector in the field. And then he would have been able to speak out, to say what was on his mind without needing to write vengeful letters to the people who ruled the planet, in particular New Zealand. They would have listened to him, he believed. The indictment of Darling would have opened Will's heart and loosened his tongue: it would have set him free.

The last known specimen had disappeared from the Australian National Library in 1972, possibly stolen, but there were thought to be one or two others in circulation, and Will believed one of these was destined to be his, that he would track one down. 'A quest,' according to the bookseller in York, 'that was a bit ridiculous, actually, when you realise the Darling contains nothing new and is of no value except to a collector. Just an empty shell, really.' But one that glittered. The bookseller shrugged.

As far as my own involvement goes, I set out on the track of Will Bodmin, but as I found out more about him, he seemed both closer and more distant, always slipping away just as I thought I had him pinned down. I saw him as a superstitious man, fascinated by ghosts and the supernatural. He believed in the most outrageous things, simply because they were trumpeted in the English tabloids. He sent his mother newspaper clippings about an American who, in 1960, had supposedly perfected a camera that could photograph the human soul. 'Priests will find their task much easier now,' he wrote, 'because they'll be able to see how corrupt or pure our souls are.' That same year, in Switzerland, he fell into ecstasies over an ancient invention on show at an exhibition in Valais. As early as 1788 a Swiss had apparently built a motorised vehicle and driven it through the city of Sion, patenting the main components in 1807. 'But nobody,' Will despaired, 'was the least bit interested.' On the 29th of May 1960, he sent his mother an article from the *Guardian* about someone finding the Abominable Snowman's jawbone. The following month, he complained that a motorboat had inadvertently cut off one of the feet of the 'poor' Loch Ness monster. He also struck up a correspondence with one Mr O'Connell, frequently mentioned in the papers as having managed to photograph said monster.

Maybe it's not so surprising that he believed in the weirdest discoveries, given that he was the son of a pretty strange inventor. Or that he deliberately looked for inventions that would be bold enough to outshine those of his father – a man he admits he didn't love, but who controlled his entire existence.

This is a story about heroes, because once we have listed every quality in them that is exactly like our own qualities, there is still some other element left over, something grandiose, like gigantic dark shadows dancing on a white curtain, making improbable gestures as they try to save themselves, and perhaps to save us too.

Christmas wasn't far off, and here it was nature's job to decorate the trees. I walked along footpaths covered in thousands of fallen pohutukawa flowers, feeling as though this new world was finally opening up to me, and I wrote in my notebook: summer has arrived, all our sins are forgiven. This was in Wellington, in December 2004, and I was planning a weekend away on Waiheke Island, just off the coast of Auckland. On the postcards I'd been sent, the island looked like a paradise of blue sea and beaches fringed by bright-flowered bushes.

At one point just before I left Wellington, I wondered about stopping in Auckland to see some Maori friends I had met in Greece several years previously. Then I changed my mind, decided to put it off until later – the island and its beaches first. But that Saturday, when I arrived by plane and then ferry to Waiheke, it was raining so hard you couldn't see more than fifty metres in front of you and the landscape, behind a curtain of slanting lines, looked like a black and white engraving. After running just the dozen or so metres from the car to the hostel – a backpackers where you had to leave your muddy shoes at the door – I was drenched to the skin. The gutters were overflowing, cars were stranded in enormous pools of water, and the warm mist rising here and there from the ground was the only thing challenging the incredible downpour.

Water, water, and more water: that night I slept fitfully, soothed to begin with by the endless conversations and laughter of the young tourists, then as soon as I started to nod off, jerked awake by huge splashing noises followed by loud cheers. What could be more entertaining, really, than diving into a swimming pool in the middle of the night, in torrential rain?

By Sunday the downpour had eased, but going for a walk or to the beach was still out of the question, and the sun didn't come out again until late afternoon, at pretty much the exact moment when I stepped onto the ferry that was to take me back to Auckland.

A weekend to forget, and suddenly I was impatient to get home to Wellington and carry on with the research that had brought me to this country, to get back to my notes and my books, my computer screen and the botanical gardens I liked so much. The plane took off into a clear sky. An hour later it was circling over Wellington, waiting for permission to land. Coming in to the airport, I usually loved to look out the window and see the runway lined up between two ochre hills and two arms of blue sea – my heart would contract exactly the same way the landscape did, suddenly reduced to a clear-cut, brightly coloured image, almost like a child's drawing in its dazzling simplicity – but this time I couldn't see a thing. We must have caught up with the storm, because the plane was being tossed about and the clouds were thick around us. Quite some time later the pilot announced he was still waiting for landing authorisation and would give us an update as soon as he had any information. The passengers clearly sensed his unease because after he stopped speaking there was a strained silence. Some of them kept trying to read their magazines, others closed their eyes, but the stress was more and more palpable as the plane vibrated, struggling

14

against the raging wind, and rain-gorged clouds threw themselves against the windows in long wet ribbons. Five minutes later the plane started climbing again and the pilot told us in a lighter tone of voice that the wind had made it impossible to land and we were heading back to our point of departure, Auckland.

As soon as the plane touched down, he cheerily wished us a pleasant evening at home. Easy for him to say. Would this weekend never end? It was like a sentence crossed out over and over again, endlessly rewritten. And when I finally made it through the crowded airport to the Air New Zealand counter, I discovered the next day's flights to Wellington were already full until mid-afternoon. While I was waiting in line, more clued-up travellers had used their mobile phones to book their seats.

I wandered around for a while, then remembered Ron and Sara, the couple I had decided not to contact before I left. Maybe they would be at home.

Half an hour later, Sara Tinkerbell met me in the terminal and walked me to the car where her husband was waiting for us. And only then, on Sunday evening, did my weekend begin, as if everything that had gone before was just an illusion, some kind of tribute you had to pay to a carnival world before you could reach the real one. As we drove through a field of light – because the sky was clear now, sprinkled with stars, and the ground was twinkling like a second sky – we talked and laughed about the sheer determination of the elements that had brought us together. Now everything was clearer, everything was making sense again, and our mingled voices wove into a comforting pattern, as familiar and reassuring to me as the even rumble of the motor.

I had met Sara and Ron in Crete several years earlier. We were tourists; we hired motorbikes and rode round the island. Since then we had exchanged occasional messages that didn't actually say a lot about what we were up to. Now on seeing

15

them again I remembered our high-spirited Greek holiday. I hadn't forgotten they were Maori, and that the name of Ron's family was to be found at the bottom of a number of important treaties between Maori and the British. He was a blue-eyed Maori – his mother was Scottish – and Sara Tinkerbell had an English mother. And that was pretty much all I knew about them, other than the fact that Ron had of course played rugby – but the reason he was driving quite fast this evening was that he was in a hurry to watch the rest of the cricket match between New Zealand and Australia. New Zealand was winning, for once, and he didn't want to miss that.

When we arrived, since I didn't know much about cricket, I started talking to Sara. I asked her where her second name came from, Tinkerbell. She said yes, it did come from Peter Pan. Her mother was besotted with the fantasy, and had always dreamed of living in the imaginary country where children never grew up. And because she could never hope to go there, she gave all her children the names of characters from Barrie's novel, such as Wendy or Tinkerbell. Sara smiled as she told me this, but I sensed there was something she didn't like about it. She admitted she had no great admiration for the 'self-centred' Peter Pan, or for the author either.

Once launched on her family history, she went on to mention one of her uncles, Will Bodmin, a collector of artefacts relating to the South Pacific. When he died he left a house full of rare books, paintings, old navigational charts, documents and other objects including over a thousand prints, some of them dating from the expeditions of the first navigators to come to New Zealand, along with an authenticated copy of the Treaty of Utrecht, various manuscripts by adventurers and explorers, and a few curiosities, such as an account in Portuguese of the death of Captain Cook as told by James Cleveley, ship's carpenter and eyewitness to the murder. The monetary value of the collection hadn't been established yet, but it was considerable.

Her uncle was an eccentric who had lived for a long time in England, where she visited him on several occasions, but also an altruistic and intelligent man she had very much admired. And who, at his death, had put her in a rather difficult situation. He had left her his amazing collection, but only on the condition that she write his biography and publish it as a book of at least three hundred pages and including a certain number of illustrations which he had specified in advance. Sara's first impulse had been to refuse: writing her uncle's life story really didn't interest her, and the collection would be better off in a public institution than at her home. At this point her mother had stepped in; since she was a published author, a poet to be exact, she offered to write it with her – they would share the profits. Other family members couldn't understand at all, and thought it was a shame that she should be even thinking of giving up such a valuable inheritance. Didn't she love her uncle? Wasn't money important to her? They pointed out that the biography was practically written already, because there were family sources and a huge amount of correspondence. Will Bodmin wrote regularly to his mother and sisters; he also kept a diary and wrote six illustrated volumes about his travels in Europe and the rest of the world. The whole thing could be polished off in six months, her mother insisted. Only Ron, Sara's husband, and her children had left it entirely up to her, and she was very grateful to them. Sara Tinkerbell hadn't yet formally declined. She had even tried to make a start on the job, but with very little progress, and as the five-year time limit set by her uncle came closer she was feeling more and more anxious about it. It would have been difficult enough to refuse, but failing without refusing was a lot worse. She had one year left.

Sara then took me into the room she had set aside for the whole business. There were cartons full of her uncle's letters, sorted according to year, stacked on shelves. Books and files were lying open on a desk alongside piles of handwritten papers. On the walls were pinned photographs and newspaper clippings, a map of New Holland and some old prints of Maori as seen by the first Europeans. A scale model of the nineteenth-century three-master, the *Red Jacket*, glowed red and white near the window. And the grey eye of the computer screen, half covered in Post-it notes, put the finishing touch to the overall messiness of the place – which was more a look of everything all crammed in together, as though Sara had given up trying to sort what had accumulated in the office, finding it more and more oppressive.

I wasn't much help really. I went on just like the others about how easy it would be to put together a biography by a kind of cut-and-paste method. People write bestsellers that way in a couple of weeks, I told her. But she shook her head, no, the problem was that she wanted to respect her uncle's personality. I don't want to write just anything, she protested. What sort of image of him should she create? She wouldn't be able to do it unless she knew why he had wanted a biography, when his collection spoke on his behalf, and much better, too, than any book could; and why he had chosen her in particular.

And besides, if she let the time just tick by and the collection went to a public library, Will Bodmin would become in his own way a benefactor of the country he had left so young and under such trying circumstances. As a conscientious objector during the Second World War he had been harshly treated, which led to his emigrating; he had retraced the route his father travelled when he left London for New Zealand in 1886. Maybe, Sara suggested, he wanted to cancel out his father's journey, or even his own birth ... You find some strange things when you study someone's life, and sometimes unpleasant things, she said, quite heatedly. Will Bodmin didn't come back to New Zealand until he retired. And yet his whole life long he loved and defended his country: he recreated it in his own way through his collection, becoming just as much an inventor of the country as he was its son. Maybe it would be better for his memory, Sara continued, if I didn't inherit the collection, because I would probably sell it off piece by piece, and it would end up scattered far and wide. All I would have left of it would be money, and my uncle would be reduced to mere coins.

Sometimes she thought the exact opposite. Her uncle had used the idea of profit as bait to draw her into the scheme: he was more concerned about his biography and his image than the future of his collection.

She had thrown herself into her work. Pushing aside her initial hesitation, she studied all of the deceased's correspondence, the various diaries he had written, and even his attempt at an autobiography. She also went through Will's notes on his experiences as a psychotherapist. In addition to being a collector, he had worked for many years in English hospitals as a Jungian art therapist.

But the more I read, she said, the harder it is to classify him, so now he seems much more complex than when he was alive, and it feels like a bit of a wild goose chase. Sometimes I think he was crazy, but sometimes I understand how necessary his craziness was.

At that point, to give me an idea of his work, she dug around in a pile of papers on the desk and pulled out an article clipped from the *Yorkshire Evening Press* and dated the 14th of February 1956, describing a major exhibition at the York city library organised by Mr William Bodmin in honour of the explorer James Cook.

The paper had yellowed, but in the grainy photograph you could still make out a slender man with a pencil moustache and a lively and pleasant expression, holding out his right arm to show off a strange-looking bracelet dangling from his wrist.

'That bracelet,' said Sara, 'was the collar worn by Captain Cook's goat.'

The collar was the key item in the exhibition. It was supposed to be proof of a detail known only to admirers of the captain: James Cook had been practically in love with a goat he dragged around the world with him, one that didn't end up on his plate. He took her back to England and, through a parliamentary vote, no less, secured a generous pension for the four-legged lady that had provided milk for the officers of the *Endeavour*. A pension such as would have been the envy of a large percentage of the population of England at the time. Cook also bought her a collar, a pretty strip of leather on which none other than the great Samuel Johnson wrote a few words in Latin.

But although the pension gave the goat the right to live out her days in the hospital where a patch of garden was already set aside for her, she passed away peacefully on the 28th of April 1772, at the home of the master who couldn't bring himself to send her away.

The story of Captain Cook's goat, said Sara Tinkerbell, is probably one of the rare romances my uncle imagined. He devoted the exhibition to this animal, and a large number of letters as well. He keeps mentioning the goat's 'faithfulness', as if it had a say in its fate! It's as ridiculous as it is touching. And here, in the photo, he's wearing the collar round his wrist as if he were binding himself to the goat as well. What am I supposed to do with this episode from his life? Turn it into something flamboyant?

Analysing everything all the time, she had ground to a halt, and the project was turning into an unachievable obsession . . .

We went back downstairs. Ron was still watching his endless cricket match, but he was losing interest. The score had changed, Australia was going to win. Ron shrugged his shoulders cynically and entertained himself for a few minutes by telling me the story of Uncle Will's homecoming after forty years' exile in England.

'We went to meet him at the airport,' Ron explained. 'He came in from Los Angeles, nothing but skin and bone, his eyes glittering, and that sharp-boned face of his making him look like a vulture. He'd travelled across the US by Greyhound bus with just the one piece of luggage, a backpack that weighed a ton but contained only a toilet bag and some old books he'd bought in Boston, Denver and San Francisco where, to hear Will tell it, the booksellers had no idea of the true value of what he bought. He'd spent his entire budget this way, and even dipped into his hotel and meals allowance. Hence the Greyhound buses, and a few nights spent on benches in bus stations. In the end he'd even thrown away his clothes because they were taking up too much space, and turned his shirt inside out so he had a clean-looking collar when he arrived in Auckland.'

I hadn't made up my mind yet whether to work with Sara Tinkerbell, but when I went into the bedroom that was to be mine for the night I was holding a bundle of Will Bodmin's letters. The room was quiet and spacious, with prints on the walls of inviting foreign scenes. To start with, a copy of a fresco from Heraklion, where we had met, then a view of Zurich in 1845. There was also an old colour print of the little island of New Amsterdam, which I assumed must be from Will's collection.

Lying on the bed, I turned on the bedside lamp and stared suspiciously at the pile of letters beside me. My weekend was rescued, to my great relief. But what was I getting myself into now?

The first aerogrammes I unfolded were from the 1960s – Will Bodmin must have been around forty at the time – and were addressed to his mother. I picked one at random, and smiled on reading that a ghost had been photographed in the York library. Will hadn't enclosed the photo.

I picked through the typed letters, which were easier to skim through, and saw that the first one was addressed to him, not written by him. It was much more recent, dated the 23rd of May 1990, and was written by a minister in New Zealand's Labour government.

Dear Will Bodmin,

Thank you for your letter of 2 May 1990 regarding female circumcision.

I agree that female circumcision is a harmful practice that has highly undesirable consequences. Thank you for bringing the topic to my attention. The Advisory Committee on Women's Health has also raised the topic with me and is considering what action is appropriate.

Yours sincerely,
Helen Clark, Minister of Health

The minister had added a handwritten note:

Thanks also for your words of encouragement on tobacco.

The next letter was from Will. He had written to a member of the Opposition in his capacity as an experienced psychotherapist.

R. W. Bodmin, DFA, psychotherapist
3 Stewart Terrace
Invercargill, NZ

13 May 1990

Mr R. J. Gerard
Shadow Minister of Broadcasting
Wellington

Dear Sir,

You will probably know that banks who hire new staff have them undergo a series of psychological tests to make sure they do not appoint confidence men, unscrupulous crooks or psychopaths to positions of trust.

For some years I have been concerned about the way TVNZ likes to show the slaughter of animals at times when they know very well that young children (too young to really know the difference between humans and animals) will be watching.

And then on 9th May they showed how to make hallucinogenic drugs from cheaply-bought ingredients cooked up in a billy over a fire! As though we don't have a big enough drug problem in New Zealand already. I have also seen programmes shown in which drug-runners are portrayed as heroes and even martyrs for liberty, and on July 22nd they even showed how common household products could be mixed to make bombs, as though we are looking forward to the day when terrorists will rule this country.

At this point I wrote to our present minister of Broadcasting to ask him if our television broadcasting staff were tested psychologically before being taken on to make sure that the better type of psychopath was not being hired – the worst sort, of course, being involved with the Courts and Prison Service. The Minister passed my letter on to TVNZ, who informed me proudly that they did not use such tests on their staff, and did not believe such tests could identify psychopaths! They imagine their ignorance will protect them! I conclude from this that the Minister has, quite simply, let the country down. I am not saying that there are psychopaths on the staff of TVNZ – it may be merely that they are too immature to have a social conscience – but it appals me that our Government will not even guard the Nation against this threat.

As you know, every country that has opted for commercial television has seen the level of violence and crime increase. Here, over the 10 to 15 years since multiple channels of commercial television, there has been a steady increase in violent crime. I think you will agree that we must act with some urgency, without any of the delays that habitually paralyse social intervention in this country.

Yours very sincerely,
R. W. Bodmin

I felt a letter like this would not have received any reply, or else just a form letter like the previous one. Are there people employed in ministries especially to dream up apparently soothing, but actually insulting, replies to all the whingers who take the government to task?

I turned my attention back to the aerogrammes. One of them revealed a strange preoccupation. Will mentioned sending from England to one of his sisters a very rare book that he wanted her to store in a safe place; but he added that he had packaged the book in a metal box he made himself, lining it with asbestos because 'New Zealand post offices are wooden buildings, and I can't risk seeing such precious items of human history go up in flames.'

So, fear of fire. I shook my head again and turned out the light.

But then I couldn't get to sleep. Will Bodmin wouldn't leave me in peace. For some unknown reason, although I had thought him a crazy old man, I was growing fond of him. An hour later I turned the light back on and read a long and quite astonishing letter. The story of a prophecy.

It had been posted from York, in 1961, and Will had written it in the psychiatric hospital where he was working as an art therapist.

It was about a young man who had been sure since his

24

teenage years that he would not live beyond the age of thirty. His horoscope and all the other predictions said the same thing. Of course his family refused to believe him and considered him dangerously neurotic. And then, the day before his thirtieth birthday, he died for no apparent reason. His brother went mad as a result and Will was treating him.

He continued his long letter by referring to other people who had predicted the date of their death. For example, the Neapolitan utopian philosopher Tommaso Campanella, who died, just as he had read it in the stars, on the day of the solar eclipse in May 1639. Or the English astrologer Simon Forman who, as his horoscope had predicted, died on the 12th of September 1611 by drowning in the Thames. However in his case, according to Will, suicide could not be ruled out. His conclusion: this isn't human. I detest people who can predict their own death!

This letter rang so many bells with me that it made me feel sick. It not only brought back unpleasant memories, it also reminded me of a story I read in the *Thousand and One Nights* that had terrified me right through childhood. A story about a child whose death at the age of fourteen had been predicted by an oracle. Obviously his parents did their utmost to save him, but it was their efforts that brought about his early death. I think he fell onto a kitchen knife. Will Bodmin might well believe in all this, because even though I wasn't admitting it outright, I believed in it myself. I had to get up and drink a glass of water, and, not wanting to read any more of the letters, I spent a long time listening to the sounds of the night, as if I might be able to decipher some explanation that would calm me down. I don't know when I finally fell asleep, but when I woke up the sun was bathing the room in a soothing, beige, unreal light. When I went downstairs, it was already mid morning and Ron had left for work hours before. Sara smiled at my embarrassment, guessing that Will Bodmin's letters were the cause.

'Well,' she said, 'maybe we'll be able to work together.'

She started showing me more of the mass of material she had assembled or written. Over a cup of coffee we talked about various things, the rest of the family, Will's father, the inventor who made us smile over his crinkled hairpin, about one of his daughters – Sara's mother – who had married a Maori, which is why Sara identified as Maori herself. She also told me that Will had initially wanted to be an artist, that he had a diploma from the School of Fine Arts in Christchurch where he had been a friend of the Angus sisters, Jean and Rita. It seemed to me that the family was spread all over New Zealand. We would have to cut things back, simplify them: this wealth of detail might paralyse us.

'We'll have to risk being unfair to Will,' I said. 'Decide what he will have to be. Reduce him.'

We would draw the line, a single line that would colour the story in its own way.

I was still thinking about this when the plane took off and I looked down over Auckland, seeing its islands, the coast, and the green water with the sky reflected in it as if it had finally figured out where to settle. I told myself it was just a matter of getting a bit of distance.

But at that point I hadn't read Sara Tinkerbell's notebooks.

STRAIGHTEN THIS
NOSE FOR ME

I can only picture my uncle surrounded by mountainous piles of objects, writes Sara Tinkerbell, encircled, invaded by his collections. In York it was books, pictures and even pieces of furniture.

We all live, she continues, surrounded by things we love, but we know how to keep them at a distance, and we imagine we are keeping a clear space apart from them. Not Will. I wouldn't like to try to guess why, but I never saw him at home not surrounded by objects he considered precious, that he had personally collected, and that were eating away at his living space, creating a thick dark shadow that hemmed him in and maybe held him together.

Before he came home from England, he sent ahead an impressive number of boxes of books. Not cardboard boxes, but heavy wooden chests, sometimes metal, arriving one after the other at his sister Winnie's house in Invercargill. Will hadn't at first planned to move in with her: he was going to stay a few months, just until he found a house for himself. He anticipated an active retirement, and had even thought of running a bookstore in Christchurch. Or else he would keep working as a consultant psychotherapist in a mental health centre.

Meanwhile, on seeing the boxes arrive, Winnie became concerned. She was a very good-natured woman, but also very neat and tidy. She had never been in paid employment, and of all the Bodmin daughters she was the one who stayed with their mother until the very end, looking after the house and the rest of the family. Fifty-four years old when their mother died, she was at last her own woman. She had soon bought a pretty little house in a wealthy suburb of Invercargill, a property that reminded me of a doll's house with its very low roof and leadlight windows surrounded by creepers – and maybe also because of the trees in the garden that had grown over the years and now hid the house, seeming to cut it off from the outside world. A charming place, but one where I couldn't imagine real family life with children as rowdy as mine.

The boxes preceded Will by several months; however others were to follow, for more than a year after his arrival. At first Winnie stacked them in her garage, but when she was forced to park her car on the street, she hoped Will would get there quickly and, as she put it, 'do something about it!'

What he did do to start with was feel uncomfortable about coming home to New Zealand, where nothing seemed to be the way it was when he left forty years earlier or, more to the point, the way he had imagined it since, and he sat back and let Winnie take care of him and comfort him just as she had when he was a little boy. But sweet-natured Winnie reacted in an unexpected way. She refused to let Will's books invade her living room. I should point out that I had warned her, told her about the house in York where stacks of books reached up to the ceiling, forcing any visitors to walk very carefully in single file; these towering piles blocked the kitchen to such an extent that you had to be a gymnast to reach the sink. They had even taken over the bedroom, surrounding Will's very narrow bed, like tall witches or fairies bending over him as he slept and threatening to collapse and crush him at the slightest breath of wind, if the window was left open.

'I won't have more than fifty of your books in the living room,' she declared. 'Of your choice.'

He was so offended he didn't bring in a single one, and, just as he had done as a child, he sulked, in the hope she would come and make it better. But she stuck to her guns. She raised the issue again by asking him to rent storage space for his boxes. Storage? A world-class collection in storage? Outraged, he rented a more or less rundown house on Kelvin Street and threatened to move in there. Then, for what he claimed were financial reasons, he sublet the bottom floor and fitted out only the upstairs. And a year later, he bought the whole building.

Winnie's home ought to have been a place where Will could breathe easy – it was small, of course, but airy, quiet and green; he ought to have been able to stretch out, be calm, let his mind run free. And yet, by June 1990, two years after his return to Invercargill, he had managed to clutter up his living environment. Except that the books had been replaced by letters. I had first seen the aerogrammes that finished up on my desk in his bedroom in the house on Stewart Terrace. They were all over the place, scattered over the bed, the chair, the floor. But they were restricted to the bedroom: Winnie wouldn't have allowed anything else. She was a plump little woman with faded blue eyes and a very sweet expression, but she wasn't one to mince words: 'Shove the lot into boxes and take them to Kelvin Street,' was her advice.

He thought she had a nerve. Wasn't she the one who had saved forty years' worth of letters?

Forty years!

Yes of course, because that's what he had asked her to do. And she had always been biddable – up till that point. For years she had done exactly what Will wanted.

As soon as he set foot in England – in 1949 – Will had written to his mother: 'Please keep each and every one of my letters, so that I'll be able to read them when I get back

29

and reconstruct everything that happened to me.' Back then his mother, two aunts and several of his seven sisters had obeyed. Since his father was dead, he saw himself as the only man of the house. An absent man, of course, but wasn't that how his father had been too?

And so when he came home, Winnie had shown him the treasure trove mounded up in several large cartons. 'We're all collectors, aren't we?' she said, with a ghost of a smile. He cleared his throat, touched. What she had collected was himself – or at least his life, his experiences. He was shocked to see this great mass of correspondence, aware now of the huge effort he had made on a daily basis over four decades. An act carried out several times a week, almost unnoticed at the time and only now revealing its enormous dimensions. There must have been ten thousand letters. Winnie had not only saved all the letters he sent to Invercargill, as well as the travel journals he forwarded twice a year, she had also rounded up the letters sent to the rest of the family, box after box, as her aunts, mother and four of her sisters died.

Will now added to this the mail he had received in England. No great shakes compared to what he had written himself, since he had kept only the important letters. He stood there helplessly, looking from the cartons to Winnie, with her sly smile. What an immense task they had accomplished together.

He insisted on sorting them before he took them away, and so they stayed put in the garage for over a year. When he finally made up his mind to open the boxes, Winnie forbade him to do it in the living room. A futile gesture, because six months later Will's bedroom was completely overrun by them, exasperating Winnie. 'I can't even get in here to clean!' Just to make his bed, Will had to walk on envelopes, which made him furious.

'Living means being able to forget!' Winnie would say. He didn't know where she had dug up this saying, but for him forgetting was not an option. He had spent his whole life, he claimed, fighting against the way time buried things, and he wasn't about to give up now. To live with his sister he had already made the sacrifice of being physically separated from his collection – he made do with going to see it two or three times a week, and very occasionally sleeping in the company of his favourite books – but he wasn't willing to jettison the work of forty years without examining it closely and learning a few things from what he called, with a touch of pride, his graphomania.

The problem was, sorting through it all was more difficult than he had thought and forced him into making unbearable choices. Chronological order, for example, muddled the themes. Each letter touched on several subjects, and to follow their development he would have had to cut up the pages. To take just one theme and make it intelligible, Will had to bring together countless aerogrammes. But every time he read a page he was drawn to other themes that were just as fascinating, and he lost himself, reading back and forth through the pile, confronted by the messy jumble that life always is. Whereas what he wanted was clarity.

And anyway, how could you follow the thread of a problem when the letters, once out of their boxes, wouldn't go back in? They all looked the same and were constantly getting mixed up. Most of them were blue aerogrammes, and on this particular morning (nearly nine o'clock by the alarm clock) they had spread themselves out even more slyly than usual: some were quivering on the window-ledge, others were ready to leap off the bedspread or had cluttered up the bedside table. And from each of them, as well as from the white envelopes scattered across the floor, the face of the Queen looked back at Will, making him feel uncomfortable. Staring straight at him. Watching him with that faint smile from 1952!

Feeling discouraged, Will thought about opening the window and letting everything fly away into the garden on the autumn breeze – papers, memories, flies, aborted hopes and regrets. His nose itched, his moustache trembled, he sneezed. Two aerogrammes slipped from his lap and floated gracefully to the floor.

He sniffed, rubbed his nose briskly, and with this simple gesture revived the question that had kept him awake part of the night – from the moment he realised, in organising his correspondence for the year 1963, that it was because of his nose that he had never married.

He had long believed he would settle down and raise a family. When he left New Zealand, he already owned a plot of land in Christchurch, on Scarborough Hill – a nice section with lots of sun and a cabin that held nothing but gardening tools. For years he had thought about building a proper house there one day, where he would live with his wife and children among the trees he had planted before he went away.

Trees – now there was something that, to his surprise, cropped up fairly regularly in his correspondence. He sent carob seeds to his mother or one of his aunts, and then questioned them about what they had done with them, wanting to know if the trees were growing well. He had even dreamed about planting New Zealand's most iconic tree, the cabbage tree, on a Pacific island, with Jean Angus. Yes, with Jean, his friend from Art School. He almost blushed to think that he had, in all innocence, told his mother about this dream. He was so proud of his skills in unmasking the deviousness of the subconscious, hadn't he seen what he was writing? Sometimes he was ashamed of himself – but this shame that made him embarrassed had its good points too: it brought him back down to earth.

All the fortune-tellers he consulted had confidently predicted marriage. In one letter to his mother, he mentioned a palm-reader he met on a bus between Bradford and York: she had seen in the lines of his hand that he would marry before he turned forty and go home to live in New Zealand, where his children would be born. Another seer had read more or less the same thing in the cards: he would marry a psychiatric nurse who would bear him two children.

And now here he was alone, in his sister's house, with the property on Scarborough Hill sold years earlier. What had he done to undo his destiny? Is it so easy to avoid predictions when they are positive?

He really shouldn't reread these letters. They gave him a distorted reflection, like a warped mirror, of a life that, even though it was his own, looked to him more like the gap between what he had dreamed of and what had happened, a kind of void, the space between two shapes. Increasingly, he would start to tremble as he unfolded an aerogramme, as if in fear of a verdict. He jumped from one time-frame to another, reliving strange episodes. For example, just after he arrived in England, he had gone to Tintagel to see the ruins of King Arthur's castle. 'I'm as happy as a lark in springtime, I recited "The Lady of Shalott" along the way for half an hour,' he had written. Rereading these words moved him almost to tears – but he didn't know why. In those days he had wanted to be an artist. He got off to a good start, making bronze candlesticks for the Holy Trinity church in Invercargill at the age of sixteen, and carving the wooden pulpit in the same church the following year. When he graduated from Art School he continued to paint, especially during the period where, as a conscientious objector, he had been forced to work as an agricultural labourer. And then without really seeing it coming he ended up as an art therapist. At the age of forty-three he had realised the prophecies of marriage had not come to pass. Or at least not yet. Sometimes fate can fall behind schedule.

He believed (as his correspondence demonstrated) that it was because his nose was crooked. A defect you would be hard-pressed to spot in photographs. People generally thought he was quite good-looking, tall and slender, with a clear, blue-eyed gaze – but people often say flattering things, it doesn't cost them anything. Only the eagle-eyed Shirley, wife of the head of psychiatry at York Hospital, noticed that he must have broken his nose at some point. Will had just confided to her that he wanted to have plastic surgery. 'But it suits you so well,' she exclaimed, 'it gives your face character!' Sweet Shirley.

He didn't really believe her; on the 16th of May 1962 he wrote to his Aunt Margaret: 'The fact is, your nose keeps on growing throughout your life. When I was at home, my nose was certainly crooked, but it was small. Over the last thirteen years it has got longer, and is now making me so ugly that people notice it and ask me how it happened. I have therefore decided to get a surgeon to straighten it.'

He expected she would help him to pay for the operation, which was going to be – as he stressed – expensive, not reimbursed, and impossible to pay for out of his meagre salary at York's Quaker Hospital, nevertheless essential for his future. When Aunt Margaret turned a deaf ear, he approached his mother. She was equally unresponsive, something Will found rather extraordinary: at least one of these women might have felt personally involved, since he had broken his nose as a small child, in the garden, one evening when one of them (but which one?) had dropped him. Wounded by this silence, he opened his heart to his sister Winnie. She was six years older, and so it was not impossible that she might have been the one who tried picking him up and caused the accident. But Winnie replied that she was quite surprised by the importance his nose was acquiring, 'out of all proportion' (sic), making Will realise he couldn't count on her either and would need to pay for the operation with his own money. By digging into his meagre savings, as he put it to Winnie, underlining the words with a thick black pen. He would sacrifice the modest collection of gold coins that he had left behind in New Zealand and that he now asked her to send to him. Since it was illegal to send gold through the post, he suggested that his sister hide the coins inside one of the large cakes she sent him twice a year, for Christmas and his birthday in April. But two cakes and a year later, the coins had still not arrived. Will, increasingly frustrated, finally suggested that since Winnie didn't dare break these absurd rules, she should pass on this 'dangerous mission' (she would register the irony) to their other aunt, Susan, whose fearlessness was well known – now there was a woman, he added, who wouldn't hesitate to take a risk to help out a family member. Stung to the quick, probably, Winnie took action at once and stuffed a cake full of gold coins; but by a scandalous and extraordinary coincidence, the parcel was lost in the post. In spite of his rage, Will dared not accuse his sister – after all, had he not incited her to commit an illegal act? She sent him a photocopy of the receipt as proof, which allowed Will to take the matter up with the English postal service, but to no avail. Even after the dust had settled, he remained convinced that the women of the house, normally so obliging, hadn't taken him seriously and were still treating him like a little boy who had no right to get married. He had already met with more or less the same lack of interest on a quite similar issue, the exact time of his birth. In spite of his repeated and urgent questioning, he was unable to discover this: the time indicated on his birth certificate was wrong, according to his own mother, who however provided no further information. In the end Will had reminded Aunt Margaret, in an exasperated letter, that 'the man who noted this incorrect time on my birth certificate made a serious mistake with regard to his own details the day he had his horoscope drawn up. And you know this as well as I do, as a result of this terrible mistake, the poor man married the wrong woman! The series of disasters that followed is well known. Proof yet again, if needed, that these things are not to be taken lightly.'

It was all in vain: no one bothered to find out the exact time he was born and thus help him to get married.

After the business with his nose had dragged on for two years, he had to make the decision to sell another treasure if he was to solve the problem. He gave up the ship's log from Captain Cook's first command, the *Freelove*. He had gone to a great deal of trouble to acquire this log, laying siege to some of Captain Cook's descendants who lived on a farm in Yorkshire. As chance would have it, they were, like him, Quakers: had this not been the case, despite his many visits, they would have kept on telling him they didn't know where the blessed log was, or which family member had last laid their hand on it. The resale of this precious document easily covered the cost of the operation and even allowed Will to make some uncharacteristic purchases of clothing when he left Penfield Hospital after a two-day stay, his nose still in plaster. Looking in the mirror, he had seen his face as a painted mask that made him look rather special and, indeed, not unattractive: hence his decision to buy new clothes to match his new expression.

What came next was, for him, a period of freedom, the extraordinary consequences of which repaid all his efforts. The anesthetic had affected him in a most unexpected way. It reawakened his memories, and lying there in his hospital bed he had an extraordinary revelation: it wasn't at two or three years of age that he broke his nose, but at thirteen. And he hadn't fallen from anyone's arms! No, he had been riding his bike with some school friends, and when he tried to do a trick, he had smashed into a telephone pole. Not only had he remembered it all with absolute clarity, he could list the names of his schoolmates as well. He wrote to one of them, who confirmed the incident; he remembered right away the street where it happened, and joked about the durability of the pole, which was still standing.

But close on the heels of this happy realisation there

followed an alarming question: why had he covered this memory with another, putting the blame on his mother and one of his aunts?

It was quite simply amazing.

After writing a heartbreaking letter to his mother, asking her forgiveness, he went in search of an explanation, to see Dr Webster, his usual supervisor at the hospital – and the husband of the lovely Shirley who had tried to talk him out of the operation.

John Webster was a good-natured psychiatrist who had dabbled in psychoanalysis but preferred to use medication and common sense. And when these remedies failed, he recommended prayer. He was, at this particular point, extremely concerned about his daughter Marion, a fourteen-year-old anorexic, and appeared grateful that Will had come knocking on his door. But instead of asking after Marion, whom he knew well, Will could only talk about the important problem of his nose and the memory that had been revived in the process of fixing it. This business was upsetting him so much, he said, that it was keeping him awake at night. Dr Webster listened, nodded, and answered by referring to 'the unknowable mysteries of the unconscious'. He added that where such things were concerned, we should maintain a degree of humility.

'A degree of humility, you think?' Will replied, biting his lip so as not to say something nasty. From his point of view, the return of this memory was like a cosmic upheaval. He had learned that this kind of reversal of perspective is one of the criteria of successful analytical therapy: the patient arrives saying something like 'I broke my nose because of my mother and aunt', but leaves singing a different tune, more accepting of his own responsibility, for example: 'I broke my nose clowning about with my mates'. Could surgery have had the same effect as a short course of analysis?

John Webster nodded, without giving an opinion.

'Although you still need to know what use this recovered memory is to you,' he suggested.

But for Will it wasn't at all a matter of usefulness; the big change was that one of his memories – one he had lived with for many years – had been revealed as false, made up, whereas the one that had re-emerged was true. That was the important thing, it was because of this new perception that he was able to think of himself as honest, although he had lied to himself for so many years. So he retorted: 'It was the lie that was useful. I lied to myself.' In the ensuing silence, he added: 'If what matters is what's useful, then the lie is more important than the truth.'

Dr Webster nodded. As if he wasn't quite convinced of Will's sincerity. And yet they were close, and he had always been able to count on Will's loyalty.

Well, nearly always.

To tell the truth – Will realised this more clearly thirty years later – Dr John Webster might well have had his reasons for not wanting Will's nose to be too straight. Because a special relationship had developed between Will and the doctor's wife Shirley, from the time Webster first arrived at the psychiatric hospital. The new head doctor liked Will straight away, seeing in him an extraordinarily good art therapist, with a great gift and flair for diagnosis and evidently very caring towards his patients. Both were contemptuous of electroconvulsive therapy, and Webster, intrigued by psychoanalysis, was curious to know what Will had learned at the Jung Institute in Zurich. The breadth of the New Zealander's interests, his scholarship, the exhibitions he had organised in the city and the occasional lectures he gave at the hospital on the South Pacific had made him especially well known. They were both Quakers, too, and loathed television with an equal passion.

Will felt he was underpaid, but he had the advantage of a

generous leave allowance that he spent travelling throughout Europe. He would bring back rare books or prints that he almost always sold on at a profit. He had managed to negotiate a low rent with the director of the hospital for a small, windowless room where, after reinforcing the door himself, he kept his treasures. He also lived rent-free in the nurses' home, although when Dr Webster took up his position he had been thinking of moving himself and his books and pictures into town.

Since he ate in the hospital canteen every day, he was pleased to be invited to dine at Dr Webster's home. Here he met Shirley, the doctor's charming young wife, and their two daughters. He shared a number of interests with John Webster, but was stunned to see how much he had in common with his wife. Everything she said seemed brilliant to him, and he was struck not only by her beauty – her eyes, her smile, the way she held her head so bewitched him that he was beyond judging them – but also by her firmly-held beliefs. She was a Quaker, with responsibilities within the church. A political activist like him, she had not only been at the same demonstrations, but was also a committee member of the Campaign for Nuclear Disarmament. And, height of coincidence, they had both taken part in the big antinuclear march in January 1960, being arrested at Hartington and released that evening. Will was delighted to learn they had been so close without knowing each other, only to finally meet a few months later, as if this were some sign of fate. And when of course in the middle of the meal she asked him if he would help her with preparations for the next celebration of the Friends – the local Quakers – he agreed at once, his eyes almost misty with gratitude, with no idea how many evenings he would be spending helping Shirley. If he had known, he would have been even more delighted. Perhaps influenced by the atmosphere of the family and the house ('the first spacious, quiet and modern house I've seen since I came to England,' he would write to his mother', Will began to talk with extraordinary enthusiasm. About art, travel, the evolution of the Soviet Union, where he had recently spent some time, and the church. Will revealed that he owned a portrait of the first Quaker to set foot in New Zealand, and indeed one of the earliest Europeans – Sydney Parkinson, the painter and naturalist who accompanied Captain Cook on the Endeavour.

That evening John Webster also seemed to be in top form. He showed a few of his canvases – he was a painter too – and declared himself very interested in art therapy and outsider art. He was even planning to go to Heidelberg in his holidays to see the Prinzhorn collection.

Will went back to the hospital enchanted; his room in the nurses' building seemed even less suitable after the beauty of the evening. He tossed and turned, reliving everything that had been said at the Websters', and several times as he was dozing off he saw a warm and glowing Shirley, leaning over him like a good fairy. She really shouldn't, he told himself, it's too ugly here.

But once again his dream was a premonition. Two days later, as he left that same building and started down the pathway leading to the splendid central block built of red brick and covered in ivy, Shirley appeared before him. With the light behind her, bathed in sunshine, she looked almost the way she had in his nocturnal vision and he felt himself blush. She stood there smiling, even spoke before he did, then pointed to the old house on the little hill to the right. 'I wanted to take a look at that house,' she said, 'because John told me that's where the trainee nurses live and one of my cousins might be coming.'

Will looked away so as not to keep blinking, on the point of suggesting he would go with her. But he didn't dare. Instead, what popped out of his mouth was the story of the little hill.

'Do you know that's where the York gallows stood, two hundred years ago?'

'You mean they hanged people there?'

She shuddered. She was wearing a sweet little hand-knitted jersey in all the glowing colours of autumn. Now that they had both turned towards the hill, Will felt more comfortable. He explained that the trainee nurses really didn't like the house because they were disturbed by tapping spirits, poltergeists.

'Really?' Shirley asked, her blue eyes wide.

'Really,' Will replied. And told her about dishes being smashed in the night, doors slamming and waking the poor girls, and even beds being turned upside down. 'These spirits,' he concluded, 'are terribly strong. The girls have a lot of trouble sleeping. They get exhausted and end up moving out.'

Shirley shook her head. 'That wouldn't be very good for my cousin. And all that going on in the middle of a psychiatric hospital with quite a good reputation. It's weird, don't you think?'

'It's because of the gallows,' he stammered. 'It's the souls of the hanged seeking revenge.'

Shirley laughed briefly. There was a moment of silence. They walked a few steps toward the little house on the hill. Then she asked him, since he knew German, if he had heard of a *Polterabend*. No, he had to admit . . .

She told him that according to an old German custom, people would smash crockery in front of the newlyweds' door on their wedding night, because the shards would bring them luck. 'It's a tapping evening, if you like.' Which, she added, had nothing to do with the tapping spirits. Except for the resemblance between the words . . . Poltergeist and Polterabend. The link wouldn't interest anyone but a fan of psychoanalysis. 'Even so. They would have us believe that these lonely young nurses are dreaming about their wedding night, when people will break crockery in front of their door and tip them out of bed. But neither you nor I would swallow that explanation.'

She was smiling, and he wondered if she was making fun of him. Then immediately he felt slightly ashamed. He should have known. Thought about it. He was the psychoanalyst. Well, almost.

Wanting to defend the spirits, he started to explain that York was famous for its ghosts. Of course Shirley hadn't been living in the area for long, but hadn't she heard about Harry Martindale, the policeman who in 1953 had seen ghosts in the Treasurer's House of York Minster? It had been in all the papers. 'It was the Roman legion that occupied York nearly twenty centuries earlier; the 9th legion, recruited in Spain,' he added, as if detail could stand in for truth.

But he didn't look at Shirley.

'And the ghosts,' she asked, 'what did they want?'

'To go home.'

Instead of laughing, and saying perhaps that the policeman was actually a young plumber, eighteen years old and overly fond of his beer, she merely added: 'Don't we all.' And waving goodbye to him, she headed off by herself toward the trainee nurses' home.

Will felt miserable the whole afternoon. In the end he vowed to be worthy of Shirley, to work so hard for her on the Quakers' party that she would have to admire him. He congratulated himself, however, that she was married, otherwise he would have avoided her, run away from her. Because although he admitted many things to himself, he wouldn't own up to being in love. He had also just realised that he couldn't completely confide in Shirley. For example, he couldn't tell her he had seen with his own eyes the Swiss army that fought Charles the Bold at Morat in the fifteenth century.

He'd seen the army one evening in Lausanne, and from

that point on he had been a devotee of Jung.

You can't say everything.

The Friends' party was a great success and Will Bodmin was congratulated by the whole Quaker community. As a reward, Shirley gave him a collection of essays by Simone Weil, translated under the title *Waiting on God*. Between the cover and the flyleaf she slipped a card on which she noted that, like him, Simone Weil was a pacifist and a migraine sufferer.

Will was now very close to the Websters, and had dinner with them a couple of nights a week. But sometimes he did go home early, in fact, because of a migraine.

The Saturday following the Friends' party, Shirley and John invited him to go for a drive to Kirkham Abbey. It was a fine day, and Shirley wore her sunglasses and put the car roof down. She said she wanted to make the most of the last of the summer. Will, sitting in the back with the two girls, pulled his coat collar up, also enjoying the wind that made them feel giddy and wrapped each of them in their own dreams. He squinted, Shirley's hair flying back and brushing over his hands as the car lurched this way and that. The touch was like an electric current flowing through him. Light bounced off her hair, the metal, the bodywork – it was magical. Gripping the steering wheel, shoulders hunched and collar pulled up, John sat behind his dark glasses, pulling his family along behind him, tackling the road like a racer, slowing into the curves and making the motor roar as he pulled the car through to the next straight. It was wonderful until the first drops of rain fell. The girls started shouting that they had to put the top up, but Shirley waved her hand, no, and lifted her face to the sky, welcoming the drops falling on her glasses as if the threatening storm merely added to her happiness, and they drove on like that to York. Will didn't realise he had caught a chill until, back in his room, he started to shiver.

He had a cold through the whole of the following week, and had to wear one of his New Zealand sweaters under a thick tweed jacket. Drinking cups of scalding tea, he reflected on the price of even the smallest pleasures.

'I'm having dinner at the Websters' again this evening,' he wrote to his mother a few days later. 'Sometimes I wish I was not on such good terms with them.'

'I realise my depressions return every five weeks or so,' he added. 'I have a couple of days when I'm really down. Luckily I have a lot of free time, because on those days I'm useless. And my migraines are back, much more frequent than they used to be.'

John often left him by himself with Shirley. The man was like some great, easy-going bear, eating slowly and speaking less and less. At the end of the meal he disappeared into his office. But once Will was alone with Shirley, he couldn't think of anything more to say, or else he felt compelled to be pedantic, to teach her about the history of the Pacific, something she seemed to welcome. But she was also skilled in drawing him to more amusing subjects. 'I feel embarrassed at being alone with Mrs Webster,' he wrote to his mother, 'because she has such a critical turn of mind that she always finds the funniest, most cutting comments to make about our colleagues.'

These were troubled times. For Shirley's birthday in March, Will arrived with a remarkable gift: a colour print he had bought in Paris, entitled *Dance of the Friendly Islands in the Presence of the Queen, Tine*. The artist, Jean-Hubert Piron, had depicted naked native women in poses copied from eighteenth-century pastoral scenes. They were welcoming two men, a European in formal dress from head to toe, wearing a hat and a blue frock coat, and a bare-chested native prince.

The Websters went into ecstasies over the quality of the

work, taken from the *Atlas of the Voyage in Search of La Pérouse.*

'Well,' Shirley said, laughing, 'clearly it's always the women who are naked.'

'And the natives,' added her husband.

'But even on their home turf, the men are more dressed than the women. They've got tattoos, at least,' Shirley insisted.

Looking at the print through their eyes, Will was suddenly aware of the somewhat ridiculous prejudices of Europeans of the time, the stereotyped eroticism of the image and its underlying contempt for the peoples of the Pacific. He felt as if he had given himself away, and blushed. Yet again he had been blind; he hadn't understood the implications of this gift that now seemed almost salacious. He tried to make up for it by holding forth about the artist, who had followed the French navigator d'Entrecasteaux in 1791.

'Oh,' said Shirley. 'Frenchmen. Well of course.'

'The Friendly Islands,' her husband murmured. And Will realised he was reading into it 'The Society of Friends', as if the print were an allusion.

Which, in his opinion, it was not.

They drank a toast in champagne. Far from being shocked, the Websters were delighted.

'I'd love to see your collection,' Shirley said.

He felt himself melting as she gazed at him.

'I'll bring you a whole load of prints,' he answered, not for one moment thinking to invite her to the tiny box-room where he stored his treasures. He had the impression she might have preferred a different response.

They had eaten the cake and sung 'Happy Birthday' when Will closed his eyes for a moment and rubbed his forehead. Little Marion – the one who was already showing signs of anorexia – looked at him anxiously and asked: 'How long have you been getting migraines?'

He was very surprised by this adult question.

'Oh, at least twelve years.'

'Ah ha!' she said, with the exact same intonation as a therapist who understands a patient. Then, turning to the others: 'Mother, I think Will has been getting migraines ever since you married Father.'

Everyone burst out laughing, drank some more champagne, then went back to talking about the South Pacific paradise as imagined by eighteenth-century Europeans.

From the corner of his eye, Will saw Marion slip out of the room unobserved, as silent as a night bird.

And his migraine throbbed even more violently.

He thought travelling might save him from his guilty affections. He left on a third trip to Russia. He returned with icons that he showed the Websters, and simply seeing Shirley again made him realise he hadn't made any progress at all. Except that he was now slightly embarrassed that he didn't declare his love.

He was rescued by events. He sent a quite enthusiastic letter to his mother in May 1962 – at a time when, beset by doubts, he was already thinking of having his nose fixed.

'There's a possibility that Dr Webster might be thrown into prison before the end of the month. It's a terrible blow. He's being called before the judge to testify in the case of an Anglican vicar who has just been charged with indecent exposure. The poor man exposed himself on many occasions in our children's clinic, and no one on the team suspected a thing. Luckily he has agreed to plead guilty, so his young victims won't have to testify. He's married and has a son, and I am glad to see that his wife hasn't abandoned him even though he'll probably get at least five years. Dr Webster is implicated because he apparently knew what was going on (which I think is completely untrue) and didn't do anything about it. That's outrageous. John Webster will invoke professional confidentiality, because the vicar was one of his patients. To give you an idea of his generosity of spirit, he called the most important members of the team together and asked them to pray not for him but for the accused.'

Here was an opportunity for Will to prove his loyalty. Nevertheless the business with the exhibitionist vicar disturbed him, and poisoned the atmosphere at the hospital. He had only to listen to the nursing staff to hear that John must have known about it and let it go on. Worse, he had sent his daughter Marion as a patient to this same clinic. What kind of experience must she have had with that pervert?

Naturally Will didn't ask the Websters a single question about it. He was convinced John had never let Marion near the priest. And if he had, that would have proved his innocence, because he would only have allowed it if he had been in the dark about the exhibitionist's behaviour. Just as he had no idea that Will lusted after his wife, and certainly no inkling that Shirley had made such direct advances to him that he had had to play dumb to avoid responding.

So there were some strange goings-on at the hospital. Things that Will had no desire to shed any light on, and that Dr Webster could not deal with.

The day the psychiatrist was due in court, he decided to go alone, without even a lawyer. Shirley simply stayed in her office to pray, and Will joined her there. When she took his hand because she was feeling unhappy, he held it tightly for a long moment. The warmth and tenderness of this contact stayed with him the whole evening, and he had to chase from his mind fantasies in which he imagined Dr Webster in prison and himself responsible for looking after the doctor's wife and children. Fortunately the psychiatrist was appearing only as a witness and was not harassed in any way. And Will remained trapped in his indecision. Little Marion continued to send him questioning looks.

John was grateful to Will for his loyalty. When, two months after the vicar incident, it was decided to convert the nurses' home into a convalescent ward, he called the art therapist into his office to tell him he deserved a lot better than the accommodation assigned to him. He was clearly far more of an expert on Jungian psychology than the hospital psychiatrists, and a finer clinician as well – which could be attributed to his excellent upbringing, since he hadn't been allowed to go to the cinema before the age of fourteen. Why didn't he come and live with them? For a modest sum, they would rent him a vastly nicer room than the one he was losing and he would dine with the Websters nearly every night as well.

This proposition plunged Will into three days of depression. His greatest desires and therefore his greatest fears were apparently being realised. He confided in his mother who, for once, told him what she thought. Normally she wrote short letters in which she refrained from making any comment on her son's life, mentioning the garden, the state of her health or Aunt Susan's, and sometimes an item from the *Weekly News* – a racist, nationalistic rag Will kept urging her not to buy. She asked him if he was sure he would be comfortable living with the Websters. Wouldn't he be better to have his own place?

His own place?

Staff living in the nurses' home would have to move out, something that was much discussed. For the most part, the nurses simply decided to move into the new building available to them. Will, who had earlier been talking about renting a place in town, was now avoiding the subject and being especially careful not to mention the Websters. So he was very surprised when young Jane Hanley seemed to know he was going to live with the head doctor. Jane was an Irish nurse, recently arrived, who had established something of a reputation for speaking frankly. She was often to be seen in one of the pubs in town where she was a supporter of the local rugby team. Will liked her casual ways and had taken her side in an unlikely-sounding episode. An eighteen-year-old girl by the name of Jenny had run away from the locked ward where he ran a painting workshop, wearing a disguise her sister had brought her. A rumour started at once that Jane Hanley had seen the runaway wearing a red wig but hadn't sounded the alarm. All the staff in the ward knew Jane and the young patient were on good terms – some even claimed they had been seen smoking together. Will had taken Jane's side, feeling she was totally honest, and when he raised the subject with her, the nurse told him the rumours where motivated by jealousy. She added:

'You know how it is. No one is spared. They're saying you'll be living with the Websters because John's wife has a thing for you.'

He had been startled, and stepped back to stare at Jane as if he had never seen her before. In actual fact he had never really looked at her properly. He smiled, running his fingers through his hair. 'Is that what they're saying?'

'Oh, I've offended you, I'm sorry,' she answered and walked off.

He would have preferred to have it out, to be reassured, perhaps. Several days went by. The affair of the runaway and her sister faded away. The two girls had unwisely walked past the police station, and on seeing the officers who had arrested Jenny a week previously for disorderly behaviour, they taunted the men, asking why they were all crammed into their pigpen when they would all be more at home in the Quaker psychiatric hospital. Of course the two girls were picked up again and Jenny returned to the clinic.

Then Jane arrived with a block of chocolate, as if she had given Will a hard time and wanted him to forgive her. Swiss chocolate, she explained, because a patient had told her he loved Switzerland. Seeing him hesitate, she produced a pack of cigarettes and asked him to choose. He relaxed and took the chocolate. He was touched, thanked Jane and no longer felt any urge to ask her questions about the Websters.

He wondered if Jane Hanley might be the nurse the fortune-teller in London had seen in his future.

The upshot was that he went to see John Webster in his office and announced very carefully, almost as if he were apologising, that he wasn't able to accept his generous offer. He would take advantage of his compulsory rehousing to find somewhere he could keep his collection.

John drew deeply on his pipe, a habit he had recently taken up, and said: 'With your family, so to speak.' There was no humour behind these words, just a touch of weariness.

'That's right,' said a relieved Will. 'My family.' At least he wouldn't feel guilty about it.

It was a wise decision, as the tragic events of that Christmas would demonstrate, in the absence of the Websters, who were away in the south of England, and of Jane Hanley, gone to Dublin for the holidays.

A fancy-dress ball had been planned to follow Christmas dinner, to be held in the main hall next to the dining room. The band had started playing dance music, and three particularly pretty and mischievous young nurses – one was twenty-two and the others were twins, nineteen years old – arrived in their costumes. They were dressed as the three wise monkeys: see no evil, hear no evil, speak no evil. This demureness was however belied by the cigarettes between their fingers. A good-looking male nurse named Peter Walker, the darling of all these ladies, was ready to party too, dressed that evening as Robin Hood. When he saw them holding unlit cigarettes, he offered them his lighter, and all three rushed toward him at the same time. In the ensuing mêlée, the synthetic fur of their costumes caught fire and the girls were transformed into human torches, screaming and running in all directions. The party-goers did their best to grab them to put out the flames, using whatever was to hand, tablecloths and jugs of water, but one of the girls suffocated and her twin sister was completely disfigured by burns. The third, who had immediately dropped to the floor and rolled, got away with only minor injuries. Will saw only the final stages of the drama, people rushing about and the dying woman being carried away on a stretcher.

Two months later, he wrote to his mother: 'They've had to reconstruct the disfigured twin, Hannah's, face. The surgeon thinks he has done a remarkable job of the skin grafts, but when the poor girl came back to see us at the hospital she was so hideous she frightened us all. I couldn't bring myself to look directly at her, and I think when she comes back to work they'll have to be careful to keep her away from children. She was the sweetest, happiest girl, Hannah.'

Fire, always fire.

In March he moved into two bedrooms and a tiny kitchen on the first floor of a house in Sandringham Street, very close to the hospital. He shared a bathroom on the ground floor with the owners. The larger of the two bedrooms was immediately taken over by his collection, and he was delighted to see his pictures given room to breathe. They needed space, they needed to be seen. He was especially proud of his recently acquired portrait of Ellen Turner, the second wife of Edward Gibbon Wakefield – the man known as the founder of New Zealand. The painting was thought to have disappeared; a number of experts even claimed it had never existed. Well there it was, in Will Bodmin's little living room, shown to advantage in the full light of day. It was a portrait of a teenage girl, with an innocent, almost incredulous look about her. She was fifteen years old when Edward's right-hand man, a certain Thévenot, abducted her from her boarding school – not exactly a heroic act, when you realise Edward Wakefield was mostly interested in her money. Ellen's family laid a complaint, and Wakefield got three years in prison for his pains. But it was while he was in gaol that Wakefield developed the ambitious colonisation projects that would take him to New Zealand. And now here was pretty Ellen Turner, in Will's home, abducted a second time in the sense that practically no one knew she had been found again. Will was going to exchange her. What else would you do with a prisoner? She would be his bartered bride.

There followed a brief period of happiness in the company of three women, Shirley, Jane and Ellen Turner, who of course were in conflict in his fantasies but essentially cancelled one another out, so there was no need for him to choose. Only one, however, when he came back down to earth, was within his reach. His nose, quite straight now that it was out of plaster, should have shown him the way to go. But it told him nothing, merely quivering slightly above his moustache, with an entirely new elegance. Gradually he admitted to himself that he had been very frightened of falling into Shirley's trap. What this trap might consist of, he couldn't clearly define, but he continued to be preoccupied by it.

A few days after Easter, he wrote to his mother: 'In the Falmouth post office yesterday morning, the staff were surprised to see a sizeable rat struggling before them. A sack of oysters had been dropped off in the post office the previous day, and during the night some of the oysters had opened. The rat went to check them out, and its tail must have strayed into one of the shells, which immediately closed. It was thus held prisoner by its nether appendage the whole night long, and of course in the morning met a tragic end.'

And as for Peter Walker, the Robin Hood of the unfortunate Christmas ball, the same letter explained that he had not escaped unscathed either. 'All the staff are upset by the sacking of Peter Walker, the young male nurse who was so well liked by patients and staff. According to hospital regulations, the girls are strictly forbidden to visit the male nurses in their accommodation. On Sunday morning, Peter was supposed to leave for a week's holiday, and his girlfriend – a trainee nurse who is still underage – went up to his room at around eight in the morning to say goodbye. This bending of the rules was unacceptable to the cleaning lady, Mrs Kelly, a Catholic and a widow, who was working on the same floor at the time. She reported the incident to the director who immediately fired Peter – despite his having put in five years of impeccable service. Several of us asked Dr Webster to intervene. His answer was that over the year four trainee nurses had fallen pregnant and that next time it would be the director who got the boot – without even having the pleasure of sinning. He added that it was essential to be absolutely unyielding in dealing with the sexual immorality that degrades our profession, and advised us to pray for Peter Walker.'

INVERCARGILL

Sitting on the edge of his bed, Will Bodmin rubs a hand over his face. Slowly. As if to wake himself up, to rid himself of the nagging suspicion that he might have made a terrible mistake. Perhaps these letters should never have come back to their sender; perhaps you should never write to yourself. Had he really believed he would be able to piece together his past? He doesn't formulate the question clearly; it is there, underlying everything, but he isn't able to reject it or accept it. How much of our energy, he wonders, is expended on barricading ourselves away from undesirable thoughts? An enormous, an unimaginable amount – that's where we could really make energy savings . . .

What draws him from his gloomy imaginings is the voice of his sister Winnie shouting through the door that it's nearly ten o'clock and there's a letter for him from Australia.

A letter!

She opens the door partway and stands there, surveying the mess again. He knows that if it were up to her, everything would be cleared away in the blink of an eye, the letters piled back willy-nilly into the cartons then sealed up with packaging tape and sent off to Kelvin Street. A clean sweep. A merciless culling.

She lets her hand hover for a moment, as if there is nowhere to put down the envelope – not the tiniest free space – and in the end holds it out to her brother. Is he not well, perhaps? Hasn't he forgotten his late-morning appointment?

'No,' he says, 'I'm fine.' Between them there is an undercurrent of competition concerning anything to do with health and illness. On one side there are Will's theories, about which Winnie keeps a pious silence because she thinks they are nothing but hot air; on the other side, the Christian Science that Winnie converted to five years ago, abandoning her Anglican faith. Since then she hasn't had so much as a cold; the eternal victory of mind over body. Illness has become a sin; it has no business even existing, because God is good.

Will might wonder why he never married, but he doesn't ask the same question about Winnie. He has never seen anything abnormal in her being always at the beck and call of her family, himself in particular. Now here they are like two elderly children in a fairytale house with ivy on the walls, the lush growth of the garden hiding everything except the roof and the garage door, which means inside the house everything is in darkness, especially the living room where Winnie had Scottish leadlights put in, like the ones from their Rockhaven childhood. Even the ornaments on the mantelpiece are the same ones Will knows, the ivory statuettes, the Empire clock: and, on one of the walls, not just an oil painting by their father of two cats playing, but also an old poster advertising Pears soap – there's a woman in an apron briskly rubbing a little boy standing in a basin. The boy is snivelling and objecting, but the woman is shouting that he's filthy. That little boy, that was you, Will, his sister told him, laughing. Surrounded and cradled by these objects from the past, how dare Winnie complain about his letters? But she could simply not have collected all this mail; if anyone is to blame, Winnie is as much at fault as he is, and has been for years.

She shakes her head, looking dismayed. 'You'd have been better to watch television.'

He thinks he must have misunderstood. Television? 'You mean instead of writing? Instead of writing . . . these letters?'

She doesn't answer, just shrugs and stays right where she is, possibly curious to know what's in the letter she brought him.

But Will is furious. That's exactly why he left the country, back then, to get away from all those women ruling over the household. And now his sister is talking to him about television! When he never watches the damned thing. He pretends, that's all. It's an act of generosity, of sociability, that leads him to sit beside Winnie on the living-room sofa and watch a programme, but he hardly ever lasts until the end. Even if he sits beside her most evenings. And she knows it. She knows how he struggles – all those cretinous TV watchers, he was in the habit of saying, who thought ads would pay for the programming, but they're the ones who've wound up paying for the ads and for programmes that are only there anyway to provide ad breaks. How can Winnie blaspheme like this? Didn't she back his tireless campaign against the introduction of privately owned channels in New Zealand? Didn't she support his repeated demands for producers and other TV employees to be tested, a bunch of psychopaths ruled by just one idea – as long as people watch it, it's good?

Of course he's only human and he has his weak moments; he did watch the wedding of Prince Charles and Lady Diana, the Queen's Jubilee and other episodes from the life of the Royal Family. He's happy to admit that. He would even go further and recognise that he owes the rapid expansion of his collection to television, along with some of his biggest commercial coups. It was in the 1970s that the first generation raised entirely in front of the TV screen reached adulthood. They had pretty much lost interest in any book that required a minimum of concentration, and entire libraries were being sold off at bargain prices by heirs who were incapable of

56

realising their true worth. He was able to buy collections that he sold off a few years later for ten times the price he paid. But in his opinion he owes this to television the same way he would be indebted to an epidemic that transformed the human brain into tripe-butcher's offal. Growing rich on the backs of the dead, he declares.

'All I meant,' Winnie continues, 'was that if you had watched TV then everything would have faded away, been forgotten. You'd be able to move on.'

But is that true? The TV worm has to get under your skin somehow, and just because it's in the flesh, because you can't see it any more, doesn't mean it's dead.

'No,' he answers, 'I'm lucky because my letters have been kept; I can read them again, work out what happened in my life.'

She rolls her eyes. At last he opens the real letter, the one the postman has just brought and that he didn't write for himself. It's from Canberra, Australia. From the National Library; Will doesn't remember ever writing to them. He unfolds the page slowly, still watched by his sister. He skims though it, and his little moustache trembles as he announces: 'Australia wants my collection.' Something inside him unclenches, his shoulders relax, he's lost in a dream now.

'That's what happened to Rex Nan Kivell,' he says.

Rex, the great collector he knew in London for over twenty years. Rex, whom he didn't like, but who was so successful.

He flaps the envelope about, puts it down on the chair, and is suddenly in a hurry. Life goes on. He'll have to have a quick breakfast. How could he have forgotten to be hungry?

'This letter,' explains Will, 'is going to help me force New Zealand's hand.' He intends to show it to the journalist from *The Southland Times* who has written two major articles about him. He can see the title already: 'A first-class New Zealand collection may be lost to Australia.' Not again! readers will moan.

Then he will be able to dictate his terms.

Now he must hurry and photocopy the Australian proposal (which is actually very vague – it's just a request for information) before his 11.30 appointment with the police sergeant.

Who said I was wasting my time? he thinks as he eats his toast. He looks through the window, staring glassy-eyed into the bushes in front of the kitchen. This Australian letter is justification for many of his past choices. 'Who would dare say I was wasting my time?' he repeats, aloud.

Half an hour later he is speeding along on his bicycle – or more precisely his neighbours' bicycle, because his has been stolen from in front of the mental health centre where he still works part-time. By a trick of fate, it was taken while he was working with the director on a project to put a stop to petty crime. The bike he lost was a good one, whereas the one he's been borrowing from the neighbours for the last four months is just a heap of junk: it's heavy, with only three gears that change if they feel like it, and it steers badly. Will is a little disappointed by it, as if the neighbours – I'm very fond of them, I'm only criticising them out of friendship – were revealing they weren't quite up to the expectations they created, not just by their appearance – quite stylish, even elegant sometimes – but also by their nearness to the Bodmins.

Pedalling furiously, Will rides past Queen's Park where, many years ago, his father used to test-drive cars on a closed track – superb vehicles, like the Reo with which he twice won the Invercargill to Dunedin race. For quite a while he also had a hot-air balloon set up in the park. His sister claims Will would have been too young to remember. But he has heard so much about it that he knows exactly what colours the balloon was; he can even see its name, *Excelsior*, in big black letters; he could reach out and touch the basket; he can hear the hissing of the burner and see his father rising up into the air; he even feels the sadness of never being invited to go with him. Even though his father took a lot of people up – including, of course, Will's idiot of a cousin, Bertie, who hasn't been shy about telling everyone about it in his many articles. No, his father never suggested Will might go with him. I was too small, according to Winnie. But was I always too small? And that Reo, I remember that car very well too, a high-powered luxury car. I never rode in the Reo either without my mother or one of my sisters, whereas my father would cheerfully take any little brat who waved at him from the side of the road. Why?

It must have been because the great Franklin Bodmin was afraid some accident might take his little Will away from him, his only son, the apple of his eye. Yes, it was out of love that he so seldom let him get into his Reo. That's definitely what his father would have said. His father, the great inventor.

Luckily this part of Invercargill is quite flat, so even an inferior bicycle will do the job.

A couple of kilometres further on, Will stops at Kelly's in the little shopping centre, a bookseller's hardly worthy of the name, more of a storage space for recent publications, scarcely in print before their price is reduced: coffee-table books, magazines, self-help manuals, in a word, everything Will considers useless clutter.

The girl behind the counter greets him pleasantly as he walks over to the photocopier. He takes out the letter he tucked away in the inside pocket of his tweed jacket, but as soon as it's in his hand he realises it isn't the right one: it's one of the aerogrammes. He turns pale, then flushes, and grumbles: Ah, Winnie. Did she give him back the Australian letter? He fiddles with the aerogramme, turning it between his fingers, does an about-face, bites his lips – which makes it look as though he's chewing on his moustache – then walks indecisively towards the door. The girl at the counter gives him a smile: 'Is there something wrong?'

'No, no, thanks. It's just . . .' He makes a sweeping gesture and continues on his way without finishing his sentence.

He sits down on the little seat near his bicycle. People come out of the supermarket with their trolleys and walk past without seeing him. Puzzled, he crumples the paper, trying to understand what has happened. Then, almost mechanically, he starts to read it. He knows it well, he wrote it just after the party they gave for his retirement.

Dear Winnie,

The big day is over, and I'm trying to adjust to being my own boss and living on a pension. A week ago, one of the youngest psychiatrists asked for my address, saying he hoped to come and visit me after I left. No doubt he'll come to ask my advice on cases he can't solve. On my last day, the party was held in the big functions room, and on the way there I wondered if I should prepare a speech or just improvise. And then I decided an overly structured speech would show I was nervous. When I went in, nearly all the young psychiatrists were there, and the three external consultants, the whole psychology department, the occupational therapists and other paramedical staff, and so many nurses the hospital must practically have come to a halt. The social workers had come too, and Dr Bateson made a nice speech about me, mentioning, amongst other things, my 'quite extraordinary insight into the sick mind'. Then I was given a large box, which I opened and found to contain a pair of Georgian-style silver candlesticks – very beautiful and well-made candlesticks, but obviously not nearly as old as the ones I sent you! Nevertheless I was extremely touched, thinking at that moment of Father, who always used to say *I would never be any use to anyone.*

People kept coming and chatting to me for over an hour, we took photos, and then I went back to work until 7 p.m.

My last case is a woman who has just been admitted to hospital. She was sitting in a foam-cushioned chair smoking a cigarette in a very well insulated house when the chair caught fire and went up like a rocket, in a ball of flame. She managed to push her four-year-old son out of the room, but instead of leaving the house he ended up in the bathroom and died in the fire. Husband and wife have gone mad.

Much love,
Will.

When he looks up again, his eyes are prickling. I'm getting old, he tells himself. And to take his mind off the subject, he gets to his feet.

Mounting his bicycle, he hurries off toward the police station. The sky is darkening, he is afraid he will arrive dripping wet. Fire and water, he keeps saying, the fire of the mind and the water of reality. Wasn't it logical for that poor smoker's son to run to the bathroom?

He stops in front of the small building with its New Zealand flag and, not seeing any bike stand, leans his against the wall without bothering to put on the lock.

Inside, he asks to see Sergeant Holmes; the receptionist tells him to take a seat in a vinyl armchair. A uniformed policeman walks past and looks at him but doesn't speak. A few minutes later a burly man with short black hair and an angular face appears: Holmes. He looks at Will as if sizing him up and asks him to come through.

He shows Will into a small, cluttered room and sits behind the desk after gesturing his visitor towards an upholstered chair.

'So you work at the mental health centre?' the sergeant asks.

'Yes, part-time. After thirty years in English hospitals.'

'At the Dee Street clinic?'

'That's right.'

'And what were you wanting to speak to me about?' He ought to know that, he has Will's letter sitting next to his phone.

'In my letter, I mentioned there are five ways of identifying a psychopath.'

The sergeant looks up in surprise, waiting for what might come next.

'Give me a case to solve and I'll show you. Do you have an arsonist in the area? I can solve the puzzle of the arsonist's personality. I have previously assisted the police in York, in England.'

'You're a profiler?'

'No, sir. Let's leave that to television. Actually, profilers have followed my example. I started this work before the word existed.'

'Hmmm . . . We don't have any arsonists at the moment.'

'My project, my aim, is to prevent arson.'

'Prevent it?'

'Absolutely. Psychopathy isn't an illness that can be cured, but we can stop it from developing.'

'Hmmm . . .'

'I have contacted our minister for social welfare about this. I explained the five major causes of psychopathy. Shall I tell you what they are?'

The sergeant hesitates for a moment.

'Anyone can understand,' Will continues. 'Do you have, or did you have a mother? Well, if you had a mother you will understand. All children see their mothers as ramparts, shields against a hostile world. When children see someone attack their mother, they naturally think the attacker wants to kill her and they think: once she's dead, I'll be the next one wiped out.'

'Hmmm . . .'

'So the child, even if its mother isn't killed, will repress this hateful image of aggression. The image is buried deep in the subconscious and that's where it causes terrible damage that may transform the child into a criminal.'

'Hmmm . . .'

'Believe me, I have forty years of experience, and all these theories have been thoroughly proven. The second cause is when the child is present during a sexual act involving its mother and believes she is being attacked when she is merely engaging in carnal activity. Are you with me?'

'Yes, yes.'

'If a child is more than six months of age, but not yet old enough to understand what is really going on, and sees or hears its mother having sexual relations with a man, it believes that man is killing the mother. The child then becomes a psychopath.'

'Is that so?'

'That's why so many terrorists come from large families living in confined spaces, sometimes in a single room, or in slums. That's precisely the case with Bobby Sands of the IRA.

'There's also the late adoption factor. A baby must be adopted literally within an hour of its birth. Otherwise it feels tricked because the bond it formed with its mother is broken without the baby understanding why. So then it decides that it must not form an attachment with anyone.'

'Hmmm . . .' the sergeant says, shaking his head.

'You're sceptical, I expected that. These things aren't well known in this country. But if you look closely, you'll see that a large number of murders are committed by victims of late adoption. Take Dally's murder of Karla Cardno, or Coulam killing that English tourist at Mount Maunganui, Holdem and Louisa Damodran, or the death of Mrs Irving and her daughter at the hands of her adopted son. I assure you, our prisons are full of people suffering from late adoption.'

The sergeant answers slowly: 'Some people say they're full because of poverty.'

'Yes, but how are you going to solve the problem of poverty? We can do something about adoption. I wrote to the minister of social welfare.'

'And what did she say?'

'That she agreed with me. Do you think we'd be having a crisis in the Middle East if Saddam Hussein's mother had given him up for adoption at birth, instead of waiting several weeks?'

The policeman is starting to smile. 'I don't really know. But you say you have assisted the English police?'

'Certainly. When there was a serial arsonist in York, I gave them the perpetrator's personality; all they had to do was pick him up.'

'Just pick him up, you say?'

Will can feel the sergeant's mind whirring like a well-oiled machine. Guessing his bemusement, he makes an extra effort and becomes even more excited: 'I've only given you three of the five causes.'

'Well, that's a pretty good start. Yours is a wonderful profession. But you know, we arrest delinquents, not psychopaths.'

'Exactly my point. They're psychopaths before they turn into delinquents. That's how we can put a stop to petty crime. Between you and me, do you know how many pyromaniacs there are in the Fire Service? Wouldn't it be better to test applicants instead of hiring cryptopyromaniacs?'

'Cryptopyromaniacs, you say? If we start arresting people before they commit a crime, our prisons will get pretty full.'

'Of course,' Will replies, 'it's not a matter of arresting innocent people. But look, I'm giving a lecture next Thursday. All welcome. If you let me put up this poster on the premises here,' he adds with a smile, 'I think it would be useful for quite a few of your staff.'

'You may be right,' the policeman says, apparently pleased that's all Will wants, to put up a poster. 'Why not? May I see?'

He looks at it for a moment, then, smiling faintly, promises Will he'll put it on a noticeboard where everyone will see it. 'Who knows,' he concludes, 'someone might find it interesting.'

As he leaves, Will wonders what kind of childhood led the man to choose this profession.

But he hasn't picked up any clues to begin his deductions. And when he gets out in front of the building again, he is stunned to realise his bike has disappeared. He is pacing up and down when a policeman – big, beer-bellied, no helmet to hide his baldness – comes out and asks him what he's looking for. 'My bike,' mumbles Will.

The policeman gestures to him to follow, and they go round the side of the building into a courtyard where three police cars are parked. The bike is in a corner, a piece of paper taped to the frame. The policeman bends down to read the paper and says: 'You've got a fifty dollar fine for leaning it against the front wall.'

'What?' says Will, furious. 'I come here to give you a hand and I'm the one who has to pay?'

'Give us a hand doing what?' the policeman asks.

'I'm preventing criminal arson . . . We'll see about this!' he says, grabbing the piece of paper. He strides into the police station and knocks on the door of Holmes' office: the sergeant, magnanimous, cancels the ticket without asking even one question. As Will tries to thank him, the officer looks at him thoughtfully. 'Bodmin,' he says, 'Bodmin. You wouldn't be one of the Franklin Bodmin family . . . the inventor?'

'His son,' says Will. 'His only son.' He stands there for a moment, biting back the rest: he used to say I would never be any use to anyone.

There's a tiny hint of triumph in his voice when he announces to the fat policeman that his fine has been cancelled. The big man shrugs: 'Next time, don't forget to put your bike in the courtyard.'

Will leaps to the saddle without answering and pumps the pedals furiously to make a quick getaway. He cannons through the alleyway and out onto Don Street so fast there isn't time to look, and he avoids the car coming from his left only by swerving sharply to the right, into a low wall. The impact throws him over the handlebars but, luckily for him, he lands on a narrow strip of grass. He checks, he's just a bit groggy and above all put out to see the fat policeman coming towards him, shaking his head the way Winnie likes to do. 'It's nothing, I'm not hurt,' says Will, struggling to his feet.

'Where's your helmet? Don't you have a helmet?'

They're staring each other down now, and Will can sense the aggression in the man in uniform. But he also knows he can't give him a ticket. The policeman merely says: 'You really ought to wear one. I know there's no law to make you, but next time it might save your life.'

Will mutters a sullen thank you. He's furious: he's usually the one who gives advice. And the worst of it is, when he picks up his bike he sees that the front wheel is buckled and can't turn because it's rubbing against the fork. So he lifts the front off the ground, pushing the bike on its rear wheel, and leaves without looking behind him at the cop who is probably still shaking his head. He sets off down Don Street, murmuring 'cryptopyros' as he passes the Fire Station. He's three kilometres from home, so there's no way he can drag this wounded beast that far, rearing up on its hind wheel, the pedals smacking him in the shins. He'll have to find a petrol station where they can keep it until Winnie can come and get it in her car – or better still, the neighbours themselves with their roomy new station-wagon. As he walks, Will broods over the stunning revenge he will take at the lecture on

Thursday. He'll talk about Hitler because that's a name even policemen will recognise. Would Adolf Hitler have ordered the burning of London, he'll demand, if his father hadn't beaten him because he wet his bed? Would he have set fire to Warsaw, otherwise? Historians have told us he hated central heating because it deprived him of the pleasure of lighting the fire himself.

He'll lay out before them the hidden causes of history, he'll talk about Henry the Eighth and focus on the great figures of the past! Great figures who, over time, have become his constant companions and no longer impress him. But he has hardly finished imagining the show in his head than a horrible thought occurs to him: we can manipulate history, interpret it, even transform it, but we cannot alter the tiniest little thing that happens to us. For example, his collision with the wall. And the telephone pole he broke his nose against when he was thirteen . . .

From time to time, he catches a glimpse of his reflection in a window: a tall, thin old man with a pencil moustache and almost completely white hair, walking along hunched over some strange contraption propped on its rear wheel. He wonders who he looks like this way, which person from history – Daumier's Don Quixote comes to mind, or maybe a centaur – but most of all he hopes no one will recognise him as the Bodmin boy looking for a workshop to repair his bike. And in the city where his father set up a famous workshop, too, Bodmin's Bike Shop – right here on Don Street, what's more; but where exactly? Wasn't there a brothel opposite? – and developed an ultramodern cycle reputed to have no rival this side of London. Even better, his father was a race-winning cyclist. Franklin Bodmin was the king of the bicycle, the motorbike, the hot-air balloon, the car, but his son Will is nothing but an imaginary rider with no mount. His father's photo comes back to him clearly – his fine moustache and wide-lapelled jacket over a shiny silk shirt, no tie – playing the banjo and singing a song he wrote himself to sell his bicycles. The salesman artiste, the sportsman artiste, the artiste advertising himself – his father. Will could still hum along to that song. It was called 'The Wheelman's Song':

Life is a wheel and when it buckles,
You feel completely stuck . . .

Ah yes, life is a wheel. He used to say I would never be any use to anyone . . . Will drops the bike off at the first petrol station he finds and takes the bus – he's strangely tired, but relieved to be anonymous again, one passenger among many.

When he gets to Stewart Terrace, he almost sneaks into the house, through the kitchen door. He's hungry again, but he'll wait a while. He can hear Winnie humming in the sitting room, busy with the jigsaw puzzle she's been working on for two or three weeks, a scene from Ancient Rome.

He drops into an armchair and complains about having to catch the bus. He announces he's going to buy himself a proper bike. The neighbours can take care of picking up this one. But he's only going to pay for half the cost of repairs.

Hearing this, his sister looks up from her puzzle. 'Why just half?'

'Why should I put a new wheel on their old wreck?'

'You borrowed it.'

'If I pay for everything, they'll just keep on living in their own little world and never face up to reality.'

'You have to know how to compromise,' Winnie said. 'I'm sure they'll come with me eventually to a Christian Science meeting. Emily anyway.'

Will doesn't answer. How can you tell her the blasted bike made him look a fool, probably made him lose his credibility with the police? Because those people never see beyond the surface appearance . . . The problem is, he knows if he pays for just half the repairs, his sister will make up the difference. Too bad for her. You can't teach some people anything.

Which leaves Sergeant Holmes.

'He's the kind of fellow,' says Will, 'who looks normal but must have had to fight his psychopathic tendencies by taking the side of the law. He must have had a mother who smoked and left him to go to work.'

'So?' says Winnie.

'Well, it's obvious he won't come to hear me talk about how to detect psychopaths. He really doesn't want to see my methods put into practice. That would be a threat to him. Yet another pyromaniac fireman.'

'Hmmm . . .' she responds.

'He also mentioned our father, the great scientist who left school before he was twelve!'

'What did he say about him?'

'Not much. He was just trying to make me feel inferior.'

But he says nothing about the letter from Australia. As he let himself back into the house, mentally rehearsing the complaints he was going to make to his sister, he found it again, mysteriously back in the same pocket as the aerogramme.

And now he can torture himself wondering why the letter disappeared, hidden behind the other one. Clearly another touch of the invisible hand.

The invisible hand . . . could you ever escape it?

He could really do with a rest, just to hide away and fill himself with television and forget, be nobody.

A GUIDING STAR

He didn't know him, Will notes in the margin of an article about his father in the *New Zealand Home Journal* in 1950. But the author accused of not knowing Franklin Bodmin was none other than cousin Bertie, the one who went for rides in the Reo and the hot-air balloon, and who, because he was fifteen years older than Will, had spent more time with the inventor than he had.

My father has always been distant, Will writes. I don't even know if I suffered as a result, because that distance allowed me to transform him into a hero. But when he came home to Invercargill, the atmosphere in the house changed at once: everyone was at his beck and call, and he made my life difficult. He despised me because I wasn't good at sport. I wasn't trying, he said. I think to be honest I would have given anything to make him proud of me. But it was beyond me: to be a Bodmin after his own heart, I would have had to beat all my friends, be first in everything, be really gifted. And since I wasn't superhuman I kept a low profile, which made him contemptuous of me. He accused me of being mollycoddled by women. Of being handicapped, taking advantage. And then he stopped talking to me, stopped seeing me. As if the sight of me hurt his eyes.

My sister Julia wrote poems in his honour. At thirteen, she had one published in the local paper and everyone

70

proclaimed her a genius. My father's real son was a daughter. Even he was full of pride in her work, because Julia had discovered how to flatter him. In her poem, he wasn't the deserter who was interested in everything but his family, no, he was an absentee, exiled for love of his family, suffering and sacrificing himself for others' happiness, 'just a lone Dad giving his life / To smooth the way for children and wife / Doing with courage stern and grim / The deeds that his father did for him.' In a way, even though it still sets my teeth on edge to say it, Julia hit the nail right on the head, because Grandfather Bodmin had actually been a hideous tyrant. But for Julia, writing was a matter of dressing up reality, making it pretty, and she used poetry as a kind of make-up. Maybe she lived in the mirror of beauty that our father held in front of her. Because he smoothed things over too. He would promise to take Julia to the US then forget his promise. He would talk about rings and necklaces, but not remember them until he landed in Auckland, where he would buy a few pieces of cheap costume jewellery. Well, Julia was proud of them anyway.

I idealised him too. But since he never promised me anything any more, I think I saw him more clearly than Julia. Still, I must have thought of him as a god because I was dreadfully disappointed to realise he was fallible – feeble, even, because you could fool him through flattery. The incident I recall in this context happened a few weeks after he died at sea. The crew of the boat he died on had sent us his trunk with his personal effects, and inside it we found a book he had carried everywhere with him for years, a thick, leather-bound volume I had often seen on his bedside table and taken to be a bible. When I opened it I saw that it was an anthology of English and American poetry, a thousand pages of the best and the worst together: on one hand Shakespeare and Keats, on the other a bunch of empty versifiers, sententious or sentimental. My father might have been a serious inventor, but he was a poet the way he was a painter, musician or athlete: he was a poser, and in poetry it was the most lyrical verses, the ones that brought tears to his melodramatic eyes, that he liked best.

When he sang, he would sometimes recite a few pensive lines between songs, punctuating them with a few notes on his guitar. I remember one poem he recited often, in which it was a matter of the 'sublime', supposedly out of reach in our narrow lives, meaning that when we shrug off 'our earthly husk' we leave behind us nothing more than 'footsteps on the sands of time'. He followed these lines with two or three gloomy chords, and there were always people in the audience who would pull out their handkerchiefs. Perhaps not my mother, because by this time she had already stopped coming to my father's soirées.

Was this poem in the anthology he took everywhere with him? Subconsciously that's what I was looking for as I flicked through the pages after he died. Instead of the famous footstep echoing in my head, I found another trace – both the opposite and the truth of the first one, so to speak – on the flyleaf. It was an inscription written by the editorial writer of the New York Times who had given him the book.

> *To my friend Franklin Bodmin, Inventor and Artiste,*
> *Beloved child of the gods, inspired disciple of Leonardo,*
> *Rival of Captain Cook, beacon of the New World,*
> *A Magician who draws from the shadows the flame*
> *of the bright future.*

Ah, the bright future . . . I was immediately overwhelmed by the certainty that out of these thousand years of poetry, this was the poem he found the loveliest and truest. I don't know what his relationship was with the journalist. Maybe he had lent him money, because greed was not one of his vices, but when I read this inscription I was embarrassed for my father, ashamed to see that he hadn't torn it out – which would have shown that the book had a value beyond that – and I remember showing it to my mother with an indignant expression. But she just shrugged her shoulders, she'd already seen it, Franklin had made sure to show it to her on more than one occasion. She no longer had any opinion on the matter; for her it was just a bit of the frothiness the world is forever producing and that it is best to ignore. It was more than that for me. Someone had ridiculed my father – seriously and deliberately – and the man, our hero, had enjoyed it, had lapped it up. I was nineteen. These days I probably wouldn't be scandalised. But back then, he disappointed me as never before. Perhaps because he had just died and I was trying to protect him.

My entire family thinks that it was I who disappointed him, and they're probably right. But didn't he push me into failure? He never encouraged me, and whatever I undertook was, in his eyes, invariably ludicrous, poorly conceived, badly executed. He didn't know the word 'neurotic', otherwise he would have applied it to me mercilessly. The more he became the great man, the outstanding inventor so vaunted by the *Encyclopedia of New Zealand*, the more inaccessible he became. He needed to prove his own greatness, even to himself, and we, his children – and I in particular, I admit – were the shining proof of his ordinariness, his peasant origins, his anti-genius. To be the genius people saw in him, he needed to go away, on a boat or in a balloon, by whatever means possible, as long as he left us behind. And I have followed his example in this respect, because the only poem I have attempted in imitation of my big sister Julia says just one thing: 'Let me board when the sun goes down / Into the sunset, over the sea / The wild sea-birds are calling me.'

But was I leaving him when I departed, or was I following him?

73

For years I lived in a kind of fear of what I might find out about him. His diary could probably have told me something about the more obscure episodes of his life, but I didn't have time to study it in detail. As soon as his trunk reached us from the ship he died on, my mother and aunts complained about how little it held. My mother even talked about theft. There was clothing, two or three boxes full of correspondence and among the few books – which included the famous anthology I had thought was a bible – was a fat moleskin-bound notebook where my father had made intermittent diary entries over several years. I opened it, not in the middle but at the end, and came across an extraordinary project: a film about his life. A producer was working on it, a scriptwriter had been hired, they were thinking of Errol Flynn to play my father. A grand finale that struck me as so unreal that I burst out laughing and rushed across to my mother, pointing at this entry in the diary. 'Where did you get that notebook?' she cried. Without waiting for me to answer, she snatched it out of my hands and looked through it, declaring a few seconds later that she forbade me to read it before she did. Speechless that my mother had forbidden me to do something, especially now that I was nineteen, I rebelled, shouting, 'I'm the one who found it, give it back!' and trying to take it from her by force. But she told me sharply that at that point I had no business sticking my nose in my father's 'private life', and I gave in.

I was so offended I left the room, swearing I would never look at anything else to do with my father. And then a few weeks later, when I had calmed down, I changed my mind and asked my mother to give me the diary. She answered that it had disappeared. I couldn't believe it. 'I gave it to Winnie,' she explained, 'and I don't know what she did with it. In any case, there was nothing interesting in it.'

By what right had she passed it on to one of my sisters, when she wouldn't give it to me, the only boy and therefore my father's rightful heir? I went to talk to Winnie, who seemed very embarrassed before finally admitting she had burned it. 'Because there were things in it,' she said, 'that were nobody else's business . . . Dirty things,' she even added. She had the gall to claim it was to protect him.

I was stunned. Who gave her permission to act this way? 'And what do the others think about this?' I exclaimed.

Well, the others thought nothing about it. We were so used to idealising our father that no one really cared about a document that might bring him back down to earth, tarnish his image and, by association, ours too. Besides which, there was no need to give credence to what was written in the diary if it contradicted what we knew about him. In reality he'd been dead to us for a long time already.

But after that little incident I began to fear the time bombs my father might have bequeathed us. And so it was that two years later an American woman got off the boat in Auckland and went to call on one of my sisters. She claimed that Franklin Bodmin had fathered her son in the United States and that he had promised her one of the Ming vases from his collection. She was sure he had mentioned it in his will and that his official family had hatched a scheme to exclude her. There was a letter from Franklin, she claimed, proving what she said and if we did not give in to her demands she would sue us. My sister showed her the door and we were never sued. Nevertheless we wondered, without daring to put it into words, why such a respectable and virtuous father had been involved, even at a distance, with a woman like that.

I became aware that I didn't know him very well, or at least that I knew only one aspect of him. I didn't even know what had become of his inventions or what they were exactly. He really was 'our father who art elsewhere'. He came home from America every two years to make my mother pregnant. But being the youngest child, I didn't see that either.

What I realised was that I was such a disappointment to

him that he didn't want to know what I was up to. Sometimes I think he would have preferred that I had never been born, even though he wanted a boy and made plenty of nasty comments to my mother over her incompetence in giving him seven daughters in a row. It might have been better for him to have an eighth girl. Then he could have considered his task as a sire was not yet complete, whereas when I arrived the cycle came to an end, and twenty years of shaky marriage were suddenly revealed in the light of day.

I mention this with a certain detachment. For many years I was totally unable to see things so clearly and it took another incident, someone I met in England when I was already thirty-five, to open my eyes a little. This was towards the end of the 1950s, when I visited the village where Captain Cook spent his childhood. And it's no coincidence that I'm talking about Cook. James Cook is the father I chose for myself in my teenage years – he wasn't any more absent than my biological father, and he was truer. So that day I had taken the train to Middlesbrough, in the northeast of England, and was sitting across from a family I found cheerful and attractive: a man about my own age, his wife, who had a ready laugh, and their daughter, aged seven or eight. I was struck by the man's good humour, by his confident happiness. I had the impression he was also watching me surreptitiously, with some curiosity.

I arrived the next day in the village of Staithes where Cook, in his early teens, had worked in the general store of one William Sanderson. I was thinking of the lovely story that some of his biographers recount. This Sanderson was apparently a short-tempered fellow, and fond of the bottle. One day when he had gone to the pub to sink a few jars, leaving Cook in charge of the shop, young James spotted a beautiful brand new shilling in the till – from the South Seas series struck in 1723 – and, finding it particularly appealing, had exchanged it for another, more ordinary one that he had in his pocket. Back from the bar, Mr Sanderson immediately checked if the new shilling was still there. On not seeing it, he accused James, who initially protested his innocence before confessing. Sanderson then fired him for lying. But since he wasn't such a bad chap when sober, he recommended young Cook to a Quaker by the name of Walker who took the lad in. Walker owned several ships, notably a collier called the *Freelove* on which Cook did his apprenticeship (I was to find the logbook of this same vessel a few years after my visit to Staithes). And so it was an injustice that led Cook to the Quaker and set him on the path to his career as a sailor. In addition – and I found this quite wonderful – Cook was able to change fathers to find one who suited him better than his predecessor. A reassuring story if ever there was one, and which, I hope, was not invented to add to the legend. In any case there I was, walking down Church Street looking for the cottage where James Cook was supposed to have lived, when I came across the family I had seen the day before on the train. Surprised, we greeted one another and at once struck up a conversation as if to make up for not having done so earlier. The coincidences that connected us were astonishing. Not only did the couple admire Captain Cook, but the man had the same first name as me and also worked in a psychiatric hospital. It turned out we weren't quite the same age: he was three years younger. Since it was almost midday, we discussed lunch and I told them I had always dreamed of being a vegetarian, but that I couldn't do it yet because I took my meals at the hospital. Once I was married and back home in New Zealand, I would live as I wished . . . So, the other Will exclaimed, laughing, you're a New Zealander? And without missing a beat he asked what my surname was. When I answered 'Bodmin', he looked shocked and asked me to repeat it. Even his wife was wide-eyed. I added that I was from Invercargill, which seemed only to disconcert him even more. They exchanged glances, furtively, and their smiles were strained. When I asked what was wrong, the other Will merely shrugged his shoulders then looked at his watch and said he hadn't realised what the time was and they had an engagement. Then they moved off swiftly towards the harbour without visiting Cook's cottage.

I was speechless, almost wounded, and it wasn't until a few minutes later, thinking about how much Will resembled me physically, that I thought I understood. I ran after them, I looked for them, but despite my best efforts, I couldn't find them. I even wondered, the following day, whether I hadn't dreamed it. And this episode became all the more unreal in my head because I didn't feel I could talk to my mother or sisters about it.

A few days later, I realised I had been afraid for years of finding myself face to face with another son of my father – a younger son, more to his taste, who would have made up for the disappointments I had inflicted on him . . .

BODMIN SENIOR

Franklin Bodmin was born in Marylebone, London, in 1869. His father was a fireman, in charge of the Crystal Palace Station; a heavy man with a face partly consumed by a dark beard, he kept his household in order with a brutality based on religious fervour. He fathered eight children, three of whom died in infancy. Franklin, the third, was eleven years younger than the first child, and this was not the worst position amongst his siblings. The oldest boy was to commit suicide barely two years after marrying, while the second son, who married very young, became an alcoholic and was sadly well-known for his brutal attacks on his wife.

Franklin later stated that he was stronger than his father, but he may have benefited from his mother's extra support precisely because he was weak. He couldn't walk. By the age of seven he was still not able to stand upright and it was feared he would remain an invalid all his life. This sickly child was a source of humiliation to the chief of the brigade, so proud of his physical prowess. He adopted the habit of not looking at little Franklin and speaking to him as seldom as possible. His sullen and unspoken hostility towards the cripple (as Franklin was called) ate away at him all the same and invariably led to his exploding with rage against the older boys. Outside the home, this brutal fireman had a reputation for bravery and generosity, especially in connection with a dog, a Saint Bernard he had trained with great care, that went with him on dangerous rescue missions and had saved a number of lives. Franklin would later confide to his wife that the dog had terrorised him. It was allowed to sleep outside his parents' bedroom door, even though there was an enclosed yard at the back of the house, and once it had lain down in the corridor none of the younger children could get by without running the risk of being bitten; with the result that those who wanted to go to the toilet – chamber pots were forbidden for hygiene reasons – could not do so without shouting or crying very loudly, waking their mother, the dog, their father, and being berated for it. Because of his handicap, Franklin had permission to call out so as to avoid wetting his bed, and he did not hesitate to do so.

He never felt he had 'refused' to walk. That term is his son Will's. Whenever he talked about it, which happened very rarely, Franklin merely said he had suffered from paralysis. But the story of his cure has been handed down in the family like a legend. It all happened when Franklin was nearly eight years old. Prayer and medical science having failed to produce results, Franklin's mother was quite desperate when she heard stories of a new doctor who was accomplishing wonders at the university hospital not far from where they lived. She wanted to consult this famous Dr Ross, but it took several months to convince her husband, who, he said, didn't want to spend more money on another charlatan. So in the end she went to the appointment with a neighbour, pushing Franklin in the perambulator which was now too small for him and left his extremities hanging over the sides like spider's legs. Dr Ross had spent time abroad; amongst other things he had studied Dr Duchenne's experiments with electricity in Paris and attended some of Jean-Martin Charcot's classes at the Salpêtrière hospital. After carefully examining the boy and pursing his lips in doubt a number of times, he withheld his diagnosis, mentioned electrotherapy (when Mrs Bodmin plucked up her courage to ask for an explanation, she was told it was simply a matter of passing an electric current through the boy to improve his nerve impulses), then decided to see Franklin again at the University College hospital. Two weeks later, Mrs Bodmin set out again with Franklin in the little pram and the same neighbour. At the hospital, she waited in a hallway until someone came for her and took her through a side door into a small lecture theatre where Dr Ross was standing in his fine black suit, and asked her to come up on stage. In front of her, the room was filled with people of all ages; she could see their pens and spectacles glittering. The doctor turned to the audience and said: 'This is the boy I was telling you about, who has never walked.' Then to Mrs Bodmin: 'Kindly leave the boy, Madam.' She stood still. The professor, like a tall, calm, black tree, called solemnly to Franklin: 'Now stand up and come to me.' And as Mrs Bodmin would later tell her husband, the boy put his feet on the ground, stood up with apparent ease and staggered over to the professor. The audience held its breath, the room was plunged into an almost religious silence, and Mrs Bodmin claimed to have become giddy and disoriented, gathering her wits again only when she saw Dr Ross take Franklin by the hand, walk him slowly across the front of the stage and bring him back to her, saying: 'We shall have no need of electricity. There you are. Goodbye, Madam.'

She left without seeking any explanation for this miracle, letting Franklin collapse into his pram before throwing herself, weeping, into the arms of her neighbour.

From then on, Franklin continued to walk. Dr Ross was so pleased with him that he came to visit the family shortly afterwards, but Bodmin senior, who hadn't been especially keen on seeing him, got home too late to talk to him. After several days of hostile silence, believing the little brat had been making fools of them, he spoke to his son only to announce he would now have to go to school.

Franklin would later play down his legendary recovery. He had walked, he said, not because of some doctor but because of himself. In adulthood no one could remember him ever spending as much as a single day in bed. And, according to Will, he showed no compassion towards the sick: fakers and layabouts! he would say angrily.

Once Will had given up the pram and his mother's arms, he needed to invent some other means of escape from paternal tyranny. In the meantime, he endured the ordeal of school. He didn't care to be with children far younger than he was, nor to put up with being treated like them. His rebelliousness led to negative comments from the teacher and thus to reproaches, even blows, from his father. At the age of twelve, he began attending the same prep school his brothers had gone to, and there his academic difficulties were impossible to overcome. When he realised his marks for the first term were going to be disastrous, he decided to run away. He managed to hire on as a cabin boy on the ship that was to lay the two ends of the undersea cable linking Nagasaki and Vladivostok. He had grown so big and strong since his paralysis years that he was able to pass for a boy of fourteen. He told the ship's officer he was an orphan – probably no more than half a lie, since he was less afraid of the outside world than of the family home. The year was 1882. Even though it was nothing like a pleasure cruise because everyone, including him, was forced to do all the cleaning, the sea voyage was like being set free. Sadly, he was picked up in Japan by the English consul. His father had alerted the authorities and the captain was obliged to hand the boy over to the Japanese police when the ship arrived in Nagasaki. Three days later, Franklin headed back to London on an English boat where he was harshly treated, like some petty criminal. He was frightened of returning to London, probably preparing in his mind for the fight with his father, but he was also overjoyed because he had already travelled further than Bodmin senior.

To his astonishment, he was not badly received. Old George Bodmin simply decided that the runaway was wasting his time at school and apprenticed him to Shand, Mason & Co, builders of fire engines. Naturally George Bodmin had contacts with the firm because they supplied his fire station, but he had not given up on the idea of turning this odd lad into a fire fighter, all the more so now that he had proved himself by running away so dramatically.

Franklin later proudly claimed he had marked out his territory and forced his father to respect him. His apprenticeship was less painful to him than school: the foreman at Shand's liked him, and was even surprised by how quickly he could grasp the functioning of the machines without referring to any diagrams. But when Franklin suggested improvements to the way the workshop was organised, the foreman laughed at him; he was overstepping the bounds of his role as apprentice. He went through a difficult period then, feeling himself falling back into apathy, a slowness that reminded him of the worst moments in his life, his childhood paralysis. The situation at home was still as hateful, even though the family was moderately well-off – a three-storey house where, astonishingly, Franklin was the only one to have his own room. At sixteen, he decided he couldn't take it any more; he was going to leave, whatever the cost. Just as he had done four years earlier, but this time it would be for good. And he would announce his departure. The day before he left, he informed his parents that he had been taken on as a cabin boy on the *Nelson*. His father, sitting at the table by himself, almost choked. But he held his tongue and let his wife ask where the young man was planning to go. 'This ship,' Franklin answered, 'sails round Africa and takes passengers to Australia and New Zealand.' His mother asked if he intended to settle there, telling him it would be a serious mistake because there was no work in those countries. In their own neighbourhood alone, two people had come home from New Zealand because of the economic situation. In any case, his father declared, people who went away had bought land or knew what they were going to do on arrival.

Franklin heard a note of near entreaty in his father's voice. But now was not the time to listen to him. He replied that he was going to work on a boat in the meantime and had no plans to settle anywhere.

His father finished his meal without saying another word. The following day when Franklin went to say goodbye, he wasn't home.

The *Nelson* sailed from Gravesend in September 1886, on a voyage to New Zealand that would take three months. The work on board was exhausting and uninteresting: Franklin had to swab the decks, polish the brass and generally do any cleaning he was asked to do. But he had no complaints. He was even happy and could feel himself growing stronger. The cabin boys organised a competition between them, which he won with ease, folding the greatest number of towels within the time limit. He would boast of this for a long time to come. Even if it seemed ludicrous to his listeners, Franklin insisted this competition was the first in a long series of successes. At the end of his life, he had progressed to claiming he had never met with failure – merely encountered obstacles that allowed him to test his skills and strengthen his determination. What didn't kill me made me stronger, he would announce.

The *Nelson* finally reached New Zealand, berthing in the Otago Harbour at Port Chalmers, where connecting trains ran to Dunedin and the interior of the country. It was late December and a lovely day. The peninsula and the islands sparkled on the blue sea, and Franklin couldn't wait to set foot on dry land, to leave behind the confined space of a crowded boat. They spoke English in Port Chalmers, and in the city of Dunedin a few miles away, and yet geographically he could not have been further from England. It was both like home – there were so many familiar things – and completely exotic. Christmas was going to be celebrated in the middle of summer, surrounded by flowers and fruit. There was a tremendous sense of freedom.

He didn't know a soul in this country, but he was seventeen years old and knew no fear. In just two days he found a job at a photographer's. He had simply gone into the shop and struck up a conversation with the owner, a dry little man with pepper and salt hair and a white goatee, who was preparing his equipment to go and take pictures of a wedding the next day. He wanted to sell two of his cameras because they weren't working very well. Franklin asked to see them and worked out immediately why the shutter on the first one was sticking. The photographer didn't seem overly impressed: he knew what was wrong too, but he didn't have the spare parts to repair it. No need for spare parts, Franklin stated, you just need to straighten the lens shutter. I can do that for you. Have you got a penknife? A penknife? A penknife and a pair of tweezers, Franklin added. After a more detailed discussion, the photographer brought what he needed and, under his watchful eye, Franklin got the mechanism in working order in under five minutes. It was almost magic. I just have to be interested in a machine, he would explain later, and I can see how to make it work. Contrary to popular belief, no two machines are the same; each has its own personality, even. Something the old goat-bearded photographer didn't seem to know. He had moved from painting to photography to follow customer demand, but had never really much cared for the mechanical side of things.

He was nevertheless sufficiently impressed by the young man from the *Nelson* to suggest he go with him the next day to photograph the wedding, an invitation Franklin gladly accepted. The following Monday, Jay Stephens took him on as his assistant, and Franklin decided to let the ship leave without him – it was illegal of course, but he knew they wouldn't find him before they sailed.

Thanks to Jay Stephens, he also learned to paint in oils. The old artist still did portraits and asked Franklin not only to mix his colours from pigments, but also to prepare his canvases, and sometimes to paint the background.

In those days there were only seven hundred thousand inhabitants in the whole of New Zealand, and the city of Dunedin was a quarter the size of Marylebone where Franklin was born. But he understood at once that he would be needed here, that the country was developing in spite of the economic situation the English newspapers were making much of. And he felt he had a gift. This wasn't just empty excitement, but a superiority he could see in his boundless energy and the skills he could draw on so effortlessly, almost without thinking, when confronted by any kind of practical problem. He had avoided all sport in England, but here he took up swimming, running, cycle racing. In a short time he became outstanding, winning his races. He trained as a light-heavyweight boxer and won an amateur title. At twenty-one, this former weakling who couldn't walk had become one of the region's best athletes. He enjoyed cycling so much that he left his photographic employment and went to work for Stedman's Cycles, where he very quickly improved the dealer's pedal and gear mechanism. He had matured: in four years he had learned not to give his ideas away if he wanted to profit from them. And when he realised there was no hope of a better position at Stedman's unless he could invest funds he didn't have, he decided to join an Invercargill cycle manufacturer where, in 1893, he became a partner. At twenty-four years of age, he was ready for new adventures.

He met Florence Harper the following year. She was nineteen and living in Winton, where she had moved with her father. This village, some fifty miles north of Invercargill, was an important rail junction, and Mr Harper, works supervisor for the Railways, had been transferred there, leaving Whanganui with some regret. Florence was only fourteen when her mother died, leaving six daughters in the care of a man who had no idea how to bring them up. Florence, the second eldest, took charge with amazing courage, looking after her two youngest sisters and assisting her father better than the eldest daughter. In spite of this devotion, Mr Harper, in need of female company, remarried two years later. Two babies were quickly added to the family, which meant the Harper family now consisted of ten people crammed into the little house in Winton, and tensions between the new wife and the older girls degenerated more and more frequently into open conflict. A hard-working, quiet man, Harper couldn't cope with this situation and turned to drink. Intoxicated, he was brutal, striking out at everyone so they would leave him be; even sober, he became increasingly morose, bloated and worn-out from over-indulgence, work and fatherhood. Then his wife fell pregnant again.

When Franklin arrived on the scene, Florence took him for a knight in shining armour. He had come to sell Sparrowhawk bicycles – the ones he manufactured with the Southland Cycle Works, of such outstanding quality they were proudly exported even to far-off England – to the Railways management. Florence's father was also amongst his customers. Franklin, a member of the Invercargill Cycling Club, was well known as a competitor in regional races, and he was wearing a blue and white striped competition jersey when he appeared one evening at the Harpers' home to complete a sale. To Florence, he was a fine figure of a man: smiling, athletic, blue-eyed, and with a pencil moustache.

Florence worked as a milliner in a small workshop, where her skills were much prized. Onto a fabric-covered base made of interwoven wires, she would sew feathers, ribbons, and a rainbow of silk flowers, sometimes fruit or birds. She hadn't yet been asked to make cyclists' hats, which were plainer, smaller, and supposed to fit tightly on the head. She was a little afraid of bicycles, or rather, they seemed beyond her reach. Of course she had heard about the exploits of Alice Bum, who had taken on the men in a race in Oamaru. But she also knew that women cyclists were often poorly thought of. They were accused of being suffragettes, and although Florence had wholeheartedly applauded the 1893 law that made New Zealand the first country in the world to give women the vote, she was aware that many men, especially here in Winton, were reluctant to see them claiming a new freedom. They were often insulted: the newspapers reported cases where stones had been thrown at them, or boys had knocked them off their mounts or literally, put obstacles in their way. For safety, some of them formed clubs. It was also quite daring for women riding in public to wear what was called 'rational dress', in other words, bloomers. No, they had to wear skirts, although these were allowed to be shorter. Old man Harper referred contemptuously to 'cycladonnas', that is to say idle women from the middle classes who neglected their households. He claimed to know for a fact that the woman who founded the Dunedin Ladies' Cycling Club was a lesbian. With a few drinks in him, his accusations went up a notch and he would talk about rich bitches who smoked and did just what they pleased, even encouraging socialism. His new wife – nothing she did or said surprised Florence any more – approved unreservedly of everything he said. Florence held her tongue.

She could see at once that Franklin Bodmin was a man of a different mindset, that he belonged to the modern world. He loved bicycles, celebrated them in his songs, and in the meantime earned his livelihood from them. He was careful not to tell old man Harper what he thought of the vote for women, but when he left, Florence managed to be outside the house as he mounted his shiny green Sparrowhawk. Instead of pedalling off, he leaned over towards Florence and asked her if she knew how to ride. Blushing, she told him no, but she would very much like to learn. The words slipped out in a near whisper. 'That should be possible,' Franklin said with a pensive look, then mentioned a show he was to take part in the following Saturday, that she might like to bring a girlfriend to watch. She would see, she said, with a shrug. But she already knew which girlfriend she would ask, a friend she could also stay with overnight because it wouldn't be possible to get home to Winton by train that same evening.

A month later, Franklin was giving Florence riding lessons, but taking her to a place not much used by the Invercargill Cycling Club so as to keep this fact from Mr Harper.

As was the case for the suffragettes, the bicycle, from which Franklin was already earning a tidy income, became the instrument of Florence's emancipation. Their future was two-wheeled. Drawing on his experience in finding advertising slogans, Franklin threw himself boldly into singing the praises of his little queen, spinning the wheels of progress and fortune, while Florence, won over in turn by the magic of the velocipede, discovered that her clumsy efforts to master this little iron machine were a reflection of her efforts in other areas. She started to talk about the wheel of the will or the wheel of the mind. Franklin went one better, composing the early form of his famous cycling song where even the sun flashes its shiny spokes. He would sing it many times over the following year, accompanying himself on the banjo, before printing it on handbills with his photograph.

Since she didn't own a cycling costume, Florence practised in a long skirt, still wearing her hat which, despite its elegance, was no match for the gusty wind – which meant Franklin frequently rode behind her to catch it. Sometimes her hair would come down too, and Franklin would see a banner of shining chestnut hair rippling in the sunshine. He was dazzled, ecstatic at the sight of her silky curls, and Florence confided that she curled them herself with an iron when she had a moment to spare at the millinery workshop. She was trying to achieve what was known then as a Marcel wave – but she could rarely say she was satisfied with the result.

Florence had only just learned to manage a bicycle when they were married, in mid summer of 1896. Their first baby, Mary, was born six months later, at the same moment that Franklin was putting the final touches to his first invention, a mechanical eggbeater that could whip egg whites five times faster than usual. They had shortened the usual timeframe for producing a child, but as Franklin would later tell his son Will, this was out of respect for a custom the first New Zealand settlers held dear, not wishing to risk tying themselves to a barren woman. Will was suspicious of this witticism. He felt that his father was yet again indulging in a witty remark to avoid the truth, and he wrote in his notebooks that Florence's pregnancy had been the main reason for the marriage: 'My father didn't dare run away.'

But perhaps Franklin hadn't really wanted to run away, even if he did very soon begin to distance himself from the household. He continued to do several things at once, working with cycles for the Sparrowhawk firm, boxing and swimming, and even painting in oils. He had a repertoire of comic songs that he sang on Saturday evenings at private parties. Florence, busy with the baby, found it hard to keep up. She didn't even have time to ride her bicycle now, and she found the long days without her husband very tiring. She was under the impression he had promised her – or at the very least allowed her to be lured by – something else. It was over this period that Franklin created the majority of his household inventions: an airtight cover for food-storage tins, a burglar-proof window, an eggbeater that didn't slip across the bottom of the bowl, a post-hole borer that made fencing easier. He also designed a hedge-clipper made from bicycle parts, which was like converting the freedom associated with the cycle into a tool. He put enormous effort into improving an environment that belonged increasingly to Florence, but that he seemed at the same time to be avoiding. Others achieved the same results through money or gifts. But it was the transformation of an everyday object that would change the course of his life. Florence loved hats – they were the only extravagance that had allowed her to escape the dreary existence she led in her father's house. Franklin remembered the times he had run after Florence's hat as she pedalled beneath the tall trees of the club grounds. Good times, to be honest. And he had promised his wife he would find a way to keep her hat on without her having to tie the ribbons beneath her chin. Well, now he had done exactly that.

He had just designed some very unusual hairpins. Up till now hairpins had been straight, and Florence was constantly picking them up as they fell from her hair. Not only did he decide to make them wavy, he also added a swivelling head with two bars that kept them in place. Even when the wind was quite strong, hats and hairdos now stayed put. 'Not the Marcel wave, the Bodmin wave!' he announced proudly to Florence, showing her one of his first attempts, an ordinary hairpin he had improved with a pair of pliers. She tried it and found it worked perfectly. Franklin's invention, deservedly seen as revolutionary, spread like wildfire through New Zealand and Australia. He applied for a patent in Great Britain that would be granted in June 1900, and in the meantime had business cards printed, proclaiming himself:

FRANKLIN BODMIN
'THE MAN WHO PUT THE CRINKLE IN THE HAIRPIN'

Their life was about to change, they were both certain of it. However, Franklin was home even less than before, adding to his usual activities business trips to promote the hairpin. When he was held up in Melbourne for over three months while Florence was expecting again, she decided to invite her two youngest sisters to come and live with her. The situation in Winton had not improved, since a new baby had arrived – the ninth of old man Harper's daughters. And besides, Florence had made a promise to her two little sisters when their mother died: thanks to them, she had played a role within her father's household that suited her well, a role that had given her such a strong sense of importance that she missed it very much.

Franklin saw no objection to the arrival of his two young sisters-in-law. The older one, Margaret, who was eighteen, would probably marry soon. In the meantime, she would help Florence, who was going to be very busy with the new baby. And as for little Susan, who was only thirteen, she seemed a gifted student and would be able to attend a much better school in Invercargill. The two girls were a bit like cats, lively but, in spite of their charming smiles, reserved. They watched everything, wide-eyed, and refrained from talking too much. It would appear they liked the house, because they never married and would spend the rest of their lives with Florence and Franklin, becoming the Aunts Margaret and Susan who were to be so important to Will.

By helping Florence, Margaret made it possible for Franklin to spend more time at home. Perhaps he felt less obligated to lend a hand, perhaps he also enjoyed seeing his sisters-in-law fussing over him. He did manage to show them he was not like their father. He got out the bicycle Florence no longer used and suggested to Margaret that he teach her how to ride it, provoking a few protests from Florence, who quite rightly felt that now she had help, she could just as well use the bicycle to get around again herself. That's no problem, Franklin replied, and gave Margaret a bicycle so the two sisters might go riding together.

He was constantly on the go. A year after the hairpin he

applied to patent another invention, equally revolutionary, he claimed. This was 'the curler of the new century', consisting of a clip and a rubber ring which would apparently curl even the straightest hair. 'You'll be able to give yourself a Marcel without a curling iron,' he announced to Florence. He could already see himself in competition with hairdresser Marcel Grateau, the father of the famous Marcel wave. And like the Frenchman, he also asserted that every woman wanted curly hair. To put his curler on the market he joined forces with one of the McKay brothers, who were noted auctioneers, and travelled to Melbourne with him. Unfortunately the result was only middling and Franklin realised that to develop his products he needed a bigger market, Great Britain or North America. People say it was the McKay brothers, personal friends of Mark Twain (whom they had met during his visit to New Zealand in 1895) who persuaded Franklin to try his luck in New York.

So he sold his share in Sparrowhawk cycles, borrowed what he could and left. In order to save the money he would need for his business, he signed on again as crew. 'At thirty-one years of age,' he later told his daughter Julia, 'I found myself in a situation similar to when I left England. But it didn't worry me; my heart was full of hope.'

He wrote little to his wife, but he did tell her he liked New York, he had met Mark Twain and set up a company with him called Koy-Lo to manufacture the hairpin: Twain was vice-president. He came home fourteen months later, his return preceded by rumours of fame and fortune recounted in a number of newspaper articles. He had the foresight to bring back trunks full of gifts that he distibuted generously. In reality he had already put Koy-Lo on the backburner and sold the hairpin patent to an American manufacturer. Nevertheless he brought home the not inconsiderable sum of forty thousand dollars, which allowed him to build Rockhaven, Invercargill's most beautiful home.

He wanted it to be of stone, in the Scottish baronial style he had found so attractive in America. And spacious: the family needed room, since Florence was once again pregnant. He hoped this time it would be a boy.

He bought a section near Queen's Park, hired an architect and had the stone shipped from Green Island. In 1906, the local paper described in glowing terms the party he threw at the end of the major construction work. Three storeys, sixteen rooms, Art Nouveau leadlights, Persian carpets and, in the great drawing room, a display of paintings by Franklin Bodmin, pending the final decorative touches. Bodmin had painted famous nature scenes for the most part – like the ones the Thomas Cook agency featured to attract its clients to visit New Zealand.

Over the next three years, the rubber hair curler was his main source of income. He opened a new workshop on Don Street, where he added to his cycles an interest in a more recent invention, the motorbike.

Already elected to the Town Council, Franklin owed much of his popularity to the hot-air balloon he kept in Queen's Park. On Saturdays, for a modest price, he would offer bystanders a short ride in the balloon. He had become an important figure, and Rockhaven seemed a residence suited to his social standing. But his family had hardly moved into the great unfinished house than he left again for the United States, where he planned to purchase not only the metal sheets from which he would construct an original ceiling for his great drawing room, but also the golden oak to be used for the mantelpieces. To those who told him New Zealand could provide hardwoods of even better quality, he replied that without the oak he would never recreate the feeling that had inspired him to build Rockhaven.

He was thus absent another year, leaving a wife, two sisters-in-law and four very young daughters. He was already beginning to reproach Florence for being a real Harper, that is to say, for giving him only daughters and depriving him of his greatest desire, a male child, a proper little Bodmin.

His American business interests didn't seem to be developing very quickly, whereas in Invercargill Bodmin was at his peak. He painted, continued to sing – now in Gilbert and Sullivan operas – but being over forty he had given up the more demanding sports such as boxing and swimming. He found it harder to give up cycle racing – heart-breakingly difficult, in fact. He was particularly upset to be beaten by a rival not much younger than he was, a man he despised because he also claimed to be an inventor. This rival, by the name of Herbert Pither, even had the nerve to open a cycle sales and repairs workshop on Kelvin Street. He was a former champion cyclist who had tried for years to build a metal airplane and who, once this was achieved, claimed to have flown it. Since there were no witnesses to this exploit, Bodmin considered it was mere boasting – to be expected, he said, of such a suspect individual.

But although he could no longer win cycle races, Franklin Bodmin was more able than ever to put his mechanical genius to work, turning his attention to the combustion engine. He invented a device which vaporised the petrol injected into the cylinders, reducing consumption and increasing engine power, a kind of early version of the carburettor, and fitted it to two old motorbikes, Clement-Garrards that he had bought for his experiments. Next he tackled a local doctor's motorbike – the huge man rode an equally huge Singer. Thanks to what was called, successively, 'the Vaporiser' then 'the Bodmin Economiser', the doctor set off at meteoric speed, terrifying half the population on his way to attend a patient, and leaving in his wake a hellish stench of burning castor oil.

Buoyed up by these successes, Franklin moved on to automobiles. He imported into New Zealand the first Reos, luxury American vehicles reserved for rich customers.

Acquiring one for his own use, he fitted the motor with one of his Economisers and challenged all the competing brands of cars to a race between Invercargill and Dunedin, over three hundred miles return on roads that were sometimes very dangerous, running through muddy stretches and along clifftops. He raced against De Dions, Russells and Minervas, beating them all. The following year, driving for a day and a night, aided by his co-driver Robert Murie, Franklin won the race again, in spite of colliding with a haycart and losing two hours.

He was now sure the petrol Economiser was his great discovery, the invention for which he would go down in history. The hairpin was simply a youthful victory; now he could see an adult triumph on the horizon. He was never again seen on a bicycle.

He decided to make a grand return to England. It was 1913, and his parents, with whom he had scarcely corresponded, had both died – something he regretted, because he now had things to tell them and achievements they would be forced to respect. He would have to make do, then, with his brothers and sisters, who would also be obliged to see him in a new light. He was now used to admiration, which he considered the rightful recognition of his talents and efforts.

In the autumn of 1913 he arrived in London, where he was warmly received by the engineers who were responsible for evaluating his device and potentially recommending it for the city's omnibuses. The tests were conclusive, the fuel savings considered substantial, and Franklin Bodmin was so sure of his success that he opened a large workshop in Kingston-upon-Thames to manufacture his invention in a range suitable for various vehicles: motorbikes, trucks, buses. He invested twenty thousand pounds sterling in the business, borrowing half this amount. One evening as he was dining with one of the city's engineers, the talk turned to diplomas, and super-talented handyman Franklin declared abruptly that he had left school at age twelve and taught himself. I'm a 'self-made man', he stated, at which his dinner companion congratulated him. But the news spread the very next day, casting doubt on the quality of his Economiser, despite its having been tested a hundred times already. Six months later, the contracts had still not been signed and the staff in his workshop were demanding wages Franklin could no longer pay. He was still hopeful when the war broke out: at this point he was told his device would not be taken up by the city of London for quite some time, if at all. For the time being, other things were more urgent. Franklin was furious, all the more so because the war should have increased the need for fuel savings. He set sail in October 1914 for the United States, leaving behind him debts, unpaid wages and a reputation as an adventurer. Hating the past, he landed in New York, where he proceeded to cover up his setbacks in London, saying simply that he had had to leave because of the war. He added that he had devoted most of the last two years in London to completing the engineering studies he had begun in New Zealand.

He was believed. He set up a firm called Bodmin Gas Generator Co and in 1918 the American army started to equip its trucks with the Bodmin Economiser. He drew from this episode in his life, as always begun in suffering and ending in glory, a vital principle: the appearance of wealth will attract wealth, the appearance of poverty will attract poverty. In other words, appearance is the only reality.

'And this is the man who claimed to be an artist,' Will complains in his notebook. 'A man who put no trust in reality.'

Whenever he was in Invercargill, Franklin continued to paint. And to sire children. His paintings were always much praised in the newspapers. After the London episode he painted for the most part large, dark oils with waterfalls, tree ferns and flowers, in an exotic and appealing style.

97

People purchased them perhaps because he was the artist, just as they listened to him singing without finding him ridiculous. But these heavy paintings that seem to curtain the landscape instead of revealing it were entirely of their time.

On the other hand, people prized Franklin's portraits less, even though he himself would admit to being dissatisfied with only one genre – his self-portraits – thereby showing a modesty people appreciated all the more because it was far from habitual. After his death, a self-portrait he had begun more than ten years previously was found uncompleted in the Invercargill house, and Will remembered it precisely because its lack of completeness gave it personality. He could see exactly how this picture would have become totally banal if it had been finished, with all the perfection of a photo touched up to appear in a magazine. For once Franklin had held back, the machine had stalled. And when referring to his father, Will thought, the word 'machine' was entirely suitable. On the rare occasions in his childhood when his father had given him practical advice, it generally had to do with ways of sidestepping reality. To draw a circle, his father would tell him: use a coin or a saucer. Will, flattered by the attention his father was showing him, would go and get a saucer and trace its outline as accurately as he could. But in public, this same Franklin would tell over and over again the story of the way the young Michelangelo proved his talent by drawing freehand a near-perfect circle. Franklin had his special technique, his shortcuts. He would begin by photographing his subject then setting the image onto a transparent plate supplied by an Invercargill photographer. Will remembered these plates, approximately three and a half by four inches, and he remembered his father using a magic lantern to project the image onto the canvas in his darkened studio. He would then trace the outline of the image with a pencil, a method that enabled him to create what he called an 'authentic' drawing of the face. And Will, who didn't at that time know that his father had been a photographer's assistant and had probably learned this technique from him, was proud to be there while his father worked – contrary to what happened in the garage on Don Street where Will was never allowed to watch him tinkering with his carburettor prototype. But here in the art studio in their huge house, he could see the faces projected onto a page and his father skilfully picking out with crayon or ink the features he wanted to emphasise. One day Franklin had even turned towards him to explain that he was working the way the great painters of the past used to, the ones who had invented perspective by drawing on window panes.

Later, when Will studied Renaissance painting at the Art School in Christchurch, he realised that his father was wrong or had lied to him. Was this the ignorance of the self-taught man? But without that ignorance he might have been paralysed. Captain Cook himself had not had much schooling.

In reality, the Rockhaven studio was often empty. Franklin Bodmin was an impatient man; only results mattered, he would say, revealing that he took less pleasure in his work than in anticipating the profit it would bring.

Reconstructing the past this way, Will was able to confirm that what happened later showed a certain justice. He had watched his father begin a self-portrait in the summer of 1929, and struggle to complete it, stopping and starting, then suddenly abandoning it because he needed to deal with other, more important things. It was November 1929, and the crisis that brought about the stock market crash impacted full force on his business, the Bodmin Gas Generator Co. Like many an entrepreneur, Franklin Bodmin had aimed too high, using bank loans to create several subsidiary companies that were suddenly failing, one after the other. Over a two-month period the whole construction came tumbling down.

When Franklin next set foot in New York, he discovered he was ruined. He was sixty years old.

Not only did he not commit suicide, he refused to admit he was beaten. He went back to work and perfected his carburettor. Seven years later he had more or less re-established his fortune of 1929. And this was what most astonished Will; his father wasn't completely useless, since he could draw on so much energy. Even if this kind of relentlessness can seem crazy, it's a craziness that keeps people alive. And when he thought about it, Will felt somewhat humbled by his father's spirit, by the former boxer who was never down and out, by this tireless man who had made his wife pregnant eight times – perhaps not a record in those days, but well beyond anything Will could have imagined or wished – by the amazing tinkerer who could invent objects the world wanted, by the man for whom in the end nothing was 'sacred', since he was able to take up art (it's all a question of technique), sport or even religion (he sometimes said there was nothing more profitable in the United States than founding a religion and that if he had been born there he would probably have done so). A man of such calibre could hardly be satisfied with a son like Will. His disappointment was the greater because his wife had produced seven girls before managing a boy. That was what he told Florence when Will was born. They had kept the telegram: 'Congratulations! After seven girls, a real little Bodmin at last!'

Will had therefore put all his efforts into frustrating his father. Not deliberately, of course, but from fear he was not living up to expectations. He knew if he tried to be an athlete, he would fail miserably; as a result, he would hide during PE classes. He loved his bike but refused to race. He was a dreamer and didn't even get good marks at school. He was interested in the arts, intrigued by them, just as much as his sister Julia, but where she showed a talent very early on for poetry and theatre, he had never produced much, other than the wooden pulpit and the bronze candle-holders in Holy Trinity church at the age of sixteen.

After high school he enrolled in the Christchurch Art School almost secretly, knowing the derision with which his father would greet this choice. 'That's a girl's education. It doesn't lead to anything, for a man.' These were his words to Winnie, who quickly passed them on to Will. The subtext was that a true artist didn't need to study. Franklin himself was proof of that.

But Will, 'that poor Will who always has a pain somewhere' – to repeat another of Franklin's sayings – had chosen to study a subject that soon revealed that his father had his own version of art history, that he thought himself above the truth, that he worked like a machine to achieve maximum output without asking himself any questions other than those that would contribute to that output, and that he had become, in short, the carburettor he had invented. In that sense he was the purest example of a self-made man, and even his death was an illustration of his life.

At sixty-seven, the inventor had in fact come into his second youth, thanks to the re-establishment of his business interests. He demonstrated this every day during the hour of organised sporting activities on board the *President Fillmore*, the passenger liner that was taking him home to New Zealand. Most of the first-class passengers spent the day lying on deckchairs, reading or playing cards, but Franklin insisted on attending the gym class, where he was undoubtedly the oldest but also the most respected. Besides, there was to be a skipping competition that day, and he was counting on doing well in it.

It was the 2nd of December 1936: they had just passed through the Strait of Gibraltar and were entering the Mediterranean. The weather had been gloomy but was now fine and by late morning several passengers were making the most of it, basking in the sun. Standing on the deck, leaning against the rail, Franklin breathed deeply and stared out to sea. After the Suez Canal everything would be very different – from that point on they would feel the call of the south, the ocean opening out before them, the winter changing into summer, they would feel themselves entering the new world.

He repeated these phrases in his head: he found them poetic and thought they would look well in his diary. Yes, the call of the south, that was a nice expression. He went back to his cabin to change for the skipping competition, but forgot to write it down.

In shorts and tennis shoes, he rejoined the group on the rear deck. Fourteen competitors had signed up, not all of them members of the gymnastics group. At least three strangers greeted him with a smile. There were also three women, but he knew them: Scottish ladies, two of them the MacLean sisters who, in Franklin's opinion, were built like carthorses and would not be able to skip for long. They were young, giggling and joking with one of the newcomers, a slender young man with a moustache, dressed in a tight-fitting vest, who was rubbing his eyes and yawning as if he had just woken up. For some reason he reminded Franklin of Will. The man introduced himself as Andrew.

Tom Harris, the gym instructor, was already there, holding his stopwatch, accompanied by a second judge who gave out the skipping ropes. Franklin was given the same one as the previous day, which struck him as a good sign because he had a handle on it already. The air was crisp, the ship was sailing smoothly, and Franklin felt relaxed in his blue and yellow striped jersey, a reminder of his first training sessions in Dunedin when he was starting to box, carrying Jay Stephens' equipment and strumming on his banjo. Of course he had filled out somewhat and was nowhere near as flexible, but he was more determined and filled with a strength, he was persuaded, that comes from the soul. The first days of gymnastic routines had shown him that in spite of his age he was the equal of the other participants.

They started with a two-minute general warm-up, skipping at a leisurely pace: right foot, left foot, both feet. Then came the competition, starting with the speed contest, which was not Franklin's strong suit. It lasted three minutes, and the younger ones whipped the rope around so fast it was practically invisible. He placed eighth out of fourteen.

Next was the real test: endurance. Speed was not a factor. Franklin knew from his years of boxing that what mattered was a regular rhythm, which needed to be automatic, so you didn't even have to think about lifting your feet to let the rope pass. Just looking at people and the way they held themselves, Franklin could tell who would last the distance. He sensed the MacLean sisters were not just too heavy but had only come to have fun with Andrew, who, after placing well in the speed section, was now looking quite casual. Franklin knew his type well: they want to win while looking as if it's all effortless; their interest is in style. Well, he would show them. Even if he didn't win, Franklin would fight to the bitter end. He closed his eyes, remembered the cabin boys' competition, his first great victory, and smiled.

Some pulled out after five minutes – puffing sissies complaining about their aching calves. Harris was encouraging the others. 'Very good, Mr Bodmin,' he said, 'your rhythm is excellent.' One of the MacLean sisters threw down her rope and sat down, panting, still moving her shoulders in time with her sister's jumping. Andrew was still going with his casual and slightly limp style, but Franklin could sense he was hooked. Other passengers with nothing better to do had formed an audience and were starting to cheer their favourites. He had the unpleasant impression no one was betting on him. When the second Scots girl tripped on her rope and conceded, she was applauded and offered a bottle of water. The spectators were smiling ironically or clapping and calling 'Come on! Come on!' Franklin refused to look at them in case he lost his focus. He heard Tom Harris say: 'Only four left, hooray the survivors!' The speedsters were not among these survivors, as if they had used up their strength in the previous competition. Franklin could feel his legs getting heavier, stiffer. But there was no question of giving up, not at this stage. He heard Andrew sigh out loud and opened his eyes, expecting to see him giving up, but no, the insolent lad was still skipping, and noisily, what's more. Franklin gritted his teeth. The boy might be stronger than me, but I will beat him because he doesn't have my willpower. In the end there were only the two of them left, he and Andrew, and the spectators clapping their hands rhythmically. It was actually helpful in a way: Franklin could focus on the sound while his calf muscles tightened, his feet became leaden and his heart started thumping; but he knew that if he slowed down, the rope would tangle around his feet and he would stumble, perhaps even fall and not have the strength to start again. He had to stick it out, jump, one foot then the other, not allow his wrists or forearms to cramp. He kept his eyes shut, stinging with the sweat running off his forehead. What he must do, he knew, was turn himself into a machine, execute every movement automatically, as if in a sort of dream – even pain can be changed into energy, into something mechanical, and all men dream of being machines. But however clearly he saw himself as one, the mechanism was about to seize up. Little spasms were ticcing through Franklin's left calf, cramp was not far off. At that precise moment, Andrew tripped on his rope, fell to one knee, swore, stood up and threw away his rope, sticking out his tongue in a most theatrical way.

Franklin carried on, alone. The last man standing, the survivor. He was waiting to be told he had won, and finally Harris stopped him. Congratulations! He stood stock still, mouth open, heart racing a mile a minute, but he raised his left fist to applause. He wiped his forehead with the towel

Tom Harris passed him, and once he had caught his breath he called out in a croaky voice: 'Champagne for all the competitors, my treat. We'll meet at six-thirty in the first class bar!' then, raising his hand again, he left. Regretting that no woman worthy of the name had been there to see him win.

He went down to his cabin to wash and change his clothes, but he kept thinking about the young man called Andrew whom he would have been able to teach so many things. Why bother entering a competition if you're not going to do whatever it takes to win? Because you don't want to grow up, is that it? The boy reminded him more and more of Will, and he had lost. Whereas he, Franklin, had won, as per usual. The way he had always been forced to do. Whereas no one had ever forced Will to survive.

He was still panting. It was a long time since he had exercised so vigorously. But I taught them a lesson, he thought. He sat down on his bed and tried to massage his calves, still twitching with painful little spasms.

At six-thirty Tom Harris and the skipping competitors gathered in the first class bar. Even the ones from steerage had been invited. Only two people were missing, including one of the three Scots lassies, who was a teetotaller and refused to set foot in such a den of iniquity. Mr Harris on the other hand was of the opinion that a true sportsman should not be afraid of a little tipple, alcohol being good for the heart.

At seven, disappointed at not seeing the inventor, some of the guests started to leave. One of them, irritated, made a joke about rich people making promises that never cost them anything. Tom Harris tried to keep them there by saying he would go down and knock on Bodmin's cabin door, but as he was already holding a glass he stayed where he was with the others, who were in no hurry to leave anyway and carried on their drinking and general merriment. By seven-thirty they were all gone and no one had knocked on his door.

It was the cabin boy who found him the next morning when he came to change the sheets. Franklin Bodmin lay curled up on his bed, facing the porthole, his eyes open and glassy, already stiff.

The doctor on board examined the body at the captain's request and diagnosed a heart attack. Franklin Bodmin was sewn into a bag and then, in the presence of four witnesses including Mr Harris, tipped discreetly into the sea.

The news of Franklin Bodmin's death – 'Tireless Fighter Dies After Final Victory', as the *Otago Daily Times* proclaimed – reached Florence and the children by telegram the next day. There was no funeral to organise, but Florence had a service in his honour six weeks later in the Anglican church of the Holy Trinity, which was full to bursting. The vicar delivered the eulogy for this great inventor and exemplary citizen, a man who had shown the highest degree of our famous Kiwi ingenuity; in addition he referred to his son Will, who had two years previously carved the rimu pulpit from which he was speaking. Thus Franklin Bodmin was not entirely dead since his artistic gifts lived on in his son.

This was such a weighty compliment that Will lowered his gaze and hunched his shoulders as if he would like to disappear. Being mentioned in church in front of so many people made him feel naked, and when he trembled it was not, as some thought, from grief for the dear departed, but because he realised he was feeling no sorrow and if he lifted his head this would be noticed. As he later wrote to his sister Winnie, his father's death had actually 'taken a great weight from his shoulders', and he was ashamed of this. He sat there staring at the floor, blinking, his lips moving, his face ticcing. He wished with all his heart that he had not inherited from his father talents that seemed to him the exact opposite of an artistic ideal. Because for Will, art is not a way of disguising things and fooling people. Quite the contrary . . . And if art is what my father thinks it is, I want nothing to do with it. At that moment, for the first time, Will became a conscientious objector – in a profound way that went beyond simply objecting to war.

In his attempted autobiography, Will emphasises this thought. 'I tried to ignore what art meant for my father,' he writes, 'and I wasn't able to.'

He hadn't become an artist. Just an art therapist, and later simply a therapist. He came to believe he had chosen this path because of his father, because of the confusion the inventor had sown in his mind.

'This,' he notes in his memoirs, 'is how I solved my problem of latitude and longitude. My guiding star was always my father. An unmoving star pinned in position on the vault of heaven. Today I can say that the picture of him painted in encyclopedias strikes me as fundamentally false, but it doesn't really matter. What does matter is that because the point my father represented was fixed, it allowed me to find my way. According to a well-known saying (I think from an eighteenth-century astronomer), it's better to not know where you are and to know that you don't know, than it is to believe confidently that you are where you are not. This opinion has no application to humanity. For years I had a faulty compass – my father – but I never felt lost. He was the one who gave me my direction, even when I fought him, even after he died.

Take his heroism. It was actually blindness, obstinacy and, seen from another point of view, an attempt to run away. I am not angry with him for the way he brought us up, but he had such an inflated idea of himself that we could never satisfy him. He liked his children only in a purely external way, as evidence of his virility and wealth, because he could afford a sufficiently large house for eight of them.

And so, in order not to feel inadequate, in order to deserve him, we created the myth of our hard-working father who sacrifices his happiness for his children. In reality he had no great respect for us, nor for women either. Over time he became more and more impatient with us all. I remember when he came home to Invercargill in 1927 – I was nine, and in those days he was still my idol. As the boat docked, the whole family was lined up on the quay, in the midst of a crowd who knew us well. It wasn't our mother waiting for him with the pram, it was Mary, already thirty and there with her two children. She was holding her baby in her arms, probably to show it to him. Father was amongst the first to appear, wearing his coat and hat because it was cold, striding easily along, as charming as ever, carrying nothing – there must have been a porter following him – and he started down the gangway. I was looking up at him, but he just waved at us, turning first of all to Mary to kiss her. Then when he turned towards our mother, he said with a tired smile, 'Not even a change in fashion can make you change your hat.' Those were his first words! Our mother's face fell, and in the moment of horrid silence, I wondered why he was angry with her. Aunt Margaret tried to smooth things over by saying: 'But look, Franklin, she's pinned it on with a Bodmin crinkled hairpin.' No one laughed, and in any case the mean remark had been swallowed up in the rush of people all around us. As always in our family, things disappeared and we believed they would never resurface.

But even Winnie hasn't forgotten. When I talked to her about it, she made excuses for Father, shrugging her shoulders and saying, 'Oh well, he was a man.' As if it weren't him, as if it were his gender speaking through him. She doesn't realise that saying 'Oh well, he was a man' is a terrible thing for her as well, because it shows she isn't capable of seeing him, she doesn't know him.

VIEWS OF ROME

Opening the third volume of his travel journal, Will saw a photo fall to the floor. At first he took it for a postcard that had come unglued. For every European country he had visited, he had sent home – that is, to his family in Invercargill – a large, hard-bound notebook like this one, containing photos, postcards and notes about the most memorable sights he had seen. In total, there were seventeen of them, making up what he called somewhat pompously his Grand Tour, and this one, the third volume, bore the title Trip to Italy.

He leaned down and picked it up: it was a photo, and even though time had faded it, he recognised it instantly. It had aged incredibly: it looked as though it had been overexposed in one corner and the sun's brightness had spread, creating a brown area that now threatened to obliterate the people in the centre.

These people were none other than himself and Jane Hanley, standing side by side at the entry to a bridge. The only mystery was how the photo had slipped into the chapter 'Rome' – the right place, because that was the city and the trip when it had been taken. On the other hand, it shouldn't have been there because Jane wasn't in the journal. Will had left her out because it was too hot a topic. Not a line about her in the whole of Trip to Italy, and he had mentioned her only in a few letters to his mother. Generally in a slightly casual way, beginning with 'I expect to meet the nurse Jane Hanley in Rome, along with one of her girlfriends. You know the one I mean, Jane the Irish nurse, who gave me the pieces of Tahitian tapa cloth.'

The previous spring, Jane had brought back from Dublin five superb pieces of cloth that had belonged to Captain Cook. 'They travelled first on the *Endeavour*, then Cook gave them to a Mr Cardonel of Edinburgh who still had them when he went to live in Dublin. They ended up in the possession of Jane's grandfather, a roofer who repaired the roof of Cardonel's heir's house. They are the only objects belonging to Captain Cook that I've been able to acquire for the moment. Once I've retraced their history, that's to say the history of their successive owners over the last 186 years, I'll have them bound like the pages of a book, along with the documents that prove their authenticity.'

What he didn't tell his mother was that he was so moved by these relics he could hardly speak, asking Jane: 'How much do you want for them?' She shook her head as if he were stupid. 'I'm not selling them, I'm giving them.' She added: 'Because you like Cook more than me.'

Such an ambiguous statement that he hadn't dared ask for an explanation.

So for the first time he was genealogically linked to Cook. It was as if Jane Hanley was opening up access to the family he had chosen for himself. After that he sometimes called Jane 'Cook's grand-daughter'. While he was waiting for his other family, his future family, the one he might start with her . . .

But he couldn't remember slipping the photo into the Italy journal.

There was Jane, standing beside him, with the blurred round shape of the Castel Sant'Angelo behind them. To the right and left of them towered two of the immense angels on the bridge. They were supposed to offer protection to the tourists, but they had been too weak and now their colours had faded as if their blood had been drained away; the reddish flames invading the edges of the photo had eaten the angels' wings and part of their heads. What remained as the focal point of the picture was Jane's radiant smile, apparently already engaged in combat with the inferno that threatened them from the edge of the sky. She was pushing it back, she was still undefeated.

Moved and embarrassed at his response, after so many years, to the carefree beauty of the moment when they had handed their camera to another tourist to take their picture together, so they would be seen together, so they would be side by side forever, on paper at least, Will put the photo away with a grimace that seemed to say: look out! an old photo can do serious harm to your image.

Other moments from that day came back to him as clearly as snapshots. They had walked a great deal through Rome, beginning with Testaccio and the Protestant Cemetery where, with crickets singing in the background, they had contemplated the tombs of Shelley, drowned in the sea, and Keats, 'whose name was writ in water'. They walked up as far as the Vatican, whose cold and lethal imperial splendours left them speechless, and when they came out they were filled with joy at being in the open air again. The world was streaming with sunlight; everything around them seemed readable, they would never be lost again, every stone had its own history. Will lent his voice to the monuments, telling the incredible adventure of Benvenuto Cellini escaping from the Castel Sant'Angelo, and talking about Bernini's angels. When they stopped at a café terrace, they even enjoyed their sore feet and their tiredness because it fitted in with their image of this excursion and its adventurousness, made them slightly more real by marking their bodies. And when Will leaned once more over the map of the city, Jane, who was watching him from the corner of her eye, put down her icy glass that seemed to sweat onto the table, and said quietly something Will would never forget: 'You didn't need to get your nose fixed.' He lifted that same nose towards her, and once his initial astonishment had passed, a great weight lifted from his shoulders. Jane accepted him with his old nose and his new one. He wanted to know – no, she said, the new one isn't wrong, it's nice, but not better. A few moments later Will's hand slipped beneath the table to hold Jane's, the first time he had squeezed her hand this way, in a confiding, almost childlike way. And as long as he was holding her hand, he had no need to say anything at all to her. It seemed to him that even the sun making him blink was passing through him to reach Jane.

They walked again for a long time, and late that evening, after the trattoria and a bit too much wine, he escorted Jane back to her hotel. Since they couldn't really end their conversation in the lobby, it was quite natural for Will to go up to her room. She put her finger on his lips, he put his arms around her, they laughed, she leaned her head on his shoulder and there was a moment of slightly giddy silence, but no awkwardness, no, not even when they sat on the mattress and began kissing. Later, as they lay on the bed without needing even a sheet over them, the night had continued to sing around them, the sound of voices and passing cars rising up from the street through the open window, foreign sounds that didn't really concern them, that rocked them like an ocean wave, that cut them off the way the laurel or olive wreaths that surround some old portraits separate them from the world. That night with no beginning and no end, Will talked about the plot of land he had bought on a hill in Christchurch before he left New Zealand. On it he had left a wooden cabin and a few trees, but since his departure all the surrounding plots had been built on and there was no longer an accessway to his property.

Jane's chest rose and fell gently as he talked; he knew she

felt his distress at being, in his words, shut outside this way, but Jane's breathing restored his courage, and he announced he would buy the sections needed to put in a new access and open up his cabin again. He pictured the house he would build there, the trees he would plant, and there would surely be a tree fern because they grow so well there.

Never before had he expressed his wishes so clearly, he thought. As if, by confiding them to Jane in the secret of this night, he was also revealing them to himself. Now they were taking shape, and Jane, sitting on the bed, lit a cigarette. He could see the tip glowing in the dark as she put it between her lips, then curving an arc to the ashtray on the bedside table.

The voices from outside were more distant, the space around them swelled and contracted with their breathing, it was listening to them, waiting for them.

Jane talked about Dublin where she had been unhappy and had no wish to return to live. Because of her family. Her mother had abandoned them – her father, her brother and her – when she was five. She didn't remember much about it, other than her father's suffering, his agitation, his rages. In any case he had sent them, her and her brother, to live with people in the country, and they came home only for special occasions and part of the holidays. It wasn't really terrible, but it wasn't good either. And then at age ten she went back to live with her father. Later she located her mother, a bad idea. An awful idea in fact, and she burst out laughing where someone else might have burst into tears.

Will said nothing, his ears on full alert. His breathing spoke for him. Jane felt his tension, and eased it by stroking her hand slowly over his face, as if she were inviting him to close his eyes, to sleep.

The next day they stayed in the centre of the city. They no longer needed to go very far nor to exhaust themselves to find what they were seeking. Shortly before midday, in the market in Campo dei Fiori, they saw a pile of empty crates burning at the foot of the statue of Giordano Bruno who had died at the stake on that spot in 1600. Will expanded on this 'remembrance fire' as he called it, seeing in it the equivalent of the Catholic communion in which the faithful eat the body of Christ on Sundays. Jane, as a Catholic, shrugged her shoulders and merely smiled. Working their way through the crowd, they went into a small restaurant where they had to stand and wait before finding a table. They were intrigued by the number of people coming and going: stallholders from the market, an aristocratic-looking young man with two greyhounds on a leash, heavily made-up middle-aged ladies, a cyclist who left his bike in the doorway, half blocking the entry, all of them hurrying past the customers standing at the counter to eat. They waved banknotes at the owner, a kind of colossus sitting in front of a box radiating a purple light that gave an unreal glow to the drops of sweat on his face and the skin of his shoulders left bare by his white singlet. He took the notes without a word, put them on his lamp and pronounced judgment: good! Not once, during the few minutes while Will and Jane were watching his performance, did he find a forgery.

The world had become light for them, amusing, even though everything had become denser. That evening, seen from the heights of the Villa Borghese, the city in the west seemed plunged into a heated mist. There was again a sound of the ocean carried by the ebb and flow of people swarming from all directions, while the night brought more odours: the scent of pine trees mingled with the spices of a kebab vendor down below, and underneath all the others, a more unusual and indefinable smell, seemingly coming from the stones and the alleys, the city's special signature.

The following day, Jane had to rejoin her travelling companion and go back to England, while Will would spend one more day in Rome before his trip to Yugoslavia where he planned to buy rare books. Leaving Rome and each other seemed impossible to them, absurd, brutal; and yet their smiles and furtive tears were positive, they were real.

Except that now, thirty years later, the memories came back to Will so strongly that it was a struggle not to be crushed by the thought that he hadn't been up to scratch in those days. Was his banknote a forgery? But where could he find a colossus with an ultraviolet lamp to check it?

RETURN TO YORK

As the train travelled north, Will started to feel regretful. He felt as if he had cheated everyone, starting with Jane. He thought about his mother a lot, and when he arrived in Florence, the city with the same name, he was nearly overwhelmed with homesickness. Would he dare go there with Jane? She might be pregnant, and then there would be no discussion: he would do as his father had done, he would get married. But could he trust Jane?

Somewhere past Florence, taking advantage of a compartment where he was almost alone, he wrote a letter for his mother.

'Dear Mother,

'All my misadventures with the shower in the little hotel I told you about last week are well behind me, forgotten, years away. They have been erased by the beauty of the history that is still present here among so many ruins. These last three days I have been on cloud nine. Meeting up with Jane Hanley and her companion was most pleasant. Jane is very generous and cheerful, and I am quite fond of her. I believe it is mutual, too, but I am not certain I can entirely trust her because she was abandoned by her mother when she was four or five years old. There are always after-effects that make such persons fragile and therefore fickle – you can see this in the fact that she smokes. The number of mothers who smoke these days is frightening, and the debilitating effects on their children can be seen every day.

'Last night I dreamed about you and Father. It was almost harrowing because in my dream I saw that all Father's inventions came from you. Isn't it true that he wouldn't have thought of the hairpin if you hadn't suggested it to him? Unfortunately I don't know most of his other inventions. It was mostly just tinkering about, wasn't it? Whatever became of his famous carburettor? Anyway, in my dream it was obvious that even that came from you. And standing in front of you, Father looked like a boy, a very small boy.

'Since my dreams usually reveal the truth down to the tiniest detail (you remember, last year I dreamed I was holding in my arms a big shiny black animal with a long neck but no visible eyes and the next day I saw the exact same photo in the *Weekly Scotsman*? It was the Loch Ness monster) I woke up feeling very uneasy. I would not like Father to have used you without proper recognition. That would be just like him, though. I will always defend you.

'I hope your health is improving. I beg you to go and see the healer with parapsychic powers that I told you about.

'Your loving son,
'Will.'

He didn't expect a detailed response. His mother's letters were becoming less frequent and briefer as her illness progressed. Sometimes she dictated them to Winnie.

The few days he spent in Yugoslavia bored him, and yet he was in no hurry to go back to England. He found Split quite pleasant and Mestrovnik even more so, where he lodged with a sculptor who lived beside the sea and where, after visiting the maritime museum, he went swimming dangerously far out from shore. He went home via Paris where he bought an old book that the bookseller tried to pass off as a translation of the Easter Island tablets. Back in England he continued his meandering, attended a Quaker lecture on East–West relations, went up to Birmingham where he located three relics that used to belong to members of Cook's crew. The closer he got to York, the greater his fear, a fear he didn't understand, a fear that made Jane almost formidable.

He was astonished by a glorious late summer's day in York, almost as if the good weather had followed him from Rome. He had been expecting a hostile climate, to pay dearly for his moment of happiness: after delight, damnation. And damnation was not being able to choose, it was the conflicting thoughts jostling in his mind. He imagined himself going about openly, courageously with Jane, asking her to marry him, but then he was haunted by threats he had difficulty defining. He was sure he would become the object of John Webster's unspoken scorn: the man was already giving him the cold shoulder since he had refused to go and live at the Webster house. Or Shirley's: she had smiled vaguely on seeing his new nose, as if to say, what's stopping you from getting married now? Not to mention the veiled sarcasm of the rest of the team, who said he was hesitating, that he wasn't *man* enough to be responsible for taking care of a woman. Admittedly, this was the era when Bob Dylan sang 'It ain't me babe . . .', but besides the fact that Will was impervious to Bob Dylan's charms and would probably, were he less marginal, have been one of the people Dylan made fun of so brilliantly, it was quite clear to him that he couldn't go home to New Zealand, start a family and build a house on his Scarborough section if, for once that he was in love – the first time in years, since Jean Angus, to be precise – he ran away.

And his fear was so undefined that it kept coming back to the insoluble question: could he trust Jane Hanley, a Catholic abandoned by her mother, and a smoker?

He must have found this questioning disagreeable, even ridiculous, since he didn't tell anyone except his mother, and even then only indirectly, without daring to admit he was drawn to Jane as to an abyss.

Just as he had delayed going back to York, he put off returning to the hospital. He spent his first afternoon in his two-room flat in Sandringham Street, enjoying being reunited with his pictures, opening the windows to give them some air. Suddenly he regretted out loud that so much space was taken up by the books, pictures and assorted small objects, to the extent that there was no room left to live in: even I, he said, I feel crowded, I slip into my flat like a thief. But he could see no solution.

He took his time opening the build-up of mail, from his sisters of course, but also replies to the advertisements he regularly placed in newspapers for his collection. Then he found a gift from Jane, a package prettily wrapped in striped metallic paper, an expensive paper he was very careful not to tear. Inside was one of his favourite shirts, nylon, no-iron – for him this was the height of progress. He didn't unfold it straightaway, touching it, stroking it, and he felt as if it were burning his fingers, that if he put it on he would always be in love with Jane.

He put it on. And in the late afternoon, he set off on foot to the hospital less than a mile away. Five minutes later, he turned back. It was better to wait till the next morning, otherwise everyone would see that he had come for her.

He was starting to wonder where he would go for dinner – he was still in the habit of eating at the hospital – when he bumped into Jane on a street corner. She was just on her way to see if he was back ... They hugged and laughed, walked for a while hand in hand, everything was becoming simple again; Will showed her his lovely shirt, they were filled with the balmy September evening, and Jane didn't ask anything in particular, except that as soon as they set foot in the flat, Will scowled as he realised that Jane could not spend the night unless he informed the landlady, since she and her husband shared the bathroom with him. And she wasn't likely to approve, he was sure of that. As for the bed, now that he saw it through Jane's eyes, it was grotesquely narrow, and surrounded by wobbly piles of books. Above it, swaying like a skeleton on a hanger, was the suit Will slipped between the mattress and the base so it would lose its wrinkles without being ironed, while he slept. They sat down at a small round table that Will quickly cleared and set with glasses and a bottle of sherry (at least he had one), and started talking about the hospital.

Jane was going through a rough patch. Once again, she said, shrugging in resignation, she was being criticised by some of the team following an incident where she felt she had nothing to blame herself for.

There was an Anglican vicar in her ward who had complained constantly since he arrived, saying he had been committed because he didn't believe in God. A faith that is not absolute, and blind, he insisted, is no faith at all, it's nothing more than a vile bargaining with God, something that God punishes. The previous week another patient – a businessman – had taken him for a ride in his car. The vicar berated him about his lack of faith. 'You can't bargain with God. God isn't a shopkeeper. You'll see. You won't get better until you let God guide you. Completely.'

'Guide me how? He's supposed to take me where I need to go?' the businessman asked, furious.

'Absolutely.'

'Like this, then?' the businessman asked, letting go of the steering wheel and raising his arms to the sky. The car ran off the road and came to a stop in some bushes down below. The driver escaped without a scratch, but the vicar, with a head injury, hovered between life and death for three days.

The medical team members felt the accident would only

strengthen the churchman's conviction that he lacked faith: God had punished him yet again. On the other hand, the businessman whose beliefs had also been strengthened, went around saying: 'He converted me, and look where it got him. It's better to do without God.'

Will laughed heartily, and Jane was astonished to see him so amused by such a dramatic turn of events. She sighed. Then the question of the medical staff had arisen, she continued. Why were these two patients allowed to go off together in a car? Jane Hanley felt she was being singled out: Dr Webster had talked about inexperience, and since she was the newest . . .

Will kept smiling, barely listening to her. He had started thinking about his patients again, whom he adored because with them he could provide the answers. He was even anxious to get back to the ones he had taught to ride a bike. Yes, with them he was an athlete. He had even bought weights and an elastic exercise band to build up the muscles in his arms and shoulders, reporting to his mother that he had increased his chest measurement by nearly two inches.

With his patients he was also an artist and, once a year, an exhibition organiser. He really liked most of those who attended his workshop and was already looking forward with some amusement to seeing Nora Baxter again. She was a woman in her forties, dressed very eccentrically (almost always wearing a turban), who would come and sit beside him as he painted, watching him with the same adoration he had shown for his father in the splendid studio at Rockhaven. He enjoyed her silent company, but after a while he would always turn to the patient who was devouring him with her eyes and ask her why she didn't finish her own work. 'But I'm helping you!' she protested, which generally led to laughter around them. Then sighing deeply she would pick up her pastels or charcoal, or go and offer advice to someone else. Will would smile at what he considered her childishness. She was the sister of a leading magistrate, and well known for her ability to foresee the future. Like me, Will thought. Each of them, at different times, had dreamed the winning number in various lotteries. But they had never had their hands on the ticket; the most difficult thing was always to get the piece of paper with the right number. And that difficulty seemed to him to hold some universal truth he was unable to quite make out.

But he did feel that this truth must also apply to his passion for collecting, since Will believed that for every rare item, there was a man somewhere ready to give a great deal to acquire it. It was only necessary to find that man; but this was sometimes so complicated that it was a bit like getting your hands on what you knew was the winning ticket. Still, the object called to its purchaser, that was certain.

In the meantime, seeing him faraway in his own thoughts, Jane fell silent, slightly frustrated at having raised to no good purpose a subject that was painful to her. She turned her glass in her hand and asked Will what he was thinking about. He jumped and looked around him. All that remained of the sunset were some red streaks among the clouds, and the shadowy room was closing in on them even more. 'I was thinking it will be difficult for me to ask you to stay the night here,' he said with an apologetic look. He seemed surprised at his own words.

She shrugged, shook her head and said nothing. They got up to leave for the restaurant. When they were out of the house Jane said: 'Now we're back here, we're like kids.' Will blushed, reading an accusation into her words. He was fourteen years older than her.

Fourteen years older, admittedly, but he looked very young, probably because he had refused to play a role in the world. 'I was a conscientious objector,' he said suddenly. 'Old age might overtake me before I grow up.'

'A conscientious objector . . . So you know how to say

no, then. And then you became a Quaker. Because they're pacifists, I suppose.'

She took his hand in hers, and when he felt its softness he wanted to run away with her, to go back and live in their Roman bubble. They decided to spend the weekend in Newcastle, taking a hotel room for two nights.

They spent the whole of Saturday poking round in second-hand bookshops. Will was initiating Jane into his great passion, but she came along only to spend time with him. She wasn't greatly interested in history, giving a strange reason: it was made by other people, it's out of our control.

Beneath these words Will thought he sensed a question: and what about our own history, what are we doing about that?

He was lucky enough to find a book published in 1828, a life of Captain Ledyard who had accompanied Cook on his last voyage and witnessed his murder. 'It's finds like this that keep me going,' Will declared.

In the evening they went to see a play, *The Imaginary Invalid*. Will wrote to his mother that he had thought he would die laughing and that it was the best therapy.

It had been the perfect weekend, and yet on the train back to York on Sunday evening, Jane went into the corridor to smoke, which Will interpreted the same way as always: abandonment, the past, her absent mother. Not once did he ask himself whether he could do something, whether Jane, by smoking, might not also be sending him a message.

The hospital swallowed them up once more in its routine, and their fears remained intact. Except that Jane was unhappy that their relationship was not out in the open – that they were belittling their history, as she put it – and that she was living in the nurses' home.

She pressed Will to explain why he didn't become a full-time collector. After all, from what she had seen (and what he had told her), he would make more money than at the hospital and he would have more freedom.

Will mumbled a reply that was neither yes nor no. Having to front up to such choices was starting to get him down. Collecting, he told Jane, is my passion. Therapy is my shopfront, it's what makes me acceptable, what I do for others.

She was flattered, imagining she was on the same side as his passion, but irritated to have confirmed yet again that for him, passion was something to hide. Otherwise, would it end? Why, with Will, did every question turn into a puzzle?

And then, towards the end of September, Will seemed to have a breakthrough: 'I'm going back to Russia to see what I can pick up there, and depending what I bring back, I may or may not become a professional collector.'

His trip took place over the Christmas holidays. Jane understood his decision, but she would have preferred him not to start by running away to Russia, on the pretext of giving himself a way to choose. She wasn't exactly thrilled either that she was dependent on a test in which she had no say. She decided to spend her Christmas holidays in Dublin.

Soon after, Will explained to her the place Rex Nan Kivell occupied in his life as a collector. Until then he had mentioned only in passing this New Zealander who was director of the Redfern, one of the most important galleries in London. Rex was a top-flight collector and Will had already worked for him; amongst other items, he had found him a portrait of Priscilla Wakefield; and now Rex was looking for prints, drawings or paintings of the *Red Jacket*, the sailing ship on which his ancestors had emigrated to New Zealand. Will had high hopes of finding one or two such images.

These words reassured Jane with their professional tone. Will seemed serious about this, in his element. More than he was at the hospital, actually. And when she imagined the success he would inevitably have if he persevered, a warm feeling filled her. For Will, she felt able to give up smoking. She had already stopped going to the pub where she used to support the rugby team. She was ready to make many changes.

THE COLLECTOR

The following weeks were among the happiest of Will's life. He felt he could rely on Jane, he had no more decisions to make in the immediate future, and everything was going very well for him. On the last weekend of September he came across a little book written by William Wales, the astronomer who accompanied Cook. He bought it for five pounds and sold it for seventy less than a week later. Towards the middle of October, through an even more extraordinary stroke of luck, he found a colour engraving in Birmingham, ten inches by twelve inches, of the *Red Jacket*. It was in perfect condition and remarkably well drawn and coloured. The clipper was a 260-foot three-master that had made her maiden voyage across the Atlantic in 1853 and ended up twenty years later in Cape Verde as a coal barge. In the image she was depicted under full sail, with her beautiful hardwood hull and prow figure – the Iroquois chief Red Jacket wearing his feather headdress, red jacket and beaded moccasins – clearly visible, as well as the carved stern and the scrolled wreaths carved on the taffrail. Cutting through the grey waves beneath a blue sky, the clipper looked like a world in itself, miniaturised but complete down to the last detail. If Will had been able to go on board, he would certainly have met the passengers who hadn't yet landed in New Zealand, including the grandfather of Rex de C. Nan Kivell.

As Will explained at length to Jane, Rex Nan Kivell had built up the most impressive collection relating to the history of the South Pacific. Will found it shameful, absolutely scandalous, that New Zealand had refused to purchase his collection. In the early 1950s, Rex sent a sample to Wellington, but the prime minister at the time, Sidney Holland, glancing at it scornfully, merely mumbled: 'Not bad for old pictures.' Holland respected only what was new, and his minister of internal affairs, not to be outdone, informed Rex Nan Kivell that the Christchurch Museum would be happy to take his collection if he agreed to finance a building suitable for housing it.

Will vigorously defended Rex, and in December 1953, sent an almost insulting letter to the director of the museum. He also alerted several New Zealand newspapers, something Rex was grateful to him for, especially since one of his letters had been published and a few journalists had had enough nerve to make fun of Holland.

And then Australia got involved. Robert Menzies, prime minister, met Rex during one of his visits to London and made him a proposition. It wasn't very advantageous financially, Will said, but Menzies was adding a decoration: Rex de Charembac Nan Kivell would become a knight of the British Empire. For Rex, the knighthood was worth many sacrifices because, as he admitted to Will, he was counting on this ennoblement to crown his brilliant career. He accepted, and the majority of his collection was thereafter located in Canberra. However, Rex was not yet a knight. Will didn't know what was holding things up; on the other hand, he knew Rex wanted at any price to acquire all the paintings, engravings and other images of the *Red Jacket*. 'My grandfather chartered that clipper,' he explained. 'It's my *Mayflower*.' The three-master made a three-month stay in Dunedin, and it was there that the man who would become Rex's father had decided not to go back on board.

127

(Just like my father, thought Will.) He bought some land, threw himself into sheep farming and married a descendant of a Marquis de Charembac, a French aristocrat who had fled to England during the Revolution. Hence the name that Rex himself had added to that of his father.

Will perfectly understood that a man like Rex would want to get hold of every authentic image of the *Red Jacket*. 'He wants to be the master of his own history; he wants the *Red Jacket* the way some people want a dream, the way I want the pamphlet written against Governor Darling. As long as he doesn't have it, his collection will be incomplete.'

Having just purchased the engraving – for a modest price, to be honest – Will could now exchange it for a princely sum, Rex's fortune reputedly being considerable. But Will didn't know what price to ask. He alternated between giving it away, giving it outright to Rex, or exchanging it for the famous Darling pamphlet, as long as Rex was able to locate and procure it. But selling the engraving at, say, double the purchase price struck him as an unforgivable lapse in taste: it was unworthy of the stakes. After all, his future with Jane was also hanging in the balance.

His business was doing so well that Jane wondered about the usefulness of the trip to the Soviet Union. You're going to be successful, she told him, that goes without saying. But Will was reluctant to change his plans; perhaps he knew that if he stayed he would have to change his living arrangements, move in with Jane, something he desired and feared in equal measure. No, it would really clip his wings. First he must go to Russia.

He organised his itinerary with care, making contact with friends in Zurich, Quakers in Berlin, an English-speaking bookseller in Moscow, a correspondent in Helsinki. Everything would have to be done over a five-week period, and he dreaded the winter in those countries.

Before he left, Jane gave him a present of five new nylon shirts, since Will had told her they were one of the best possible bargaining tools in the Soviet Union. He was also taking a number of other items with him, including an illustrated book on boxing that he knew he would be able to exchange for an old work. Jane observed yet again that beneath his eccentric exterior he was a clever negotiator. What a pity he didn't have more self-confidence!

'Yesterday, Tuesday December 10th, I started out on this journey that is so important, and fell asleep on the train,' Will notes in a journal dated 1962.

'There were four of us in my compartment, one of them an overweight businessman in his fifties who started sweating early in the morning, in spite of the season. He was carrying a pile of newspapers that he opened greedily, plunging himself into them as if he might find the meaning of his life, or perhaps his death sentence there. I could see his lips trembling. Sitting opposite, a man of my age, on the thin side, kept tapping his foot nervously, probably in time to an obsessive rhythm running through his head. The third was a teenage boy who got up occasionally to smoke in the corridor. And then me, asleep, perhaps so as not to keep seeing them, perhaps because the train was rocking me.'

These notes, Sara Tinkerbell tells me, are the first of a series that were written in stages on Will's journey to Switzerland and Russia, and his return via Finland. Everything indicates, she says, that this tour of Europe was a turning point in her uncle's life. It wasn't just one of those trips to France, Switzerland or Italy that he was in the habit of going on whenever he had a bit of free time – in this respect, Will was a precursor, one of the millions of migrants who would crisscross Europe from the end of the twentieth century onward – it was the journey that was to bring stability to his life. Increasingly, Will was a man from nowhere, citizen of an imaginary homeland. Living in a psychiatric hospital was probably a way of preventing himself from putting down any roots. And as for travelling in search of what would allow him to stop travelling – that rare object, that unique and life-changing item – this is also a matter of putting yourself in the hands of fate, of the absurd. Rex Nan Kivell told him all of this, in his own way. 'My dear Will,' Rex even concluded, referring to his years of experience, 'we collectors are damned souls in search of a body.'

But when he fell asleep in the train on the way to Kings Cross Station in London, Will dreamed, strangely, that he was face to face with his landlady, Mrs Norwick, arguing with her about the noise he made walking around upstairs without slippers. He emerged from his somnolent state just before London, straightening his head which had been flopping to one side or onto his chest, his ears still ringing with the curses he had shouted at Mrs Norwick. He knew of course – and would note it in elliptical fashion in his journal – that he was unhappier with himself than with that woman. He felt he had never been disrespectful towards the Norwicks, an elderly couple huddled beside a big electric heater, shivering and scrimping endlessly on the heating bill. He even felt sorry for Mrs Norwick because she had recently had to have an operation on her insides – since then the word cancer had floated in the air, although it was never said. And good old Mr Norwick, usually a touch frantic-looking, his hair wild, would walk around with a rag in his hand, or a screwdriver, as if he was about to do some little task he couldn't quite focus on. And always in slippers, day and night.

Will had dined the day before at the hospital canteen as usual. He realised now that, for this last meal, he should have invited Jane to a restaurant. If need be, since he earned so little and had to put money aside to buy rare items during his trip, they could each have paid half. But he hadn't thought of it. So he had found himself in the canteen at six-thirty with a meal on a tray, and when he went to sit beside Jane, Kenny Randall was already there. Kenny, a nurse who had arrived at the hospital at more or less the same time as Jane, was barely thirty, had the gift of the gab and was proud of his athletic build. Will found him tedious because he was also the type of person who talks at length about the TV programme he watched the previous night. Jane seemed to enjoy listening to him, though, and before her relationship with Will, she occasionally went to the pub to have a beer with him. Will sat down opposite them and tried to look both intent and distant, as if what he had on his mind was preventing him from hearing Kenny's remarks – he was talking about sport – and he took care, when he did make a few passing comments, to address them in a near-murmur to Jane only. With the result that Kenny, miffed, finally hissed: 'Apparently the two of you have things to say to each other in private.' He said it jokingly, and Jane smiled, but Will's face was stone. Kenny turned his attention to his dessert. Will and Jane got up at the same time and left. It was dark outside, and cold. Will had wrapped himself in his duffel coat, Jane was wearing a hat and scarf – they weren't going to be able to wander along the paths in the park or risk any contact more intimate than holding hands like schoolchildren. And Jane was wearing gloves anyway.

Damn Mrs Norwick, Will grumbled, what a guard dog she is! But Jane didn't react to his complaint, which made Will wonder: if I can get rid of that imbecile Kenny Randall, why can't I get the better of my landlady? Why do I have to be always above reproach? But in the end he gave up the idea of taking Jane home with him. They said a fond goodbye: he would write to her, she would be back from Dublin before him, she would miss him, he would miss her.

Will hadn't realised how furious he was until he was back in his two-room flat, after he had put on the slippers required out of respect for the waxed wooden floor. Fur-lined slippers

131

in fine leather, whose shapeless ugliness reminded him of the landlady, their comfort very quickly turning into increasingly unbearable discomfort. Will could feel his toes curling, twisting, trying to work their way through the fur, to poke right through it. He lay down on the bed and watched his feet moving, stretching the leather out of shape, creating dark, hard, painful lumps. But the thought of getting rid of the slippers didn't cross his mind. And when he closed his eyes, he saw an Invercargill breakfast scene – he was ten or twelve – when his two aunts were discussing his sister Julia, the so-called poetess, who had 'run off' with a young Maori postmaster who played the violin. 'It's disgusting,' Aunt Susan was saying. 'Can you imagine having a man beside you in the same bed?'

'Eeuuw,' said Aunt Margaret, 'imagine his feet, his lumpy feet! His toes, his toenails!'

'Horrible,' Aunt Susan said, spreading Vegemite on her toast.

Well, now Will had lumpy feet, and he was showing them: until he made holes in his slippers if need be.

Finally he undressed and lay down quietly, but he slept badly because he was excited about his journey.

Which is why he was tired on the train – perhaps.

When he walked into the Redfern Gallery, he still hadn't made up his mind what he was going to ask from Rex de C. Nan Kivell in exchange for the print of the *Red Jacket*. The young man who came to greet him at the door, very fashionably but casually dressed (halfway, Will thought, between artist and dandy, exactly the kind of young man Rex went for), knew who he was: he was expected. He went off at once to tell Rex, who came from the back of the gallery, holding out his arms as he saw Will and shaking his hand warmly. A tall, handsome man with silvery hair, wearing a dark suit, he looked something like a more intelligent

Harold Macmillan. Rex's manners were exquisite – you would have lent him money as soon as look at him. He took Will off to see the gallery's latest acquisitions. In addition to the usual artists, he was showing a few canvases from the major exhibition that had been organised recently with the Galerie de France. There were works by Alechinsky, Zhao Wuji, Hartung and Soulages that made an impression on Will, maybe because he had dreamed of becoming a painter and wondered what would have happened if he had really given it a go. He asked Rex, who in becoming an upper-middle-class Englishman had lost his New Zealand accent, if he ever exhibited Antipodean artists. Rex admitted he did not, and added with a touch of irony, that's all too new. Will smiled. Rex was playing up the complicity that is expected between compatriots in exile. He had also once again invited Will to stay in his spacious apartment, but Will had refused, preferring to stay with another New Zealander, Tad Jensen, who worked for Lloyds Bank. He had turned down Rex's lovely flat, he felt, because he wanted to be able to negotiate the price of the print without feeling obligated for anything else. In fact it was mostly because Jane had sown the seeds of doubt in his mind. She didn't like Rex, whom she didn't even know. But his story, as Will had told it to her, didn't fill her with confidence. For starters his visiting card, with the 'de C.' inserted between his first and last names, seemed pretentious to her. Not to mention the words 'knight of the order of Dannebrog' in small print beneath the name, something that Will had not been able to explain to her. But he had smiled at Jane's naïveté; she came from a background where there was no contact with that type of personality. If only you had seen my father's business cards . . ., he had replied. Although he didn't put it into words, he was also a little embarrassed by Nan Kivell's taste for pomp and ceremony. It wasn't very New Zealand, to be frank. You only had to look at the letters Rex sent from the Redfern Gallery: he invariably added to his signature the typed word 'Director' that he then crossed out by hand. Wouldn't it have been simpler not to type the word? But perhaps it was meant to underline his consideration: for you, dear Will, I'm not the director, I'm just myself.

He's a complicated man, Will concluded.

Don't be taken in, Jane had said.

Here in his office, Rex was himself. More than a director, a great collector. His walnut desk had been taken over by objects in studied disarray: papers, brochures, a rolled-up poster, a telephone with scraps of paper stuck to the handset; on the walls, a few beautiful pieces of abstract art.

And more than a collector, an emotional man: Rex was looking at the print of the *Red Jacket* with moist eyes.

'This clipper,' he said, 'was my great-grandfather's. When you think that it ended up as a coal hulk, a gutted hull somewhere in Africa . . .'

'I thought it was your grandfather,' Will said.

'It was my great-grandfather. If you like we could do an exchange. For . . .' He thought for a moment. 'For the pamphlet – one of the originals – where Eliza Fraser tells the story of her shipwreck on the *Stirling Castle* in 1836.'

Will felt himself blush. This shipwreck was one of the great moments in Australian history and it was a magnificent offer. Eliza Fraser's pamphlet was worth a hundred times more than the print.

Rex waited for his response with something heavy in his expression, something close to suffering. Will told himself he had only acquired all of this, his gallery, his reputation, his collection, by devoting his life to it, his blood, by giving up his youth. But this was no time to weaken.

'I need the pamphlet,' Will said, 'against Governor Darling.'

There, he had said it, it was out in the open.

Rex looked at him, and his face split in a wide grin.

'Well of course,' he said, 'if I had it . . . Unfortunately, I don't know where to start looking for it. You're better than I am, in that respect.'

He held out his arms. 'Ask me for something else.'

Will remained silent. Rex continued.

'Let's suppose I find it, I don't know how. It's worth a great deal more than that print. If I had it, I could buy in one go all the pictures of the *Red Jacket* that have ever been produced, all the paintings, all the drawings.'

'Not really,' Will said. 'If I don't agree to exchange my print for anything except the pamphlet, then they're worth exactly the same.'

Rex nodded slowly. Then, with a sad expression: 'You haven't brought it to me to tell me you won't sell it to me, have you? That would be absurd.'

'No, it's not absurd. I can ask you, and only you, for the pamphlet, because I believe you have the means to find it. I'm sure of it. I can add some other pieces, if you like.'

'Other pieces,' Rex said in a disillusioned voice. 'What if I had it, this pamphlet, and I gave it to you. It could be the death of your collection, Will. I'm telling you this after forty years of experience: a piece as rare as this should only come at the end of a career. Otherwise it might stop you in your tracks. You're on your way to becoming a great collector, Will, perhaps the only one capable of outdoing me, and not vegetating in a psychiatric hospital. Don't compromise your future.'

The words 'great collector' electrified Will. He could feel his hands flapping about. He knew the value of Eliza Fraser's pamphlet and was also aware he hadn't paid very much for the *Red Jacket* print. And as for compromising his future . . .

'I can help you track down your famous pamphlet,' Rex continued, 'but to do that I have to consider you an ally. What if I found it before you – it's not very likely, I agree, but let's suppose. Why would I sell it to you when you refused to help me to complete a collection that concerns my personal life, my innermost self? Imagine, Will, that the *Red Jacket* is my real home, I even see it as my cenotaph.'

'But I'm on your side!' Will protested, thinking of the letters he had written in New Zealand in support of Rex.

And he gave in. For Eliza Fraser's pamphlet and the promise of Rex's support.

He immediately felt he had done the best deal possible. Yes, he was an excellent negotiator. As for Rex, since it was closing time at the gallery, he produced a bottle of whisky and they drank a toast. To their searches, to their friendship.

'*Excelsior*!' declared Will. 'That was the name of my father's hot-air balloon.'

'*Excelsior*!' Rex responded, raising his glass. 'An excellent device. Let us try to go higher. You've had your nose straightened, haven't you? It suits you. In my case, I've had to straighten my entire life.'

They drank again. Will was mildly perturbed to learn that Rex had spotted his operation. Unless he had heard about it on the famous New Zealand bush telegraph. But he was so delighted at having won the esteem of Rex de Charembac Nan Kivell that he could forgive him anything. A classy ally who thought he was a great, a very great collector. His equal.

At the Jensens' he saw a different kind of happiness. They were a family like the one Will had sometimes dreamed of, like the one he might have one day in New Zealand if he got a move on. Or most likely not, he would probably never have two such sweet children, a boy and a girl, the boy at five years old sitting in the bathtub and flooding the room because his mother didn't come when he called. She had good reasons for taking her time: her husband Tad was deep in a discussion with Will Bodmin about Rex Nan Kivell.

Looking closely at the 'original' Eliza Fraser pamphlet,

Tad had said: 'I wouldn't be surprised if that was a fake.'

Will almost jumped out of his chair. His first thought was that Tad must be jealous, because he too, as much as his work at the bank and his family commitments allowed, collected objects related to the history of the South Pacific. It was an epidemic among expats, this maniacal urge to know everything about their place of origin.

'If it were a forgery,' Will protested, 'I would have noticed at once. I can tell the paper from that period, and the ink. Without a magnifying glass.'

Tad nodded.

'Yes, but I know Nan Kivell. He was one of my first customers when I came to London.'

Probably because, like him, Rex was from New Zealand, Lloyds had assigned him the account to manage. Will knew the basic facts of the story. There had been a dispute, Rex had left Lloyds and Tad hadn't got the promotion he was counting on. Impatient Tad, who wasn't even thirty-six at the time, hadn't come to this country to sit around and wait.

Will continued to defend Rex. Who could deny what a great collection Australia had been gifted because of New Zealand's crassness? Tad raised his hand to stop Will. 'He wanted a knighthood, that's all. In New Zealand, that wasn't possible because of his conviction.'

His conviction? Will had never heard of it. What was this story? For pedophilia, Tad went on, then added that personally he wasn't shocked that Rex was queer, but . . .

But. Will was stunned. 'I didn't know', he said. And blushed, because Tad burst out laughing and raised his beer glass to drink Will's health.

'You remind me of a woman I used to know,' he said, 'who claimed to be a philosopher. She only realised her future husband was queer on their wedding day, when she saw all her husband's friends arriving in trousers so tight you could see their genitals.'

137

'Tad!' his wife cried.

And she rushed into the already flooded bathroom.

Will was angry, and agitated. He insisted Rex had no need of a knighthood of the British Empire because he was already a knight of the order of Dannebrog. Perhaps he was baiting Tad to get him to say a bit more, because he did react, instantly, saying he knew all about that order: one of his customers was actually a member of it.

'Actually? You mean Rex . . .'

'Is not a member. No, he isn't on the list. He made up the honour the same way he made up the name de Charembac. We had his birth certificate at Lloyds.'

'But his collection exists,' Will persisted. 'And his gallery as well. That's what really counts, isn't it?'

'If you like. It's just the man behind it who doesn't exist. You can imagine it caused me a few problems when I was managing his account. I shouldn't really be talking about it. For me, Rex de C. Nan Kivell is as real as a playing card, nothing more, nothing less.'

There was bitterness in his voice, and Will didn't insist. The atmosphere had become awkward, and Tad, who was more irritated than the discussion should have justified, took it out on his son for flooding the bathroom. Until little Tom, his little blond head pathetically drooping, lifted his chin and announced with a menacing slowness:

'When I grow up, I'm going to be a Negro.'

In the moment of surprised silence that followed, and before his mother could reprimand him for using the word 'negro' in front of a stranger, Tom stared at his father and added: 'A big one! A very big one!'

There was no need for him to clench his fists, the adults burst out laughing. For Will, it was as if he had stated: 'I'm going to be queer.' The atmosphere lightened at once. There were more important things than Rex.

*

But Will would not forget Tad Jensen's accusations. As soon as he got back from Russia, he wrote to one of his sisters, a bookseller in Christchurch, to ask her for details about Rex Nan Kivell's family. This is how he came to have a copy of the *Red Jacket* passenger list. He would later meet a Birmingham collector who had known Nan Kivell since the start of the 1920s and, over time, he would piece together Rex's history which, of course, had very little in common with what the man himself had told him.

No Nan Kivell had ever disembarked from the *Red Jacket* in New Zealand, nor had any Nan Kivell ever chartered the ship. Although Rex was indeed born in Christchurch in 1898, his father was unknown. His mother, the daughter of a grocer who scraped a living on the Canterbury Plains, had been seduced as a girl by a handsome young man who talked of taking her to Christchurch, or even to England. He abandoned her as soon as she fell pregnant, and she in turn left her baby, entrusting him to her parents' care. Rex's grandfather had thus been a father to him, which probably, in Will's mind, explained why Rex confused his father and grandfather when telling the family story. His second drama had been to discover as a teenager that he was homosexual in a country where this was a crime. He had therefore covered up his inclinations by being passionate about 'virile' sports such as rugby, and by an aggressively militaristic stance. As early as 1916 he took advantage of the threat of war to enlist in the New Zealand Expeditionary Force sent to England. To do this he had to lie about his age.

He was to stay in the army for three years. Contrary to what he later claimed, he never saw action and never even left English soil. He served in such places as the New Zealand Army Hospital at Brockenhurst and the New Zealand Command Depot at Codford. And always in low-level positions. His military file makes no mention of any distinction; rather the reverse. It records his insolence, his lies, the fact that he forged leave documents – for which he spent time in prison – and impersonated an officer by wearing the uniform of one of his friends.

Rex had started to experiment with new identities at a very early stage, in a desperate struggle against his unfortunate birth. Discharged from the army in 1919, he boasted of heroic deeds in combat and claimed to have been a victim of mustard gas. At the same time, rejecting the dullness of his family tree, he invented an ancestor in the form of the fictitious Marquis de Charembac. These disguises assisted him in taking on a world he was sure would have rejected him if it had been known he was an illegitimate child who was abandoned by his mother and brought up surrounded by sheep. He worked as a volunteer on an archeological dig in Wiltshire. The Late Iron Age objects he unearthed there established the beginnings of a reputation, and it appears he was able to dispose of enough of them on the side to be appreciated by a few major collectors.

From this point on, he aimed steadily higher and further in the art world. He started work at the Redfern Gallery in 1925, rising to the position of director in 1931. After several decades of cunning and persistent effort, he managed to blend in to the English upper class and to begin a tentative return to his origins, duly reinvented to suit the new social status he had created for himself. The only thing missing was to become part of the nobility, or at least to be knighted and be able to use the word 'Sir' in front of his name.

Where New Zealand refused to ignore his criminal homosexuality, Australia set it aside, although with a stubborn slowness. It would be some twenty years before the promised title eventuated: Rex Nan Kivell did not receive his knighthood until 1977, just a year before he died. In the meantime he had become one of the country's greatest cultural benefactors. The distance he had created between the little New Zealander of his origins and the renowned

English collector was now so great that he was never able to bring himself to return to the South Pacific and thus never again saw the New Zealand he had left in 1916. He had fled his country, but he had also reconstructed it in the same way he had built Rex de C. Nan Kivell from his hopes and fears, the way he had made himself the entrepreneur of his own life, the way he had become – in spite of what he saw as common and ignominious, even working class, in the term – a self-made man.

One final note: the name on his birth certificate was not Rex but Reginald, and the family name was written as one word, Nankivell, a Cornish name of no particular distinction.

Once Will had pieced together this history – several years after his stay with the Jensens – he did not blame Rex for it. He couldn't help but admire this achievement because it was on such a grand scale. What suffering, he told himself, what constant, enormous suffering, must have pushed him to deny himself so consistently, in order to become more himself. For someone as religious as Will, suffering deserved respect.

Rex's struggle against reality finally led him to harbour delusions of grandeur. During the last conversation he had with Will, in 1972, he presented himself as the most important artist in the Redfern Gallery. 'The painters I exhibit,' he said, 'are simply pawns in a game they don't understand. I can replace them and move them as if they were ordinary soldiers. I'm the one pulling their strings.'

He liked conceptual art, though. 'I'm not interested in objects these days, just in the ideas of objects.' And then, by the end, the mere idea of a work, unencumbered by any concrete form, was enough for him. This may have been the logical extension of the separation he had always made between his fantasy self and his real self – a fantasy that his fortune had allowed him to maintain. His young associates accepted this new penchant with humour – they joked about it among themselves, saying as Rex got older he was losing his taste and was now trying to eat the menu instead of the meal. But when he became sufficiently enthusiastic about what he called Belgian artist Marcel Broodthaers' jokes (he had loved the artist's interview with a cat that answered him in meows) to want to bring his work into the gallery, his colleagues refused to even discuss it: it would destroy fifty years of tradition at the Redfern. This wouldn't have bothered Rex in the least, since he now felt himself to be above tradition and even above the idea of art, something he found as fluid and vague as the concept of ordinary identity.

'When I really think about it,' he told Will, 'I have, quite unwittingly, turned my life into a work of art. Are there accidental artists, the way there are saints who don't know they're saints? I'm not enough of a theorist to reach any conclusions, but I believe their existence is a necessity.'

Will saw him enclosed in a bubble, a fine sphere of vanity designed to protect him; inside it he shone, rather like an old baby. And soon the bubble would burst.

Rex wasn't going to help him find the anti-Darling pamphlet. Too bad. Where he had been fiercely disappointed by his father's lies, Will never expressed any anger against Rex. He felt sorry for him.

THE BREAK-UP

He came home from the northern snows like Father Christmas, except that Christmas was over a month ago. 'Your art-therapy group has been waiting for you for ten days,' Jane told him. 'And demanding you: they're bored with your replacement.'

She didn't complain on her own behalf, didn't say she had been worried and had wandered around the hospital that seemed even more gloomy than usual. She found Will changed by his travels, more serious. He was wearing a *chapka*, and his thick coat was heavy with odours of ships and distant cities. The first evening in his flat on Sandringham Street, he started unpacking his bags while Jane put the water on for tea. The bags were full of parcels done up in paper that wasn't brightly coloured Christmas paper, but each object Will unwrapped made his eyes shine like a child's. And Jane smiled at the sight of him. She didn't dare hope for a gift of her own.

'Look,' he said, brandishing an icon, 'here's what kept me two days longer than planned in Leningrad and made me miss my boat to Helsinki.'

It was an icon of the Virgin, dating from the early twentieth century according to Will. He had been offered others, older ones from far-off regions where, he was told, they wanted to send them to the West to 'save' them, but he had refused,

143

incapable of hiding them at the Finnish border. But this one hadn't cost much – practically nothing compared with what he could get for it in London. In the pale lamplight, dark lines stood out against the gold and red background with all the strength of a faith that will no longer hold back. Jane was fascinated.

'The Slavic soul,' Will said. He had paid in dollars, but it was his nylon shirts that had sealed the deal. Money is not what matters most in Russia.

And off he went, praising the Russian people – even the horrible barracks-like buildings the Stalinists had tried to park people in like cows on a factory farm, even those hadn't broken the Russian soul. It was indestructible. Everywhere, in the underground and on the buses, you could see people weren't interested in their own little personal profit, like they were here, but in the greater good.

Jane shrugged. She wanted a cigarette and didn't dare. She wondered out loud if Will loved these people because they couldn't afford to stop the cut-price sale of their icons to foreigners.

He shook his head, as though he couldn't understand where such a prosaic point of view could come from, and carried on emptying his sack of goodies.

Two Persian miniatures, painted on wood, in frames. One was of a pheasant under an apple tree, the other showed two children, a boy and a girl, holding hands on a flower-bordered path.

'A fantastic bargain,' said Will.

He was talking about money, she was picturing a fairytale Christmas, like in those children's books where you see *isbas* in the snow with little lanterns swaying above heavy arched wooden doors, and sleds . . . Did he see a sled?

No, he had stayed in the city, and on Christmas Day he went looking for a church. Ah, Slavic spirituality! He had gone into a monastery. Contrary to what the propaganda here said, some were open, and all afternoon he listened to singing that transported him into another world. That was better than riding in a sled. 'People are poor,' he concluded, 'but dignified. It's not like Jamaica or Panama, believe me.'

'You might have written to me, sent me something,' she said suddenly.

'But I sent you a card from Helsinki. Didn't you get it?'

'No.'

'And from Zurich, I sent some vegetable-peelers to my mother. They're the best in the world. I bought them in Baumgartners. Every time I go to Switzerland I send her a dozen.'

'To your mother, yes, of course. What's so special about these peelers? Can you show me one?'

He looked surprised. No, he hadn't thought of bringing one back. Why would he?

'Perhaps we might want to cook something,' she said, resigned.

Now he came to his big find, the highlight of his trip. It was the story, written in German by Admiral Adam Johann von Krusenstern, of the round-the-world expedition he had led on behalf of Russia between 1803 and 1806 – the four-volume edition published in Saint Petersburg in 1812. Will had acquired this extraordinary work for a ridiculously low sum, compared to what it was worth in England, and he had even managed to get the price considerably reduced for volume II because there were three missing pages (he knew where to find them and would get them copied and inserted in the right place).

'The poor bookseller,' laughed Will, 'his problem was he spoke English.'

'His problem was,' Jane interrupted, 'he needed the money. Maybe he was worried because he had Christmas presents to buy.'

Will was quiet for a moment, not understanding why she was being ironic. She was sitting at the little table where she had set down the teapot, warming her hands round a large cup.

'My idiot of a landlady didn't have the brains to put the heating on before I came home,' he said.

'But no one knew when you were coming back.'

'Yes, perhaps. But getting back to the Leningrad bookseller, I didn't take advantage of him. Absolutely not. If it weren't for me, he might not have sold these books until who knows when, and probably for an even lower price. Believe me, he was happy. So happy, even, that for two dollars – two dollars, do you hear? – he threw in a book in Latin he had no idea of the value of.'

He held it out with a flourish. The bag was lying slackly on the floor and looked almost empty, but Will's face had a certain mischievous glow.

'This book,' he said, waving a red-bound volume about, 'is entitled *Batavia*. It's a history of Holland in Latin, published in Leiden in 1588. I'm going to put an ad in the papers, and I bet you I can sell it for two hundred dollars.'

And so it was. As for Krusenstern's *Voyage Round the World*, bought for four hundred dollars, he was reluctant to part with it, kept it for fifteen years and finally sold it on, just before he left for New Zealand, to an American dealer who offered him thirty thousand dollars.

Now he was stroking the copy of *Batavia* that he couldn't read because he didn't know Latin, but which on its own would cover half the cost of his trip.

This was his pride and joy, not so much the financial gain as the opportunity to prove that he could manage, set off with practically nothing and come back with something: the journey itself provided the wherewithal to make it, it wasn't an expense, as it was for the majority of people, but a way of making a living, and even a source of deep pleasure.

The rolling stone gathers no moss: for me it's the opposite, the opposite!

Jane forgave him for not bringing anything back for her. The promise was not in the gift but in the trial itself: would he be able to live off his searching and dealing? He had succeeded magnificently, and she expected him to say so, expected them to move on to the next stage. But he continued defending himself, as if she had judged him to be immoral. 'It took me twenty years to acquire the knowledge I have now. My collection isn't founded on money but on my expertise . . .' And finally: 'These books, these objects are orphans and I find them a home. Shouldn't this service be paid for?'

She agreed with him a hundred times over, she approved absolutely of what he was doing, she was delighted to hear that, even though they had been abandoned by their parents, they didn't frighten him. It was just that she was expecting something else, the next step.

'I saw Nan Kivell in London,' he said. 'He'll help me find the anti-Darling pamphlet. If I can get my hands on that, everything is possible . . .'

'You won't need the hospital from now on,' she said.

She looked around her. Now that he had emptied his bags, she felt trapped by all these objects, unable to move. Like in a warehouse. If she stepped back without looking, she might knock something over. While Will was away in Russia, she had done the sums. They earned enough to rent a house where the collection could spread out. She would pay half the rent and it wouldn't cost Will any more than living here. Probably less . . . He would be able to travel.

'Oh yes,' he said, dreamily. 'A house. That's true, it's the best thing. As soon as I have the pamphlet, we'll even be able to buy it.'

Jane frowned. Was he going to make their life together secondary to such a fanciful quest? She would have liked to tell him he would be in a better position to search if they rented a house. But since she would have shouted, she held her tongue, instead taking out a cigarette.

'Ah,' Will laughed, 'I thought of you for Christmas. I nearly bought you a little earthenware pot – it looked a lot like a tiny tagine dish – where you burn incense to get rid of the smell of smoke. And then I decided it might get broken on the way.'

The miniatures behind their glass weren't broken though. Jane got up to get an ashtray, stepped back and felt something crack beneath her heel. One of the miniatures! Will had put it on the floor.

'What a disaster!' he cried, throwing himself down on his hands and knees.

Jane stood paralysed with shame, then lifted her foot, bumping her knee against Will's shoulder. She almost fell, clutching at the table. He was carefully picking up the pieces, unafraid of cutting himself on the shards of glass. 'The miniature is fine,' he shouted in triumph. 'It's just the frame and the glass! What a stroke of luck!'

He stood up, cupping the pieces in both hands as if they were a wounded bird.

'All the same,' he said, 'if you didn't smoke . . .'

She no longer felt like following him every weekend, but she went once to London with him, and while he was skimming through the second-hand bookstores she bought a few clothes.

He arranged his weekly hunting trips according to the train timetables, and sometimes remarked that if he had a car he could do everything much faster. Jane didn't have the heart to point out that they could have afforded a car if they were living together. She tried not to feel resigned. At the hospital, everyone knew about their relationship now, and Jane felt she was putting up with the disadvantages – notably that she was less at liberty to go to the pub – without getting the advantages she would have liked. She believed her colleagues felt sorry for her because she was still living in the nurses' home.

A month later she accompanied Will on a tour of West Yorkshire bookshops. On Saturday they went from Leeds to Sheffield and Birmingham. It was a grey day, and in a Sheffield bookstore Jane was talking to the owner, a young and cheerful fellow who seemed new to the trade. While Will poked about among a new delivery of books that the owner hadn't even quite finished sorting – there were several cubic yards of all sorts of 'printed materials' from a house that the heirs were keen to clear as quickly as possible – Jane asked the bookseller for the publication date of a brochure with a torn cover, a pamphlet about emigration to Australia. It would surely be of interest to Will, she thought. The young man glanced at it and said cheerfully that it must be early nineteenth century but that he had some that were in better condition. So he would give her that one for practically nothing – a pound, say. Saying this, he made a dismissive gesture, meaning 'Please, take it away.' Then he offered her a cup of tea, since he had just made some for himself, and Jane was happy to take a seat at a little table right beside the counter where the bookseller carried on sorting documents. From time to time he stopped to swallow a mouthful of tea and make a remark to Jane, who was trying to read her pamphlet. They soon started to talk about rugby. They liked the same clubs and shared their criticisms of the English team in the Five Nations tournament. Their laughter seemed to disturb Will who on two or three occasions raised his head from his cartons and, like a bird, stared at them with burning eyes, as if lost in some distant vision.

Finally, he popped up beside Jane and looked at his watch. 'Let's go,' he said, grumpily, 'we need to get to the station.'

Jane held out the pamphlet with the torn cover that she had put down beside her. He glanced at it suspiciously and paged through it. 'What's this worth?' he asked the bookseller.

'Depends whether you're interested in it,' the young man said, somewhat ironically, then added: 'To you, one pound.'

Will seemed not to care for his smile, and answered: 'I don't think it's worth that,' before turning his back to leave.

Jane followed him outside, embarrassed by his rudeness, waving to the bookseller. But this little act of jealousy from Will wasn't entirely displeasing to her. It was a sign that she could be at least as important as a packet of old books.

They had planned to eat dinner in Birmingham and then see a film. In the train, Will cheered up and was jollier than usual all evening.

It wasn't until Monday morning that he came to see her at the hospital, in her department, with an anxious expression, his face pale and gaunt. He took her out into the corridor to speak to her in private, staring intently at her in a way that made her uncomfortable. He had dreamed about the pamphlet she showed him in the bookstore in Sheffield, and in his dream it was clear the pamphlet was about two convicts named Sudds and Thompson. Could she confirm that?

Yes, she could. It was about two British soldiers in Australia who had been very badly treated: one died, and the other went mad. Yes, that must have been their names.

She watched Will turn even paler. He had to phone the Sheffield bookseller urgently.

He managed to reach him late in the afternoon. Of course the bookseller remembered him and his wife. How might he help?

Well, it was about the pamphlet with the torn cover they had talked about. Now he wanted it. He had thought about it and felt it would fit with his collection.

The bookseller was silent for a moment. He didn't know if he still had it. He would look. Could Will call back the next day? If he found it of course he would keep it for him.

That night Will tossed and turned, convinced now it was the anti-Darling pamphlet. The next day he called in sick at the hospital and took the train to Sheffield. When he arrived at the bookshop he saw it wasn't the same person behind the counter, but an older man. No, his young colleague hadn't mentioned a pamphlet with a torn cover. But . . ., insisted Will. The bookseller offered him others in better condition that also dealt with emigration to Australia.

Will went through them all, he searched through the books on the tables at the back of the shop. The bookstore was a series of separate little rooms, and what might have been a delicious browsing expedition became a nightmare. Will went back and forth, back and forth, and after he had messed up the shelves, moving the steps around to reach the highest ones, the owner's patience was finally exhausted. To calm the man down, Will bought two books that he wasn't especially interested in but would be able to sell on. If only he had thought to ask Jane where exactly she had found the brochure, in which room, his search could have been a little more methodical. As he paid for his purchase, he complained – with a smile – to the bookseller that the shop was 'very disorganised'. The man shook his head but didn't answer.

When Will phoned again the next day, the young man answered, to his great relief, but told him he didn't recall selling the pamphlet. On the other hand, it might very well have been part of a job lot he had sold to a bookstore in Leeds whose address he supplied. But why, he asked, was the pamphlet so precious?

Will answered that it was just a question of collecting, that it was a piece he was missing. But since it wasn't an especially rare pamphlet he was almost certain to find it quite quickly somewhere else, and probably in better condition.

Once again the bookseller said nothing for a moment.

The following Saturday Will went to Leeds on his own; Jane had refused to go with him because they'd had a fight. He had tried to get her to say where she found the pamphlet, and since she couldn't remember he suggested taking her to a doctor who, by hypnotising his patients, enhanced their memory to the point where they were able to recall details they didn't realise they had noticed. She told him he was mentally unbalanced.

In Leeds there was no trace of an undated pamphlet with a torn cover, dealing with emigration to Australia. Will had to widen his search, revisit all the bookstores he had gone to over that tragic weekend, because, touched by madness, he believed he had bought the pamphlet in Sheffield for one pound, and then, unaware it was the famous anti-Darling piece, had left it somewhere, unless he had swapped it . . .

Then he pulled himself together and accepted that he hadn't bought it; however, he was increasingly convinced that he hadn't recognised it because he had been blinded by the jealousy Jane had triggered in him.

The thing he had always feared – incompatibility between a woman and his quest – had just materialised before his very eyes.

Too worked up to sleep, he went down with an unexplained fever and took sick leave. When Jane came to see him, she found him incoherent. He grumbled that he didn't blame her for anything, but the next minute he became agitated, said he was unable to discuss it and wanted to be alone. Then he went to bed for two days. He tried to read, but the noise of the Norwicks' television reached him though the floor and irritated him to the point of rage. The set seemed to be on day and night and to mock him in his weakness. He could just imagine those two old imbeciles huddled between the heater and the TV set, unwitting representatives of an existence he considered unworthy of humanity. He went downstairs to announce to Mrs Norwick that if he kept on hearing the deadly racket of their TV he would leave.

She defended herself, arguing that at her age she had every right to a bit of entertainment and that he was lucky enough to have an interesting job. For at least half a day, the Norwicks turned the sound down. But since they were hard of hearing, they gradually turned it up again, probably without even realising it.

John Webster appeared late in the afternoon two days later. Will opened the door in pyjamas and dressing gown, with a scarf round his throat. His pallor and his drawn face revealed his state of health. John glanced furtively, almost guiltily, into the room, which looked as though it was about to be swallowed up by the objects it contained, a room made even less welcoming by the sickly smells of bed and food. He said it was a friendly visit, not a professional one – what mattered most was for Will to take his time getting well; everyone understood, but people were a bit concerned all the same. 'I'm happy to see you,' John concluded.

Will had the impression that was true. John walked forward cautiously between the piles of books towards the chair Will was pointing to – the only unoccupied chair in all the mess. To clear another chair, Will started to gather up scattered garments and stuff them into a laundry bag. 'My landlady is supposed to do my washing,' he said, 'but she hasn't come upstairs this week.'

John had heard he'd missed out on a very important piece for his collection.

'The opportunity of a lifetime,' Will said bitterly. 'It's unforgivable.'

'Now you know it exists, you should be able to find it.' John took out his pipe, an unmistakable sign of unease, and without lighting it, gripped it between his teeth. Then he pulled it out again and said: 'What's bothering all of us on the team is that Jane Hanley isn't well.'

Will thumped his laundry bag to compact the clothes. He stood up, holding it by the neck like some potbellied marionette. He was waiting for what was coming next.

'Some of her colleagues caught her sniffing ether. Is that usual for her?'

Will almost dropped the bag. No, he had never seen Jane

sniffing. He would never, could never have imagined . . . It was as if he had been betrayed.

Dr Webster sucked on his unlit pipe.

'So it's just an isolated incident, then. That's good.'

Above their sagging pouches, his tired eyes swivelled about. Not a bad chap, John, never had been . . . But what had happened to their old closeness?

'That department has a lot of problems,' said John, 'always the same ones.'

'What do you mean, the same ones?'

'It's always about sex. We might have expected better from adults.'

There was a long silence. Will bit his lip, thinking of Shirley.

'I'm amazed to hear Jane has been taking drugs,' he said.

'You just told me it was a one-off.'

Then John got up, heavier than ever but taking good care not to bump into a pile of books. It was a delicate balance – the true nature of balance. Will felt as if he could read what John was thinking, something like: I have seen inside Will's psyche, he externalises it in his flat.

Then he stood there for a second looking at Will in his too-long dressing gown with his scarf pulled up to his slightly trembling moustache. Which, in this light, had reddish highlights.

'What's to be done?' Will asked. 'Will you speak to the director about it?'

John gave him a cynical smile and slowly shook his head. They wouldn't even raise the issue within the department. Too dangerous.

'Will we pray then?' Will asked.

John looked at him for a long time, as if he had a mountain to carry.

'Pray,' he said.

MOTHERS

'Dear Mother,' Will wrote on the 13th of April 1963, 'something has happened at the hospital which made me depressed all of last week. Jane Hanley, the nurse who was with me in Rome last summer, was caught sniffing ether at the hospital. John Webster, our department head, was wise enough not to spread the news around, but Jane is aware several people are in the know and I think she must have had some discussion with Dr Webster. No one knows how to sort out this sad situation. I think for Jane the bottle of ether represents a substitute for the maternal breast. Since she was abandoned by her mother when she was very small, I don't think she can do without a substitute. That's the kind of doubt that prevented me from forming a long-term attachment to her. Because otherwise she's a charming young woman, intelligent and caring. But my profession does have a tragic side: it forces me to see more clearly than others. And I pay the price for that.

'I know what you replied when I told you I couldn't rely on someone who had been rejected by her mother during childhood. You said that wanting to live with perfect people isn't realistic, to do that you would have to believe you were perfect yourself. No, I don't believe I'm perfect, but nor do I want to follow the road to ruin.

'The headaches and depression I had last week are gone

and that's mostly thanks to my patients – with them, I feel useful and that's also why I wouldn't want to swap my work at the hospital for a more lucrative career as a collector. One of the patients I mentioned to you already, Mrs Nora Baxter, can foretell the future. It happens that last week I was depressed to the point of even thinking about leaving the hospital, because my relations with John Webster, and now with Jane, have become too difficult. Well, when I went into the department on Monday morning, a nurse rushed over to me and asked me if I was going to resign! I was very surprised, but responded by protesting that there was no chance of that, and then she begged me to go and reassure Mrs Baxter, who had been weeping for hours on the grounds that I was on the verge of giving notice.

'How could she have known about my doubts when she'd had no contact with me for over a week? Or was it perhaps because she hadn't seen me that she thought I wanted to leave? No, I think this second supposition is too easy an answer, and I'll tell you why. Mrs Baxter has already foretold events that would happen to me. In February she told me I would have an accident: she saw me lying on the ground with an injured leg and face. Her vision disturbed her so much she came to warn me during the painting workshop. Be careful when you ride a bike, she said.

'The following Tuesday my bicycle slid on a patch of ice and I went flying, scraping my shin. At that exact moment Mrs Baxter, who was in the ward and therefore couldn't see me, cried out that I was hurt! An hour later, I was happy to announce to her she had got it slightly wrong, because my face was fine.

'Then on the Wednesday one of our patients, a poor young girl, ran out into the park, barefoot and wearing only a nylon nightgown in spite of the bitter cold. The Australian male nurse and I caught up with her and as we were bringing her back, each of us holding one of her arms, she suddenly became angry and shoved me hard, so that I fell forward into a brick wall. I cut my left eyebrow open and bruised my face exactly as Mrs Baxter had predicted.

'This week I can tell her she got it wrong because I won't be leaving the hospital. But sadly, this comes at the cost of another resignation. Rumour has it that Jane Hanley has decided to move to a different institution and would be leaving anyway at the end of this month, April. I haven't yet had a chance to discuss it with her, but if it's true I think people in the department will be relieved, in spite of being very fond of her.

'I'm sending you in a separate parcel a packet of fennel seeds. Plant them in the vegetable garden. You haven't mentioned how the carob trees are doing that I sent you before the start of summer.

'To get back to Mrs Baxter, she's a patient who is very dear to me. I feel as if what I experience with her is the same as what happens between you and me when I dream about what is happening to you. It is a great comfort to me to know there's a link between us that is much faster and much more alive than airmail!

'I would like to come and see you in New Zealand and help you recover. I beg you, please ask Julia or Jill to contact that healer in Auckland I told you about. His name is Dr Stone, he is amazing and a religious man. If he comes to Christchurch, you really must not miss him.

'Your loving son,
'Will.'

His meeting with Jane the next day was a stormy one. She wore a mocking expression and, far from denying she had sniffed ether, seemed proud of it. Will was silent; it didn't even occur to him to suggest she should take back her pieces of Tahitian tapa cloth. In the end he said: 'The hospital will be empty without you.'

157

She laughed, short and sharp, and answered that she was quite certain he would be staying on. Not for the reasons he stated – his so-called therapeutic success rate – but because he was served two meals a day at a modest price and because the routine allowed him not to notice time passing.

His only comment was a smile, in the belief that he was avoiding discussion in order to spare her. She sneered and said, finally, 'I gave it a try, I failed.'

'No, no,' he thought it best to reply, 'you didn't fail.'

Then he saw tears running down her cheeks, but couldn't tell if they were tears of rage or sadness.

Jane made as if to say something, then changed her mind, turned away and walked off towards the nurses' home.

He stood for a few seconds on the path through the park, one hand on his bicycle. Then he left too.

On the 3rd of May he wrote to his mother: 'Now Dr Webster is resigning. He has found a position in London and I hope we will part on good terms. His time here hasn't been the most profitable, he knew nothing about psychoanalysis. Jane Hanley isn't here any more and she has left a major gap. She's a very strong personality.

'I've been looking after a young patient for the last three weeks, a boy of twenty with whom the psychiatrists have not had much success. He lives in the past, he is much more focused on history than I am, and consumed by the impossible desire to go back to bygone days, which he believes were better than the present.

'In particular he knows all about Queen Victoria, and the mere mention of her death makes him weep and plunges him into a despair that only I am able to calm. Unlike the psychiatrists, I don't try to reason with him, or to prove that the present is our only reality. Because I don't believe that. You know about my Jungian experience, you know what happened to me in Switzerland; well, these things make me feel very close to the young man.

'My diagnosis is that his attachment to the past comes from the trauma of his birth. He could not bear the idea of leaving the warmth of his mother's womb and coming down to earth in the cold reality of the world. He was a premature baby and was put in an incubator. And so he wants to return to the uterus. It's impossible, but that's not something he can be forced to accept . . .'

Further on, he adds that he is fighting off a relapse into depression. 'Ever since the anti-Darling pamphlet slipped through my fingers, I feel lost. I've decided to go back into therapy with Dr Gunther, a Jungian in York.'

At the start of June, however, he shows a complete change of mood.

'Dear Mother,

'You can't imagine how happy I am. I feel even freer than in those happy days when we spent our summer holidays at Riverton beach. And this is all due to Dr Gunther's therapy. We have established that my dissatisfaction and nervousness go back to when I was about four. I don't remember anything before that age, but as far as I know, my early childhood was very happy. And then at four, you remember, I developed a facial tic. (Did I have any other problems? I really must know. I beg you, please tell me.) I don't know where the tic came from, or why it went away either. But it caused a regression in me: I wanted to go back to the comfort of where I was before I was born. I must have repressed this obviously impossible desire in my subconscious for forty years! I believe the boy I told you about recently, the one who is so attached to Queen Victoria, must have helped trigger it in me again. In any case, about a fortnight ago I dreamed I was in a superb garden where everything was exquisitely sweet and the sun shone wonderfully warm. Although there were no houses or streets around it, I understood the garden was in *Florence*.

'Since that's your name, Dr Gunther of course recognised the desire to return to the uterus, and when he revealed it to me all my anxiety fell away. It was as if walls that were too solid for me were crumbling away and suddenly I was able to stand up and reach out my arms. My happiness is indescribable, I get along well with everyone, young and old alike. If Jane were still here, I think I would be able to reconcile with her.

'Everything is becoming clear. I understand now that time is simply a veil cast over the mysteries of life by our conflicts.

'Yes, everything is getting clearer, and I have something important to tell you. I have decided to come and see you. It won't be easy, but God will help me find the money and the time. I will be there in August.'

Two days after sending this letter, he received news of his mother's death. It took him completely by surprise. And if he hadn't already been in therapy, he would probably have suffered a major depression.

A month later he left for Portugal. A photo that Sara Tinkerbell found in the travel journal he wrote on his return shows him beside a country road with a pack on his back and another, bulkier and probably heavier, sitting at his feet. In the background, high dark hills are outlined against the sky: perched here and there on one of them, the white walls of a village look like chalk marks.

There's no doubt Will got there by hitchhiking. In a letter to his sister Julia (who condemns hitching as too dangerous), he talks about it as 'a way to save money' and says he stays in youth hostels as often as he can. He wants to keep his expenses down, so he can put aside enough to pay for binding the books in the bag at his feet. Because, as he explained to his sister, he has been given the address of some excellent binders in Lisbon who charge about a third of the price they do in London.

He also has in his pocket a letter from Rex Nan Kivell

inviting him to come for a few days' holiday in his house in Tangier, described by him as a lovely old house in the Moorish style, built on a cliff above the sea, surrounded by ancient trees and superb gardens, and with five terraces for sunbathing!

When Sara Tinkerbell refers to that summer, she talks about heroic misery. This is the moment in my uncle's life, she says, when I feel the saddest for him. The bag stuffed full of books that he drags through half the countries in Europe like a ball and chain, he claims he's carrying it to save a few pennies, but he is just about to inherit money from his mother and therefore from his father. He's about to become a wealthy collector.

No, Sara protests, I can't let myself be taken in by my uncle's financial arguments. I'm sorry to resort to what might be considered pop psychology, the kind of mechanical interpretations that have been so criticised in the Jungian method, and which my uncle abused to the point of making himself ridiculous, but the bag seems to me to be a substitute for Jane Hanley. Will is carrying his failed relationship around with him, and the Portuguese binders are obviously not going to be able to repair it!

Sara is sad to see Will's life running on like a dream he can't control. That's what she stresses when she says the mention of financial reasons is a subterfuge that allows Will to cancel himself out. More than ever, he allows questions like 'how much is it?' and 'how much will I make from it?' to dictate his behaviour. Sara doesn't shrink from talking about infantilisation. Will lost contact with his own desires to follow a financial imperative which, while it looks rational, is a form of madness.

She mentions regression again when she sees him becoming younger. He dresses like a young man, he travels with a backpack and stays in youth hostels (what a contrast with his Roman holiday the year before!), he hitchhikes. Perhaps he is also dreaming of more plastic surgery. His mother's death has thrown him into disarray, and made the effects of his break-up with Jane dramatically worse. Alone, and behaving like a teenager again, he accepts the hand Rex extends to him, since he can no longer seduce women.

It is this Will, plunged into an almost childish innocence, who travels through France, then Spain and Portugal, in search of his fortune. He describes himself as a rolling stone, but he also wants to gather moss. He is forty-three years old.

From Spain, he sends Winnie a letter marvelling at the miracle of Olivenza he has read about in a Spanish newspaper. 'It's a miracle like the loaves and fishes,' he writes. 'In a university cafeteria in Olivenza, the cook made a mistake in his order and had no food left when a crowd of students arrived for lunch. All he had left, in one large pot, was a stew made from a kilo of rice, a few chunks of meat, an onion and three bay leaves. Desperate, he fell to his knees to beg the Lord to help. And his pot became bottomless: every time he dipped his ladle into it, it came out full. He was able to feed more than one hundred and fifty people in this way. He said he had ladled so much out that his back hurt. I saw his photo in the newspaper with the miraculous stewpot that he wants to offer to the church as a holy relic, once the bishop has blessed it. The students testified that it was a genuine miracle.'

That he believed in this type of story, according to Sara Tinkerbell, is proof of his weakened state. But after this episode where he speaks of divine grace, he pulls himself together and for the rest of the summer he makes no more mention of divine intervention, ghosts or apparitions.

On the other hand he makes some important finds. In his heroic misery, he develops his other option, the collector's path; and that summer it will be his salvation.

His letters from Lisbon are no more fantastic than the

ones he normally wrote from York. In them he talks about happy days, he likes the Bairro Alto and its narrow streets, he enjoys walking for hours and returning exhausted to the youth hostel. Even without knowing any Portuguese, he feels at home here, because home for him is always where he feels slightly foreign. Living incognito takes him back in time but also allows him to search, to be lost in order to find himself again.

'I love this city,' he writes, 'with its hills and its narrow streets that suddenly lead out into unexpected open spaces. An iconic image of life itself. I'm convinced that a vital discovery awaits me here. The light in Lisbon, the warmth of the nights and above all the constant whispering of wind and sea speak to me of something that is suffering because it is not understood, taken up and spoken out loud . . .

'In the youth hostel I feel comfortable so long as I am not with other tourists. The first night, there were four of us in the room – in bunk beds, and the three others were English – and it was only when I woke in the middle of the night that I realised what had brought me here. I got up and went to the half-open window. There was no one on the street, but I listened anyway because I was trying to catch a murmur of prayer, to see an army marching into view. I expected this because that's what happened to me fourteen years ago in Lausanne. I even felt in my pockets for a cigarette, though I haven't smoked for a long time. I know I would like to go back to that moment in Lausanne that set the pattern for all the years to come, that showed me the strength of Carl Gustav Jung's ideas. I know if I could go back to that moment, I might be able to change it and alter the course of my life. Then I wouldn't be here this evening in Lisbon, I would have faded away in front of this window on Andrade Corvo Street, and I would have escaped my destiny once and for all.

'But nothing like that happened.

163

'There is something else awaiting me, something greater perhaps.'

The fact is that a binder he gets along well with – who speaks some English – puts him on the track of an extraordinary map. It was drawn in France in the sixteenth century and the antique dealer who has it shows it to Will and explains that it was based on the reports and maps of the Portuguese navigator Cristóvão de Mendonça. Will knows there is debate around this question. But he is unable to say if this map (which isn't one of the so-called Dieppe maps that are often referred to as proof that the Portuguese arrived in Australia before the English did) is authentic. He can see it's a fairly accurate representation of the coast of southeast Australia and looks old. But where has it come from? Was it really drawn in France in the sixteenth century? He is confused by what the dealer says in a sort of English he has trouble understanding. He already knows that a Dutch navigator went to Australia one hundred and sixty years before Cook, but he is almost shocked to hear the dealer state: 'Your James Cook wasn't the first European in Australia. Mendonça got there two hundred years before him!' The asking price for the map is so high he gives up the idea of buying it, and leaves the shop feeling very irritated: he has to walk for three hours to calm down. Is he on the verge of a major discovery, or are they trying to put one across him? The most painful thing for him is the thought that anyone might want to destroy Cook's image. After all, Cook honestly believed he was the first European to land in Australia. He didn't lie. Can you be angry with a man for believing his wife was a virgin? There you are: you should never want to be the first. Anywhere.

Losing Jane, then his mother, and now having to defend his spiritual father, it was asking a lot, too much . . .

From a café terrace, he writes to Winnie:

'I am experiencing some extraordinary things in this

city. I saw a map today that would seem to prove the Portuguese discovered Australia two centuries before Cook. Is it nationalism that makes them believe this? I don't have the means here to prove the map's authenticity. Or its true provenance either. It is much too expensive for me, unless it is authentic – in which case it is priceless.

'The Portuguese apparently covered up their discovery of Australia because according to the Treaty of Tordesillas the land in these regions should have come under Spanish control. And then the original maps disappeared in the great fire that ravaged Lisbon in 1755.

'This business reminds me of Hawaii. The Spanish navigator Juan Gaetano went there as early as 1527, two hundred and fifty years before Cook. But since Spain wasn't in a position to take possession, it preferred to keep the existence of the islands secret so no other European country could take control, and Gaetano's maps were so well hidden that no one knew where they were. Worse still, even the memory of the discovery disappeared. It wasn't until England proclaimed its sovereignty over the islands (then called the Sandwich Islands) that someone in Spain woke up and found the archives containing records of Gaetano's voyage. And four more years to lay hands on the famous maps. Too late!'

Unable to invest in a map that might have somewhat undermined Captain Cook's glory, Will leaves with a consolation prize that may be even more exciting. Understanding his passion for the English explorer, the antique dealer offers him the Portuguese version of Cook's death as related by an eyewitness, James Cleveley, ship's carpenter on board the *Resolution*. Will knows that Cleveley is the creator of a number of drawings that his brother, the painter John Cleveley, used, notably as the basis for his *Death of Captain Cook*, and he also knows James Cleveley wrote a memoir of his voyage and the events in Hawaii. Unfortunately, this memoir disappeared long ago. If a Portuguese translation

165

exists, that would be an astounding discovery. Although he is stunned, Will is careful not to reveal to the dealer that the English original no longer exists. On the contrary, he quibbles, asks if the translation is accurate, if it's really Cleveley's text, afraid, since he doesn't read Portuguese, of buying a pig in a poke.

But the dealer sings the praises of the work, saying it shows Cook did not die, as the English legend maintains, from a blow to the back of the neck as he turned away to ask those on board his ship to cease firing on the Hawaiians. Nothing of the sort! No, he took a Hawaiian chief and his family hostage and things went wrong from there. He apparently also killed a native with his own hands. 'I can't swear to the accuracy of the facts,' the dealer says, 'I wasn't there. But that's what he claims, the witness. It's an extraordinary story.'

They continue their discussion, each half-understanding the other. This is the third day they have met, and the dealer, either tired of negotiating with Will or, on the contrary, having grown fond of him after all this time in his company, finally lowers the price by half. 'It's been sitting on my shelves for seven years,' he admits. 'It would be better for it to live out its life elsewhere.' Will is very touched to hear another man speaking the way he does about the life of books. As soon as the bargain is struck, the dealer invites Will to lunch so he can find out about English antique dealers, because he's planning to go to England the following year.

'He wasn't wasting his time,' Will reports. 'I know the important dealers well and I explained to him what they offer for sale. But I have to say this enchanting book (I will have it translated when I get back) was sold to me for a price not much higher than the cost of the lunch. And since the dealer was paying, I could say I got the book for practically nothing.'

That, according to Sara Tinkerbell, is an example of a

satisfaction she has trouble understanding. Why is Will so proud of acquiring an object 'for practically nothing', when he talks all the time about 'a fair price' and honesty? It's as if he was owed something, something greater than the object he acquires. What is he lacking, really? Sara concludes: 'The law applies to marriage, it can never guarantee love.'

Will stayed longer in Lisbon than he had planned, but when he left it was not to head south to Tangier. The little book by James Cleveley in his luggage prevented this. Too bad about the blue sea, the terraces under the trees and the sunny mornings, he couldn't risk talking to Rex about the book before he had it authenticated. This is what he told his sister, and this is something else his niece doesn't accept. Because, she says, he could have gone to visit Rex without mentioning the book. No, she believes two major obstacles prevented the trip. First, Will no longer needed the protection of the great collector: his Portuguese discoveries had restored his self-confidence, and he was less tempted to succumb to what she calls homosexual conniving with Rex.

Next, to go to Tangier he would have had to cross the Strait of Gibraltar and therefore pass close by the place where his father died. Facing up to his father's death at a time when so many important figures in his life were disappearing, when even Captain Cook was no longer what he had been (and Will was carrying a little volume that told of his death) made the journey difficult, perhaps even impossible to attempt. Will was in the habit of avoiding failure by explaining his behaviour in terms of external imperatives. Again on this occasion he writes to his sister Julia:

'In Lisbon, I didn't notice time passing. The bindings cost me more than I had anticipated, and I bought a number of extraordinary books, but I'm not sure that any one of them is sufficient to pay for my journey. It would therefore be better for my finances if I go slowly back to England.'

This idea of journeys that pay for themselves, says Sara, leads us to think that Will is looking for a free passage through the world, rather like a stowaway.

BROTHERS

The world had turned while he was on holiday in Portugal, and the hospital was no longer in the same place. Not quite. The things most familiar to Will had disappeared: Jane's voice, John Webster's worried expression as he sucked on his pipe, the thrill that went through him whenever Shirley appeared unexpectedly. And he could no longer take comfort in writing to his mother. The castle has sunk beneath the waves, he murmured, and will reappear in a hundred years. Sometimes he would open a door without thinking, a comment to Jane on the tip of his tongue, and then he would freeze because he was face to face with someone else, an unknown woman or a head nurse. His words would vanish into thin air before he had even spoken them.

His first shock was as he went into his office: that dazzling, bare whiteness . . . It took him a second or two to be sure he hadn't got the wrong room. Repainted, it had been repainted in his absence, without waiting for him, without asking his opinion. The paintings and drawings by his patients that had covered the walls – a permanent exhibition including a bark-cloth drawing from the Philippines – were piled up on his work table. And his plants, where had his plants gone, his philodendron and his potted cabbage tree? When he leapt out into the corridor to ask for an explanation, he came across a new nurse, young and smiling, who along with the occupational therapist, was running the painting workshop while he was away and who told him she was very pleased to meet him, as if he were the one who had just been hired.

The really nasty surprise was yet to come: there had been a change of department head. The new man, Stanley Owen, was a cold-seeming psychiatrist, in his thirties – quite a lot younger than me, Will noticed, slightly shocked – who greeted him casually and informed him the hospital needed to make serious savings. A matter of survival, he declared. What Dr Stanley Owen called 'the consultant psychoanalysts' would be reduced in number from now on because they were much more expensive than psychotropic medications and antidepressants. The range of medications available these days was marvellous, he went on, and we're not making full use of it. Mentioning these two types of treatment this way seemed monstrous to Will, and he steeled himself in preparation for the inevitable, an attack on art therapy. It didn't come directly. But there was a silence between them, Owen also apparently expecting something from Will, some answer that didn't eventuate. He drummed his nervous fingers on his desk, as if to say: let's not waste our time with silence.

When he left without having really talked about his work, Will realised suddenly that Owen hadn't mentioned prayer, which didn't cost a whole lot and up till now had had a very good reputation. But then he wasn't a Quaker.

He focused on his workshop. This wasn't a tactic, it was a chance to lick his wounds. There, surrounded by pots of paint, easels and sheets of drawing paper, he felt at home. Even the patients seemed to be better in this room with its big, ivy-framed windows where they came together to draw, paint, make collages or small sculptures. They joked, drank tea, compared their work and even managed to talk about something other than themselves for a change. 'We're together,' Will liked to tell the participants, all present of their own free will, all generally in better health than the average patient. And he wasn't lying. And it was also here, through these long afternoons when he felt sheltered from the world, that he was most easily able to write to one of his sisters or jot down a personal thought in his notebook.

Although he was on staff, he had always had a position slightly apart, and this now became even more marginal; it was closer to the ghostly existence of the patients. But he was not referring to them when he wrote 'I live with the absent.' No, he meant Jane, Shirley and John Webster. At least with the patients he could see them, sometimes touch them, laugh with them. But when he wrote that he felt himself sliding 'into a black hole' instead of using the usual term 'depression', he was borrowing that expression from one of the new patients in the workshop, Jack Diggs. The man who had talked to him about black holes and whom Will referred to in a letter, curiously, as 'my brother in arms'.

The man he had made it his mission to protect, because the new department head wanted to send him away.

Jack Diggs had been hospitalised at his own request because he was afraid he might kill himself. The psychiatrist who admitted him – Dr Minkowski – had mentioned a paranoid breakdown: he can't run fast enough, he added jokingly, to get away from his wacky ideas.

And yet if anyone gave the impression he was making an effort, it was certainly Jack. He sweated in Will's workshop as if he were fighting giants, when there was just a canvas in front of him and his only weapons were brushes. He was a tall man, brooding and massive, in his thirties, and every day in the workshop he fought a battle Will knew nothing about. Will sensed that just one defeat, one lost fight might be enough for his whole life to fall apart, but up to this point Jack had always succeeded. Except at weekends, of course, which he apparently spent at his parents' home and where he must experience some strange things, because Jack came back on Mondays in a complete state, agitated, pale and very weak. It was painful, for the nurses as well as for Will, to see this mountain of a man trembling like a child, and they were quick to stuff him full of medication.

But in a team meeting Stanley Owen had decided that outpatient care would have to do. 'He's avoiding responsibility here,' he declared. In the silence that followed, Will thought he detected the current ideology – people should pull themselves together, not cost the community so much. In particular he thought he saw a criticism of his workshop. Nostrils flaring, moustache trembling, he replied: what took responsibility away from Jack, in his opinion, was the antidepressants.

'In my workshop, he takes control of his fate every day.'

'Oh yes? What does he paint?'

'The black hole he's trying desperately not to fall into.'

Silence.

Dr Minkowski, Jack Diggs' referring psychiatrist, nodded his head as though he understood.

'He has some very interesting ideas,' Will stammered.

Smiles. No one disputed Jack's 'interesting ideas'. The young man had studied physics and even worked in the laboratory of the famous Professor David Bohm. The problem, as Minkowski pointed out, was his other ideas, the ones that had prevented him from pursuing his research and even, in the end, from finding work. And he concluded that prolonged internment might well impair Jack's ability to take responsibility for himself, although to be honest getting him to a point where he could do this would be a stretch . . .

The decision was therefore postponed until the next meeting, at which Dr Minkowski would be happy for Will to present Jack's case as he saw it. After all, he was the only person Jack Diggs confided in. Full of pride at these words of recognition, Will promised to cast some light on this business.

*

Jack had in fact spoken to him at length on two or three occasions, each time after one of his painting sessions that left him close to exhaustion.

Whenever he came into the workshop, Jack seemed very determined; without speaking to anyone, he planted himself in front of his canvas from the day before, shook his head as if dissatisfied and attacked a new one, always in the same way. He would start by covering it in layers of paint that looked like giant snail tracks. Then by endlessly painting over them with other colours, he subdued them, stiffened them, making the edges lumpy, crusty, bristling with defensive blisters. The whole thing became heavier, darker, until it looked dirty, but from this ugliness there arose a strength, a threat – like a trap or a prison. On this particular day, Jack had been struggling for two hours, and his agitation, working its way up from beneath the fog of medication, was visible in his trembling. He seemed close to breaking point.

'Stop,' Will advised him. 'Let it rest. You'll work better once it's dry.'

Jack raised his head, dazed, blinking.

'I can't do it,' he sighed.

The drugs, Will thought. And said nothing.

'It's the black hole,' Jack said. He rubbed his forehead with the back of his hand, leaving a dark blue streak.

Will took a step back to see the painting better. What Jack had painted was a kind of magma of no recognisable colour, but it didn't look like a hole. 'It must be hard to do a black hole,' the therapist said. 'There should be something around it that isn't part of it.'

Jack swallowed. 'A black hole,' he said, 'is when gravity is so strong that even light is its prisoner. It turns back on itself.'

He said this slowly and with real suffering in his voice, as if the imprisoned light was affecting him. At the same time, he pressed his right hand against the canvas, and when he

173

lifted it off it was stained red, black and green. He stared in astonishment at the mark on the canvas, then leant closer as if he was looking for a solution there.

Will held out a rag. Jack wiped his hand carefully, but it was still dirty: he would need some turpentine. And his forehead was still streaked with blue. He explained that he had struggled against the black hole. 'Our eyes,' he continued, waving the rag. 'They say our eyes pick up the light of dead stars. It's the wrong way to think about it, because it measures the stars out there with a clock from here. We would need a universal clock, but there isn't one.'

Tears ran down his cheeks as he lamented the lack of such a clock; you'd have thought he had announced that God was dead.

Will nodded. He understood that Jack might be drawn to the black hole where everything disappeared, grief as well as memories.

Mrs Nora Baxter, who didn't like to see Will monopolised by another patient, popped up beside them. She was wearing a green silk turban and looked up at Will with an anxious expression, her brow furrowed. 'Jack has a problem with his painting?' she asked.

'No, no, of course not,' Will answered.

She pulled at his sleeve and he turned towards her. She whispered in his ear that he was going to receive an inheritance. 'But I know that,' he protested. She shook her head. 'Ask them to look and see if your parents put some money into a fund that starts with the words *United Friendly*. Look there, the money's there.'

And back she went, looking authoritative, to sit in front of the little easel where she'd been doing practically nothing for the last hour.

It was Will's turn to feel puzzled. *United Friendly* . . . united and friendly like good parents. He banished the thought from his mind, but it was back again within a few minutes. Then again an hour later, like a little lamp that kept turning on and off in his head. United and friendly. And then the black hole. The two are in opposition, like Jack Diggs and Nora Baxter. Like his parents. Who had been united for him.

As the patients were leaving, he kept Jack Diggs back. He had been sitting on a stool for several minutes, as if inert, his head bowed, not making the slightest attempt to clean up his equipment.

'I'll clean up with you,' Will said.

Afterwards they had a cup of tea together and chatted for quite some time, Jack Diggs having suddenly come to life.

That evening, Will wrote to his sister Winnie:

'The very far-sighted Nora Baxter told me about an investment fund beginning with the words *United Friendly* that our parents apparently put money into. Can you have a hunt?

'On the same subject, I did receive the copy of the will and I see the lawyer mentions the sale of Mother's jewellery. I'd like to know how much this might bring me, even if an eighth share is probably not a lot. But there's something more important. Mother promised me her paternal grandfather's sovereign, the one with the head of William IV that has a hole drilled near the edge so you can hang it from a watch chain. It's the only thing that was handed down from that great-grandfather, and Mother promised it to me so often that Father told me: you should ask her to put it in writing! Unfortunately I never did. If someone else wants the sovereign, I'm ready to do a swap. I just hope it hasn't disappeared. I really want to find it. Do please let me know as soon as possible [. . .]

'Once again, I have a surprising patient. He doesn't tell the future like Mrs Baxter, but he showed me that instant communication – of the sort I sometimes had with Mother – is not a physically impossible phenomenon. He's a physicist who used to work with the famous professor David Bohm.'

During the night he had an unpleasant dream. He was marrying Nora Baxter, they were walking forward over the green carpet in a great hall, and people were laughing at them because she was decked out in a long red dress and a grey jacket with a white fur collar that made her look like a queen in a pack of cards. She had a big belly, a lot of make-up, and she was walking clumsily.

When he woke at five and couldn't get back to sleep, he started writing the history of Jack Diggs.

Jack Diggs, wrote Will, says he had a happy childhood in one of the nicer suburbs of York where his father, who was manager of a small accounting firm, owned a comfortable house. 'I remember playing volleyball on Sundays with my father,' Jack says. 'Sometimes my brother Stuart – he was two years younger than me – joined in. He wasn't very sporty, but he was a happy lad.'

At around the age of fourteen, Stuart became interested in the occult; he started dressing in a very affected way, preferably in black, and doing astrological calculations. He became a real night owl. He was also studying numerology, which brought down upon his head the sarcasm of his father, for whom numbers referred to more concrete realities, notably money. One evening at dinner, Stuart announced in a choking voice that his astrological calculations predicted he would die at thirty. To be exact, he was going to die on the day of his thirtieth birthday. 'We stopped talking,' says his brother Jack, 'and stared at him. He was so pale Mother asked him if he had a fever. He hadn't touched his food. Without waiting for his answer, which would in any case have been a very long time coming, Dad carried on talking about the cricket results. Stuart sat there saying nothing and a few minutes later he went to his room. Two days later, Dad asked him casually if he always believed his astrology stories and Stuart answered that it would be impossible for him not to: he was going to die on the day of his thirtieth birthday, it was a dead cert. Dad shrugged and told him he would do better to predict share prices, which made me burst out laughing.'

Stuart became more and more withdrawn. At the slightest remark, he would reply that he wasn't going to live past thirty. Irritated, Jack told him that wasn't so bad. His mother tried to persuade him to seek help, but in vain. And his father, a strict Anglican, suggested Stuart go back to the church and get involved in sports, because, he said, prayer and sport solve all life's problems.

The atmosphere in the home soon became impossible. Meals were eaten for the most part in silence. Their father would sometimes get up without a word of explanation and leave, even though Stuart seemed not to have said anything – or perhaps only muttered something inaudible. 'Seeing my father leave like that was unbearable,' Jack remembers. 'It was as if he was doing what Stuart threatened us with. I began to hate my brother, I fought with him several times, yelling at him: "You stupid bastard, I'll kill you before you're thirty! That way your prophecy won't come true!" Of course my mother blamed me because I was stronger than him.'

Once Stuart finished high school, his parents rented a bedsitter for him in town. For a year or two things went back to normal. Stuart came home for special occasions: he had found a job in an insurance company, and the family was starting to forget the difficult years. Jack was already living in London where he was studying physics, and he didn't miss his brother one bit. 'As long as he was getting by,' he says. 'I thought he must be happy enough, because he was still with the insurance company and he had a girlfriend; they moved in together and there was even talk of marriage.

'And then last year, just after his twenty-ninth birthday,' Jack continues, 'the whole family got together for Christmas lunch. Stuart arrived with Mary, his girlfriend, but he looked strange, his face was blotchy, as if he had been drinking the day before. There was a tension between them, and during the meal, Stuart hissed at Mary: "In any case, in a year's time I won't be here and you'll have plenty of peace and quiet."

'Mary shrugged as if he had said something silly,' Jack goes on, 'but in front of everyone it was hurtful all the same, and when she saw my face and our father's, she realised we weren't treating it as a joke. Only our mother carried on as if there was nothing wrong, cutting cake and passing it round with a smile.

'My father looked at his plate without touching it. He had lost his appetite. I was so disgusted, I was so ashamed of our family that I had to get up and go into the kitchen to calm down. In fact I drank a couple of glasses of the sparkling wine that should have been served with dessert.'

After this, Jack had no news of Stuart until about a month before his thirtieth birthday. 'The whole family,' he says, 'was dreading the fateful day, but I was the one who was most anxious about it. I couldn't stop wondering: what can I do so my brother won't die? I was restless, and in the end I phoned him to find out what he was up to. He chuckled, then asked me if I wanted to be mentioned in his will – which struck me as a pointless insult because he owned hardly anything. I tried to stay calm, but then I counterattacked by suggesting he should find a hideout. Here, in your Quaker hospital. "Go and stay with the Quakers," I told him, "and you'll be close enough to God that you won't need to actually go to heaven."

'Of course my making fun of him stopped him from seeking the protection I was suggesting. And then he disappeared three days before his birthday. Mary called the police at once, but as soon as she mentioned the prophecy they took her for a loony and stopped listening to her. Nevertheless, they called her on the day after Stuart's thirtieth birthday. He had been found dead in a hotel in Leeds. Since there was no apparent cause of death, there was an autopsy, but it was inconclusive, and we still don't know why Stuart died. This is a very important point, because to my great astonishment I learned he had taken out a life insurance policy with the company he worked for, to the tune of one million pounds, naming me as beneficiary. The news took me completely by surprise, and the police even interviewed me about it. I was ashamed of having misjudged my brother. I understood what he had suffered, and now I feel the terror he felt, faced with that prediction, faced with his inescapable death. He was the brightest in the family, the most innocent. Why had he wanted to leave the money to me and not to Mary? He loved me, and I thought he detested me.

'There's one more thing: if it's suicide, the insurance company won't pay out. I'm sure, absolutely sure, that it isn't a suicide, but I don't know whether I'll take the case to court, whether I want the money or not.'

Will had thought long and hard about this story; he found it all the more terrifying because it had reduced Jack to such a pitiful state. And to oblige Jack to react, not to remain a victim in this business, to the point of wanting to follow his brother in death, he had tried to get him to admit that Stuart had blackmailed the family and then committed suicide so as not to lose face. 'If your brother didn't kill himself,' I said to Jack, 'then you killed him. But you didn't kill him, therefore he killed himself.' He rejects this argument, even though it's the logic he's following when he accuses himself of killing his brother. His position vis-à-vis the insurance will be an important test. I see a paradox there: if Jack fights for the money, and if he gets it, he will have to believe his brother died for him – and thus, in his own mind, he will have killed him (the way we killed Christ). If he refuses the money, he'll be disowning his brother and washing his hands of him; that's his only possible way to freedom. Well now, in the name of common sense, several members of our team feel that Jack would be *mad* not to take the money: that would prove he is completely out of touch with reality. Owen of course is of this opinion. 'If Jack can manage to get the cash, he'll have succeeded in taking on reality,' he has said. 'Staying poor would be condemning himself to live a fantasy life.' He even said something that went down very well and seems destined for a bright future with our Philistines: 'Who would remember the Good Samaritan if he hadn't been rich?' It's a measure of the small-mindedness of the team: the whole debate is about the money, whereas the real mystery, the real heart of the question, is to be found in the connection between Jack and his brother Stuart.

A week later, Will returned to the subject of instant communication, so dear to him. 'I've just read in *The Times*,' he wrote to Winnie, 'the story of twins so closely linked that when one of them was being operated on under anesthetic in a London hospital, his brother was writhing in pain at home at the precise second when the scalpel cut into his body. He had to be given powerful pain medication. According to Jack Diggs, the physicist patient I mentioned earlier, quantum physics shows that two protons can be connected in such a way that what happens to one of them is instantly reproduced by the other, even if they are thousands of kilometres apart. He studied instant communication in Professor David Bohm's laboratory. Einstein knew of it and called it 'ghost-like action-at-a-distance'. So there are ghosts, as I have always maintained, and I'm happy to see physics finally admitting it.'

Will had become so involved in Jack's case that no other patient had ever occupied his mind to the same extent. He saw the man as another self and, disregarding the rules of therapy, attempted to tell him about the vision he had in Switzerland that had decided his future. He hoped Jack would be able to provide him with the explanation he had been searching for in vain for so long. But when he tried to talk about it he lost the thread, his memories were jumbled, he started laughing, and Jack stared at him with a brooding expression as if he wondered what was wrong with him. Will beat a hasty retreat, afraid he had forgotten the concrete details of his vision, and decided to write it down before it changed and became completely obscure. To do this he referred to the journal he kept at the time.

THE BATTLE OF MORAT

In June 1949, writes Will, I was in Zurich, where I had started a course of Jungian analysis with Frau Hunziker a few months earlier. From there I travelled across Switzerland on my bike. I was planning to go to France, to Ferney, where I was to visit Voltaire's chateau. On the evening I arrived in Lausanne, exhausted from a long day's ride, I went to stay at the People's Palace. In the room they gave me I found a strange little fellow lying on one of the two beds, wearing a white singlet and cotton trousers and smoking in the semi-darkness. I turned the light on and introduced myself, but he barely responded. He wasn't hostile, however. He was in his fifties, short and gnarled, with a curly beard and a deeply lined face. The strangest thing was the smell that permeated the room: something sweetish, almost sickly, and I couldn't help but comment on it as I went to open the window. '*C'est mon fromage,*' my roommate said. Since I spoke only schoolboy French, I had to ask him to repeat it, and that's when I realised that the enormous round package sitting on the chair near him, wrapped in a grey cloth, was a cheese – a Limburger that gave off a smell of the stables, something warm and organic that made me feel as though I was surrounded by a herd of cows. The man, who told me he was a fisherman, not a farmer, held out his pack of cigarettes. 'Smoke,' he said, 'it covers the smell.' I took one of the yellow cigarettes – corn paper – but as it had no filter I soon found myself chewing as much tobacco as I was smoking. Between puffs I struck up a conversation. I could see my clumsy French was irritating the fisherman, who, perhaps thinking to speed up our discussion, switched to a kind of bastardised German. 'Present,' he said, patting the cheese as though it was a pet animal. 'Geschenk. Princess, Geschenk für Prinzessin. Ich King fisherman. Capito?'

No, I didn't understand how he could offer this stinking cheese to a princess, but I was getting used to the smell and when mixed with fresh air from the window and the strong smell of tobacco smoke, it became quite bearable. Pleasant, even. Suddenly exhausted by my hours of pushing the pedals, my eyes closed and I fell asleep. The cigarette fell from my fingers and I had just enough time, before I lost consciousness, to see the fisherman pick it up and stub it out in the ashtray. Merci Mensch, you're a good man.

I woke up in the middle of the night, suffocating, my stomach in knots. That blasted Limburger again, probably. I sniffed at the warm air laced with bovine mustiness – unless it was the old fisherman suffering from serial flatulence, the way cows do – and got up to get a breath of air at the window. I saw the moon shining high above the rooftops, and when I looked down I could see by its light something unusual going on in the street. The lamps had gone out, but countless flaming torches lit up a silent crowd that had gathered beneath standards among which I recognised the Swiss flag and the flag of the city of Bern, with its bear climbing diagonally across a band of orange. Then I noticed the people were wearing medieval costume: multicoloured hoods, tunics over hose and pointy-toed heuze boots. They were soldiers, some of them knights, who had dismounted and taken off their helmets, and stood with the light from the torches reflecting on their armour. White crosses were clearly visible against the silvery metal. A forest of lances reached skyward, and then I realised there wasn't a horse in sight, and that most of those present had lowered their heads, or were down on one or both knees. Some had put aside their swords or crossbows to fold their hands in prayer. I was mesmerised – was this one of those famous Swiss carnivals? The strangest thing was the silence that had allowed this army to rise up out of nowhere. A terrifying silence, until I noticed the prayer. It began as a scarcely audible vibration that grew to a murmur, then a buzzing that rose towards the sky, reaching my window and entering the room to blend with my roommate's snoring, amplifying it as if the man were some kind of wind instrument. As I watched the fisherman's chest rise, a long moan emerged from his mouth, and the entire room started to groan. The prayer continued to swell, becoming a roar, thundering against my eardrums; it was going to explode, to ring out in the fearful din of war, in a clamour of shouts, the neighing of horses, the cries of the wounded. Everything whirred and whistled around me, and harsh words, aimed as precisely as bullets, in a language I didn't understand, came firing out of the old man's mouth. The whole room, floor and walls included, was shaking, threatening to break apart, and I panicked for a moment, thinking about the sound waves from loudspeakers with enough power in their bass notes to burst people's lungs. I shouted to the fisherman in German: 'Wake up! Come and look!' He stopped snoring and raised his head, but in the darkness I couldn't make out his eyes.

I repeated: 'Come and look!'

He lay there, raised up on his elbows, his white singlet standing out in the blackness, and while I was watching him the noise stopped.

The fisherman let himself fall back again without answering. Looking out the window I saw the soldiers get to their feet and pick up their weapons, marching off in silence below me and disappearing, leaving the moon to shine down on an empty street.

I was very excited, even agitated, and the regular but noisy breathing of my roommate was driving me crazy. I stepped out into the corridor, but all was quiet, as if nothing had happened. I went back to bed and tossed and turned beneath the sheets before I managed to fall asleep. The next morning I tried to question the little fellow about the night's events, but he just shrugged his shoulders and left, carrying his heavy cheese like a globe of the world and leaving me with no explanation whatsoever.

In the room where breakfast was being served, I asked two students sitting next to me what last night's procession of people in costumes had been for. Apparently they knew nothing about it. When I kept asking, they called over an older man who turned out to be a history teacher from Neuchâtel. He spoke English well, and was delighted to talk to a New Zealander; he immediately referred to our country's great military achievements in Greece and Italy. When I finally got the chance to ask him about the midnight procession, he told me he was very surprised to hear about it and would not have been able to see it anyway because his window looked out over a different street. I wouldn't let it drop, and gave him such a detailed description of the flags and clothing that he became thoughtful and questioned me further. Each time I described with absolute precision objects and uniforms I simply could not have seen. He decided that it was the Swiss confederate soldiers, and he even mentioned a battle the Swiss won against Charles the Bold, Duke of Burgundy, in the fifteenth century. Afterwards, looking concerned, he went to ask the manager of the People's Palace if during the night there had been any kind of procession of troops in medieval costume. The manager shook his head, and the teacher came back to announce with a broad smile that it must have been a dream.

When I insisted on the reality of my vision, he explained pompously that something seen by only one person is obviously a dream or hallucination. Then he excused himself and left. I was slightly ashamed to be taken for someone who hallucinates or confuses his dreams with real life. But today, fifteen years later, it's the rest of my trip that seems like a dream to me, and my nocturnal adventure that has become the reality.

I left, feeling slightly put out, counting on my therapist to clarify things for me a few days later. Had I been the victim of a hallucination? Over the last fifty kilometres to Ferney I kept asking myself this question; I reached the French border having noticed almost nothing on the way. On arrival I realised I had left my passport in Zurich, and I had to negotiate with the police, who finally decided I was some sort of harmless Brit. But there was another disappointment in store for me when I reached the chateau I had been dreaming about for a number of years, as an admirer of Voltaire's life and ideas. I discovered it had passed into private ownership and wasn't open to the public on Thursdays! I had to pester the guard for quite some time before he would let me into the grounds to photograph the building. I might perhaps have convinced him more easily if I had shown him a banknote. But I was travelling cheap, and I came from a country where we don't tip. When you explain this to French people they just can't believe it. They think there's some kind of subterfuge involved, because they can't imagine we might have people in a position of authority who, although they are all too often stupid and inflexible, are seldom corrupt and would resign if they were shown to have wrongfully pocketed the smallest sum of money. Such honesty strikes them as complete madness.

I left Ferney late in the afternoon, and as I pedalled towards Lausanne I knew I wanted to go through the city without stopping – and never wanted to set foot in the People's Palace again. To be honest, the mere thought of it frightened me.

Since my legs felt like lead, I stopped for a short rest and ate some soup and a slice of ham in a little roadside restaurant. When I came back out, it was already evening: I would need my lights on, using the dynamo that rubbed against the rim of my wheel and slowed me down. The road verge was losing its green colour and glow-worms were starting to glimmer in the grass. I picked one up and tucked it into the hollow of a little leather buckle hanging from my handlebars. I liked its radiance: its independent light shining out in pretty contrast to the mirror of the lake on my right, which was growing gradually darker and duller. Then I got a puncture in my rear tyre, and discovered I had no patches or tools. So I had to push my bike to the nearest service station. I was on the outskirts of Nyon, where I was lucky enough to find one still open; the manager was happy to lend me the tools to repair the inner tube myself. A triangular nail had made a hole in the tyre, the kind of metal cleat used on the soles of climbing boots, and I thought a hiker had tried to slow me down. This is a universal law: everyone, by the mere fact of moving, tries to impose his own rhythm on others, and it takes an extraordinary amount of energy to resist falling into step with everyone else.

In any case, night had fallen and here I was still standing outside the garage – a summer night so bright I could have travelled with no light except the glow-worms – and I needed to find somewhere to sleep. The manager of the garage, as obliging as ever, told me about a forest where camping was allowed and I could spread my sleeping bag. I had no trouble finding it, and in the shadow of some tall trees I settled myself on a carpet of leaves so thick that I didn't need my little foam mattress. I fell asleep quickly, lulled by watching wisps of cloud drifting across the moon, only to dream about the Duke of Windsor being beaten up by a ghost who had cornered him in a small library in the castle and was punching and slapping him around. I woke to the noise of tree branches knocking together, like giants silhouetted against the sky, and when I heard a roll of thunder loud enough to burst my eardrums, I decided I would be better out of there before lightning struck. As it flashed across the sky, I made out several tents around me, and realised I wasn't, as I had thought, alone. However as soon as it started to rain, I would be the most exposed. So I sallied forth on my bike. A couple of kilometres from the forest, the road passed in front of a farm where the lightning intermittently lit up a restaurant sign. Heavy raindrops were by now hitting my head and back, and I hurried into the courtyard, heading for the light I could see filtering through the gap between the shutters. I knocked on the door, and since no one came at once, I opened it and stepped into a large kitchen. Three men and a woman were sitting around a long table. I explained my situation as best I could, but they kept shaking their heads and saying no, no, we're closed – it must have been two in the morning – and I could tell they were as drunk as skunks; wine bottles littered the table along with the remains of what must have been an especially copious meal. A slender young man with a long nose above a thin moustache stood up and explained they had worked very late and were exhausted, but he swayed on his feet as he spoke. The others whispered among themselves, and when the woman rose in turn I could see the fear on her plump, rosy face. They kept asking me if I really was alone, if someone had sent me, and my answers didn't seem to satisfy them. When they finally understood that I just wanted to sleep on the piles of hay in the barn because of the storm, a second man came over to me. The two of them, he and the one with the moustache, started to search me so clumsily that I doubt they would have found a weapon if I had been carrying one. In any case they weren't looking for weapons but cigarettes and matches, and while they were patting my pockets the woman held up a packet of tobacco so I would understand. They must have been afraid I would set the barn on fire. Eventually the young man led me outside, lighting the way with a lantern he had taken from the windowsill and managed to light. When we got to the barn door, he told me I could go in with my bike and all my gear – that's the word I remember, 'gear', he said, meaning what I was carrying on the rack and in the saddlebags. He showed me the ladder to the upper level of the barn where the hay was stored. He gesticulated as he spoke, the lantern flame rising and falling, throwing huge shadows here and there in the dark interior, and I was of course afraid he might end up dropping his lantern and causing a fire – maybe the others in their drunkenness would accuse me of doing it. But everything was fine, and I had only just stretched out in the hay when the storm broke, and thunderclaps went crashing across the sky.

When I woke up, the sun was shining in under the roof and I went back to the kitchen to thank my hosts. But there was no sign of life, other than someone snoring in the next room. So I wrote a thank-you note in my bad French and left it on the table.

I have no memory of the rest of my trip. But I do remember returning to Zurich to my analyst, the formidable Frau Hunziker, whom I had compared a short time earlier to Saint Francis of Assisi because she was so uninterested in money that she didn't charge me for my sessions on the weeks when I didn't earn anything. She didn't even have a bank account – which was the reason, I suppose, for wanting me to pay in cash.

My adventure at the People's Palace didn't impress her much. She also wanted to label it a dream, which irritated me a great deal. 'How could I have dreamed so precisely of events I had never seen?' I asked her. 'Was I tapping into the collective unconscious?'

Her reply was that I had probably had this dream to please her, to show her I was a good student thoroughly

189

versed in Jungian theories. According to her it's a common phenomenon. In the same way, people involved in Freudian analysis have dreams that match Freud's ideas.

For the first time since I began my sessions with her, I told her I disagreed. What she was saying implied that we are responsible for our dreams, which would be horrendous. At that point I quoted the famous anecdote, as told by Plutarch, about the tyrant Dionysius of Syracuse, who had Captain Marsyas put to death because he dreamed he killed the tyrant. Look what happens if we are made responsible for our dreams! You can't live. To be fair, I should have added that it was Marsyas who had the terrible idea, hard to understand, of telling Dionysius about his murderous dream.

To which Frau Hunziker answered sharply that Marsyas condemned himself to death for reasons we cannot hope to understand. My lesson had had no impact. I wasn't satisfied, but I said nothing more.

At the time, I was taking Jolan Jacobi's classes on the representation of the unconscious in art. In addition to studying the work of painters such as Hieronymus Bosch and Bruegel the Elder, we were analysing the output of patients in psychiatric institutions. One idea kept coming back: that great creators and madmen alike are able to draw on the unconscious, which Jungian psychology shapes and forms like raw material. I liked the idea, found it soothing. I had drawn from this source, in my vision: perhaps I too was becoming a great creative artist.

Except that my artistic output was zero. I never touched a pastel, a brush, nothing. And then one day, in the Institute library, I came across a book in which I recognised the scene I had observed from the window of the Lausanne People's Palace. There was a reproduction of *Confederate Soldiers at Prayer Before the Battle of Morat*, a painting by the Swiss artist Bachelin, dated around 1870. It was all there: the costumes, the weapons, the prayer, even the same faces and their expressions. This discovery may have been an even greater shock to me than my vision itself, because it was confirmation that I hadn't been dreaming. I was certain I had never seen the painting before – or a reproduction of it – and I had never been to Morat, where it was on display in a hotel. Nor had I ever even heard of Bachelin or the battle of Morat, that glorious moment in Swiss history when the confederates repulsed Charles the Bold in 1476 and killed more than ten thousand Burgundians for a loss of only four hundred and ten of their own men. There was no doubt that such an important event would remain present in the collective unconscious, and now by some unknown mechanism this memory had infiltrated me, invaded me. I could not have dreamed it. Either I had gone back in time, or the past had reached out to me. The fact that it had reappeared in the form of an existing picture could, however, give rise to a great deal of conjecture.

I curbed the panic rising in me at the thought I might be mad. I remember that I ran from the library without even a glance in the direction of the students I knew (I was afraid of letting them see my anxiety), and I buried the whole story deep within me. When I realised I wasn't able to tell Frau Hunziker about it – I didn't dare – I knew there was no point in continuing my analysis with her.

As quickly as I could, I got a certificate of attendance at the Institute and went back to England, where I now felt able to work with patients in psychiatric hospitals. I understood them.

Will was never able to tell the story of this adventure in detail. He tackled the question again with Jack Diggs, making a joke of it: 'I've seen a fifteenth-century army, in Switzerland,' he said. Jack turned and looked inquiringly at him again, wondering whether he was taking the mickey, pretending to be like him. No, Will wanted to know if it was possible in theory, since clearly it was in reality. And Jack told him that formal logic rules out that kind of thing. If you went back in time and prevented your parents from meeting, for example, you would destroy yourself on the spot; as a result, you wouldn't be able to go back and prevent your parents from meeting. To go back in time is a paradox which, in logical terms, always negates itself. But, he later affirmed, Aristotelian logic is merely a formal, superficial description of phenomena. It accounts for only a part of reality and when we force ourselves to respect it we turn ourselves into sad little machines. Then, taking a deep breath and avoiding eye contact, as if he were confessing something, he explained that instant communication isn't even an exception, but the basic rule. Reality, in his opinion, is like a poem: if you change the first word you've already altered the last one, even if it hasn't been written down yet. And if you change the last one, you change the meaning of the first. Everything we do affects everything else, but we don't know how. And the past doesn't disappear: it has an effect here, and we have an effect on it. What you saw, he told Will, you might also see differently at some other time. And maybe you wouldn't recognise it even though it is your past.

These words comforted Will; he felt as if they supported him, told him he was right in spite of all the Stanley Owens of the world. But he was careful not to report them to Dr Minkowski, who would only have taken them for babble and entirely symptomatic of Jack's illness. Will remained convinced that Jack was speaking the truth. Except that, in this instant communication where everything was connected, instead of being in contact with the whole world as he should have been, he felt terrifyingly alone and misunderstood.

Jack left the hospital suddenly, of his own accord, before the treatment team could make a comprehensive decision about his case. He had overcome his fear of suicide, and even if his departure showed that his time in the department had not been wasted, he left a gap that people tried to fill by talking endlessly about his brother's suicide. Right to the last day, Jack had refused to explain how he planned to settle his dispute with the insurers. Perhaps, he said enigmatically, he would leave it in the hands of fate.

He promised to keep Will informed. So Will waited for a sign, a card, even a dream to inform him. Nothing came.

It was painful to start with; he had lost a lifeline. Sometimes he woke in the night with the thought that he hadn't understood the first thing about Jack, that the story about his brother was a smokescreen, a shell hiding more than it revealed. There was something more – but what? Sometimes he still had the impression Jack had been sent to tell him something and that he hadn't been able to decipher the message. To tell him what? That he was a lousy therapist? The question roared so loudly in his ears that he had to fight it with the same energy Jack had used against the black hole in his paintings. From that point on, he never once asked himself that question again: he was a great therapist, end of story.

HOME

And so the Diggs affair ended inconclusively, without a winner or a loser in the treatment team, although Will was convinced Dr Owen would return to the attack. Between them there was still a kind of indifference tinged with hostility. Stanley Owen had just decided on a campaign to give the patients pets for therapeutic reasons. This was an old established tradition in the hospital that no one would contest, but one that had faded away because of the considerable constraints it imposed on the staff. In itself, it was no threat to Will.

He saw in it, nevertheless, a new rejection of his workshop. In one of his notebooks he wrote: 'Dr O should remember I managed to get rid of John Webster.' A generous overestimate of his powers, but one that reveals his fears and his desire to counter-attack. For a pacifist, his tactical instincts are good, drawing other pacifists into his offensive – the Quakers who run the hospital. He proposes, within the circle of the Society of Friends, a series of lectures where he will talk about what he calls 'the natural way to mental health'. As might be expected, this 'way' turns its back on medical techniques and instead promotes a combination of psychoanalysis and religion. He is mixing a dubious cocktail in which he makes numerous references to Jung and clumsy use of Freud, having read him little and badly, and attempting against all odds to pass him off as a supporter of religion. But Will knows how to regale his audience with moving anecdotes and stories of spectacular recoveries, winning over people who in any case have no knowledge of psychoanalysis. Will has bet that Owen, who is not a Quaker, will refrain from picking a fight with a prominent Friend, and this turns out to be the case.

The unexpected success of his lectures goes to his head a little: he comes to think of himself as the herald of 'the true science' that Jack Diggs told him about. It's a science based on intuition, shortcuts and daring interpretations: the importance of symbols, thought transmission, prophetic dreams, instant communication – these are a few of the elements he invokes in challenging what he calls (but only in his private correspondence, for he is a careful man) 'the Procrustean breeding grounds of the laboratories and the dim drudges of behavioural psychology' who try to explain our behaviour as genetic and our thoughts as chemical, 'as if a plane were no more than a pile of nuts and bolts and a poem just a bunch of words'.

In his enthusiasm, he ventures into even more dangerous territory. He attempts to rehabilitate ghosts, the forgotten ones of science, in his opinion. This is an undertaking that haunts him like a longed-for revenge. The fact that ghosts have a limited degree of autonomy, that they are neither entirely alive nor entirely dead, does not mean they do not exist, he declares. Quite the opposite. He even seeks supporting evidence in the tabloids: photographs of the Loch Ness monster, and others supposedly showing ghosts caught in the library of an abandoned school. Nothing seems to surprise him these days. Sometimes he justifies these strange phenomena in terms of scientific ignorance, sometimes he refers to nature's unruliness, her rebellion against mankind's aggression. He sends his sister Winnie an article from a local paper telling of Scottish rabbits that climb trees. There's a photo showing some rabbits up a cherry tree. These mutant rabbits, he claims to know, are the result of radiation emitted into the atmosphere by nuclear testing.

The more he develops his thinking, the more he gives the impression he believes the world is unconsciously seeking its own destruction. Increasingly, he compares conventional ('fraudulent') science to a driverless train hurtling blindly towards death. To continue on its wild way, it must 'disguise its death drive as a quest for progress'.

Given his reliance on the Bible, quantum physics and Jungian psychology, he could be taken for a crackpot and he begins to realise the danger he is in when some of Dr Owen's ironic comments are reported back to him, referring to his ideas as twaddle and poppycock. At first he just laughs, but an alarm bell finally rings when he learns that the director of the hospital, even though he's also a Quaker, seems to share the doctor's opinion. And his audiences are dwindling and starting to express doubts. In a completely unexpected reversal, Will Bodmin wonders – and writes it in his notebook – whether he might not be in the process of provoking his superiors to get himself fired. 'Am I too a driverless train hurtling blindly towards destruction?' He adds that if he loses his position at the hospital he will have to focus on his work as a collector. Isn't that what he secretly wants? Isn't that his vocation, neglected for over a year – since Dr Owen's arrival, in fact? Now, he adds, it's important to save yourself for enemies who are of equal stature: 'This Lilliputian Owen is not on my level, I have picked the wrong enemy.'

In the meantime, he hadn't even tried to get James Cleveley's story of the death of Captain Cook translated back into English. He now decides to go back to his collection: it will keep him from losing his place at the hospital. His logic may be hard to follow, but it turns out to be correct. As soon as Will gives up his lectures, he finds a new zest for life and the level of tension drops noticeably at work.

His flair for collecting is as impressive as his psychological theories are woolly. 'I've been lucky enough,' he writes to his sister Julia in 1966, 'to come across *The Ships of Tarshish*, the first novel ever written in New Zealand. These are the ships, according to the book of Isaiah, that enabled the lost tribe of Israel to depart. The author of the novel, a surveyor by the name of Edwin Fairburn, believes Maori are that lost tribe – a myth taken up by the Mormons, unless they invented it independently to convert a large number of Maori to their religion.'

Shortly before Easter he mentions five Australian gold coins dating from the gold rush era, for which he paid one hundred and fifty pounds each. 'I read this morning in *The Times* that a woman sold an identical coin at auction for five thousand pounds. I have five of them. If this price is genuine, I will with one purchase have earned enough to buy a house without taking on an enormous mortgage.'

A house! He has always vaguely dreamed of owning a house, even though he kept putting it off and resisted whenever Jane tried to talk to him about it. But this time he will take action. What is pushing him is a dispute with his landlady, Mrs Norwick. He had been seething with resentment since his break-up with Jane, blaming the landlady's surveillance – 'like keeping watch on an underage child' – for preventing him from developing his relationship with the young nurse.

'Dear Winnie,' he writes – in 1966 again – 'I think I told you already that Mrs Norwick is seriously ill, and, out of concern for her condition, I have refrained from any criticism, even though I was saddened to see her the victim of a slow and pitiless lobotomy, sitting glued to the TV the whole afternoon watching programmes stupid enough to drive a donkey to distraction. A dual lobotomy, I should say, because her husband, who is always slopping about in his slippers, is assisting her in this brainwashing operation. Three days ago, I made up my mind – for the good of my health – to point out to her that the TV must also have ruined her eardrums because she has the volume turned up higher and higher, which is a considerable disturbance for me. Sometimes I even think that she and her revolting TV set have come right into my room. Can you imagine the horror I feel then? It becomes impossible for me to rest, and I need all my energy not to make irreparable mistakes with my patients or to get caught up, because of fatigue, in some transaction that would be disastrous for my collection.

'My comment, although it was moderate and absolutely true, made her angry. Yesterday she came up to tell me the house had rising damp and she was afraid my books were causing it! I was speechless at such an underhanded approach. (Do tell me, please, if it is a peculiarly female trait to try at all costs to have the last word.) I made her sniff the shelves and piles of books, I pulled out every volume she indicated and stuck it right under her nose. Not the slightest trace of mould – on the contrary, the sweet smell of the wax I order specially from the British Museum to rub into the leather bindings. In addition, I air my books regularly and keep the temperature high enough to get rid of any dampness. It is distinctly warmer here, among my books, than it is on the dark, damp ground floor where the Norwicks live. But such is human nature. Once the mind has been corrupted by television, once the brain has been softened, only being weaned off it for several years can restore them to full function.

'I have decided not to have Mrs Norwick do my laundry from now on. In any case she didn't dry it properly and has permanently discoloured, probably from misusing bleach, the only 100% nylon shirt remaining of the ones Jane Hanley gave me. And she shrank it as well. God knows how. Such a lovely shirt, now unfit to be worn in public! I wonder if Mrs Norwick might have done it on purpose. I admit it made me so furious I couldn't sleep for two nights, thinking about it. I don't know where Jane found the shirt, but in the shops now all I see is cheap cotton or a nasty polyester mix.

'No, I can't stay with people like this. I must buy a house that's roomy enough for my collection, a place of my own where I won't be subjected to the moods of a sick woman with a damaged mind.'

Two months later, he announces he has set his heart on a six-roomed house in Bishophill, on the other side of the River Ouse. There is also a garden with a shed where he can keep his bike. In order to buy it, he puts in not only the money raked in from recent profitable dealings, but also the remains of his inheritance, as well as the proceeds from the sale of 'one hundred and fifty manuscripts to the National Library of New Zealand, four antique maps and a Gobelin tapestry. So,' he adds, 'I didn't need to borrow much. All the same, I realise that my monthly payments will be so high I'll have to stay on at the hospital.

'The house is superb, but it has been closed up for the whole winter and I will have to get new central heating before I move in. You can believe me, Winnie, when I tell you there will be no dampness, no mould in my house.'

He sends his sister a detailed plan of the premises and explains what each room will be used for. The living room on the ground floor will be converted into a small gallery and reading room for maps and manuscripts. Upstairs he is setting aside a very small space where he will squeeze in a double bed, a sign he hasn't given up hope. The room next door is to be a library; he also plans to set up a corner to do gymnastic exercises, including an apparatus that will build up his pectorals.

He moves in in March and mentions happily the 'airy' feeling his new residence gives him. But it would seem he can't bear that feeling, because he immediately proceeds to buy a mass of objects that will fill the house. Since his sister has not managed to find the investment that started with the words *United Friendly*, as seen in Mrs Baxter's vision (he is not upset with his patient, on the contrary, he has spent a long time thinking about the deeper meaning of what she said and is sure the legacy exists somewhere in some other form), he sells his Australian gold coins and buys some antique furniture and Maori weapons from a London dealer. Over the same period, he picks up entire series of Victorian novels, sensing that their prices will skyrocket – which is exactly what happens two years later. He tells Winnie some young people have sold him 'a whole attic full of old books for peanuts, since the ignoramuses had no idea of their value. They were delighted to have me take them off their hands and watched in amusement as I filled my backpack and went to and fro like some ancient beast of burden. Well, I'll be onselling their collection for twenty thousand pounds sterling! I wonder why I am having such good luck, when I still can't get my hands on the anti-Darling pamphlet.'

These numerous acquisitions are piling up and gradually taking over the available space in his new house. Will decides to send a few rare items to New Zealand, packed in cases he lines himself with asbestos. In spite of this, just a few months later he notices the space around him has shrunk 'like a badly washed shirt', and sees he is going to have to sacrifice his bedroom. More precisely, the double bed will have to be exchanged for a single. 'Otherwise, I would have had to give up the desk,' he writes.

The walls are now lined with crowded shelves and display cases overflowing with bric-a-brac. Mobile shelving units full of paintings are cluttering up almost all the corridors. Even the beautiful old maps Will had hung in the living room are starting to disappear behind pieces of furniture he has been meaning to repair but which, also filled with pamphlets and prints, cannot now be moved. And yet in what strikes the visitor as an impossible jumble, Will is able to find the smallest object in a matter of seconds. He knows exactly where everything belongs and has been careful to separate the items he wants to keep, the ones he expects to sell, and the ones he wants to send off. But whatever he does, his universe continues to shrink, which has a disastrous effect on him: his own activities will eventually suffocate him. Perhaps this is why he starts feeling irritable again, his phobias returning along with his old recriminations against the ways of the world. When Winnie complains that a thief had the nerve to steal a tree in a pot practically from her doorstep, he answers:

'I am sickened that you have been a victim of such a theft. But you must understand that since women started smoking, children have felt from birth that they were getting a raw deal, because a mother who smokes cannot bring them up properly. They take their revenge as best they can. This revenge reveals itself as a thirst for profit that leads them to take whatever they want without regard for anyone else, and that in the long run will see them destroy the planet.'

Or: 'Petty crime is reaching terrifying levels in England. Opinions are divided between those who maintain the lead in petrol fumes has damaged the brains of young people and those who put it down to the consumption of refined sugar.'

He even comes to doubt the usefulness of knowledge. 'If I hadn't known what Jane Hanley's abandonment at a young age would lead to, I would have married her in ignorance. Would I have been stepping on a mine, or would that ignorance have been bliss?'

He says he is haunted. By what? This man who accuses television viewers of shutting their souls away behind the screen and watching them parade about outside, cheapened and commercialised, seems to be going down the same road – he sits there, as if walled in, with his collection and his obsessive thoughts instead of television. His letters grow more and more sombre, fixated on catastrophes of every stripe.

On the 17th of May, it's the story of a patient, a young woman who went hunting with her father and accidentally shot him in the face. 'They have cared for the father as best they can, grafting on the face of a dead man, but he's a fearful sight, drooling endlessly, and his daughter, now unable to sit across the table from him, has had to be hospitalised here.'

When he mentions his own family, Will notes that his parents married too young, lacking maturity, and that in any case his inventor-father had 'such curious character flaws that today he would be in psychiatric care.'

Predictably enough, this battle against an enemy he is unable to pin down eventually makes him ill. He writes to Winnie: 'I would never have believed it, catching a cold in the middle of May that kept me flat on my back in bed for four days. I ought to call it flu because I had a fever and treated myself with gallons of tea and whole bottles of aspirin. The explanation for my cold is simple: I wore a shirt that wasn't properly dry. Since you can't get 100% nylon shirts any more, I have to buy cotton ones, but cotton is tricky: you can never tell if it is completely dry. So you must always iron your shirts. But I buy so-called no-iron shirts because I don't have time to waste ironing. Which, as I have learned to my sorrow, is a mistake. I am a victim of false advertising. But Winnie, how could an advertisement not be misleading when it tells you something to cover the hidden message, which is: give me your money?'

By the next week, however, he has completely recovered, and is delighted to announce a ray of hope: 'A patient told me that they still sell nylon shirts in Barbados, and he even gave me an address. I've written and am waiting impatiently for a reply, as you can imagine. If it works, I'm going to order six shirts at once. And if they're good, I'm going to buy them till death do us part!'

He decides suddenly to make contact with Jane Hanley during one of his trips to London. After hesitating for some time over writing to her at the hospital where she is nursing, he sends a brief letter, trying for a casual and amusing tone, without suggesting outright that they meet.

There is no answer from Barbados. On the other hand, his letter to the London hospital is returned to sender: Jane no longer works there.

Over the following year, Sara Tinkerbell remarks, Will gives the impression that he is sticking to a routine: his job at the hospital, about which he reports nothing spectacular, and his methodical collection work, through which he makes a number of minor discoveries. The Darling pamphlet, however, remains elusive.

As far as the hospital is concerned, Will hardly ever mentions Dr Owen. He merely notes some small changes in the workshop. For example: 'A new nurse is supposed to assist me, along with a woman psychologist who believes she can read the patients' symptoms in their drawings. I don't need to tell you how tense this woman makes the atmosphere. Some of the patients, probably in terror, produce things especially for her, work that looks like Rorschach tests, and she's delighted by it. I'm always surprised at the patients' enormous capacity for pleasing the staff [. . .]

'And the nurse, a chunky young woman with a piggy face, is taking classes in town in the evenings, with an American woman who teaches how to catch a rich husband. The nurse was talking about it to the psychologist this afternoon. Here are some of the topics: Where to find the wealthy. Don't be fooled by a skinflint. Spot the millionaire beneath the surface. The charming loser, etc. In the meantime, the nurse is paying good money to listen to this rubbish (I think there are even exercises and homework assignments) without ever asking herself why the American hasn't found a rich husband to spare her the trouble of selling her nonsense. I didn't much appreciate that the psychologist and the nurse spent an hour squawking like a couple of magpies over this tripe. But perhaps it keeps them from doing mischief elsewhere. I hear Dr Owen has suggested to management that my workshop be wound down. For financial reasons, apparently.'

That is in fact what happens six months later. Luckily, Will Bodmin is not the only one to be affected by a downsizing plan that covers a whole section of the staff. Far from being downcast, he finds a new energy that allows him to land a new job in under two months, at Darlington Hospital. Of course he has to take the train every day – there's no question of moving now that he has his own house – but he feels the welcoming atmosphere of the new hospital makes up for the effort of commuting.

'I should have left sooner,' he writes to Winnie, 'instead of wasting my time fighting Owen.'

GHOSTS

Although Will Bodmin tried for a number of years to rehabilitate ghosts, he still claimed not to believe in the occult sciences, spiritism or astrology. Ghosts remained intermediaries, in his opinion, only slightly material, unable to be either completely alive or entirely dead. Sara T. pointed out to him one day that this made them like a lot of us, but the only response she got was a polite smile, as if he didn't understand her objection.

He threw himself into giving ghosts their autonomy, trying to prove they existed independently of our imagination, and that is perhaps why he put so much energy over several years into photographing them. It was as an expert in 'ghostology' that he was invited by one of his old acquaintances, Kate Lawson – she had helped him put together his Captain Cook exhibitions and attended a couple of his lectures on 'the natural way to mental health' – to come to her home and get rid of some troublesome ghosts. Or, more accurately, to determine whether the noises that seemed to come during the night from the living room where her ancestors' portraits were hanging, could be caused by spirits.

'It's a lot like calling the pest exterminator,' remarked the smiling friend Kate had invited along as well.

Will looked up at her. He had been sitting drinking tea with the two women for almost an hour, avoiding making eye contact with Liz Gillespie, whom he found statuesque and even overwhelming. Her comments were gentle and always accompanied by a smile, but he didn't know whether she was being sincere or ironic. This time, however, the reference to pests was verging on mockery.

Bravely resuming his explanations, Will summarised a few of the main points for the two novices. In many cases, he explained, a ghost is a dead person who can find no rest because of a misdeed that has not been atoned for, and he cited as an example a case he had studied, on location, at Nannau Hall in Wales. A ghost haunted this old manor house for hundreds of years until the eighteenth century when, in a violent storm, lightning split open the trunk of an oak tree in the park and a skeleton fell out which was easily identified as the remains of a Welsh prince named Owen Glendower. A fierce opponent of Henry IV, he killed a number of men in his fight against England, until he in turn perished, assassinated in 1416. Since his body was never found, he had no grave. And then at last the storm returned him to his family. Three centuries after his death, he was given a Christian burial and never bothered anyone again.

There was a moment's silence. Will looked down at this cup of tea. Empty.

'Owen, now there's a murderer's name for you,' he said with a laugh.

As if she hadn't heard, the stately Liz commented: 'So, ghosts are Christian and the climate, like the Lord, works in mysterious ways . . .'

Kate Lawson added in a quiet voice: 'If I want to know who the ghosts in my house are, do I have to trace the history of its occupants? Until I find some misdeed? Wouldn't that be like the confessional or one of your psychotherapy sessions?'

'No,' replied Will. 'Not at all. No . . . well, perhaps a little.'

206

The women looked at each other. 'Don't talk to me about confession,' Liz said, shaking her head. 'I used to know an exorcist, and he was a very grim-looking fellow. Thin and yellow as if he had a diseased liver; I felt as though he was the one possessed. Nothing like you, Will.'

This rather large lady intrigued Will, especially since she had once been a Catholic nun, in Bar Convent, which she left after several years. Kicked out, to be blunt.

And now she had started on the gin already – maybe because it was evening and the hour, she said, when spirits come out of the walls. When she talked, her necklace of square glass beads glittered against the bare skin of her throat, distracting Will from his thoughts.

'How do you bait ghosts?' she asked.

'Sorry? What?'

He hesitated. 'You take them by surprise,' he said.

How do you bait them? With food, yes, of course. Liz had thought of that because when she was thrown out of the convent it was because of her greediness. A deadly sin that the Church authorities had taken seriously. She would take other people's desserts, empty the fridges in the night, gorging herself, Kate had told him. She became enormous – the woman who had wanted to feast on spiritual things had never swallowed so many earthly delights.

'Or I should say,' Will went on, 'I try to take them by surprise. With my camera.'

He had believed – he still believed – ghosts were sensitive to photography. He had managed to get in touch with James Henderson, a famous ghost-hunter whose photographs appeared occasionally in the newspapers and who had even, quite recently, succeeded in photographing a female ghost in Stonegate, in York. Will had carefully cut the picture out of the paper, but when he was finally able to talk to Henderson the man was evasive, refusing to reveal his techniques. Still, it was after their meeting that Will bought his Hasselblad.

He hadn't had much luck and his photos never showed anything very clear, but just as he was about to give up, a novel invention brought him renewed confidence. In February 1974, he read an article in *Time* magazine about an American who had developed a camera capable of photographing the auras of human beings. Aura? Will had at once identified this as the soul, which he assumed was even more difficult to capture in a photograph than a ghost. He wrote to the American, but received no reply. Still, the fact that he knew such an apparatus existed was encouragement on the highest level. Maybe one day, Will thought, I'll meet Jack Diggs again and we'll be able to put together a similar, or even better piece of equipment.

'So,' Liz Gillespie asked, as soon as he said a few words on the subject, 'it was that invention that sent you down this path? You didn't consider taking inspiration from Allix's "astral trunk" – a long tube you place behind the skull, reaching up to the planets and allowing us to converse with the spirits of Saturn, as Flaubert tells us?'

But Will had never read a single line of Flaubert. 'He wrote novels,' he replied, 'but I'm talking about serious things.'

'Oh, how right you are.' She had a tinkling voice, and Will was having trouble not staring at her cheeks, her bare arms with their silver bracelets. For the first time in ages, his eye was drawn to a woman's flesh, he was mentally describing it as silky, fresh, supple, pink and even whisky.

Whisky?

He jumped. Kate Lawson was offering him a drink. He accepted.

The conversation continued. They felt a touch giddy as they returned to the subject of the unburied dead, the millions of people killed in bomb attacks . . . Do these dead come back to haunt us?

Will was of the opinion that ghosts remained attached to places: they don't travel around. On that note, he swallowed a second whisky.

They discussed the best time to hunt for them. In the evening? According to Will, paying too much attention prevents them from showing themselves. They are fearful, it is better to observe them in a slightly distracted manner. 'I've noticed that sometimes they can be attracted by a convivial atmosphere. People sitting round a table, eating and drinking late into the night; the noise they make allows the ghosts to come unnoticed to warm themselves next to the living.'

'I didn't know they were sensitive to the cold,' Kate said. 'But did you bring your camera, Will? It would be so wonderful if you could get one or two on film.'

'Oooh yes,' Liz agreed.

Will drank a third whisky and admitted humbly that he hadn't thought it appropriate to come with his Hasselblad.

'What's the use of a man without his Hasselblad?' shouted Liz.

'Oh Will, you'll come back then, won't you?' begged Kate. 'And next time you'll bring it?'

'You'll come to tea with us?' Liz asked, sounding innocent.

Will vowed he would. His head was spinning slightly, but he was happy, gazing at the paintings Kate was pointing to behind her. Her ancestors – there they were, getting in the way, wandering about all over the place. And yet they looked well-behaved enough, in their heavy gilded frames.

He tried to draw Liz out on the subject of the library at Bar Convent and her collection of religious books, but she started to laugh and told him about the seventeenth-century astrologer John Case who invented a black box in which he showed anyone who was willing to pay for the privilege images of their late parents.

Instead of being annoyed by the comparison, Will laughed with her because he found Liz's ignorance harmless, and especially because after four whiskies he felt quite sure the two ladies held him in very high esteem. He no longer wanted to leave, he had no problem drinking – besides, ghosts don't make you nervous when you've been drinking. Wasn't that what he had just explained? Dutch courage, said Liz. It's my courage, mine, Will retorted, standing up, and his chest swelled with it, it warmed his heart, brought a glow to his cheeks, set his moustache a-tremble; and when he finally left at nine o'clock in the evening, he took the brisk wind to be his ally, blowing him along. It feels like midnight, he muttered as he climbed onto his bike, come on you ghosts, show yourselves! He was pedalling as fast as he could, speeding along, whistling, singing – but the headlamp was feeble, no glow-worms this time, nothing but an imbecile of a driver catching him in his headlights and honking, scraping past him, almost knocking him over. Will found it funny, and for perhaps the first time since he was a boy he shouted insults at the rotten driver, happily, even cheerfully: 'Idiot! Boozer!', laughing heartily and zigzagging all over the road.

The following day was Sunday, the day he dreaded most, when he couldn't go fossicking in bookstores and fleamarkets, and he woke with a headache that meant he couldn't go out. But he wasn't in a bad mood, far from it. For once he knew what had caused the pain that gripped his skull like a vice. The ghost of the wine, he muttered.

He took two aspirin and pottered about, something he didn't make a habit of, because doing nothing made him anxious. And then towards five in the afternoon, he felt as good as new and was even hungry. He decided it was too late to go into town to eat and thought it might be an idea to check on his photographs of ghosts. He wanted to perfect his technique before he went back to Kate Lawson's. He had a whole box full of them. Initially he had given them to a neighbourhood photographer to develop – the same place he had bought the Hasselblad – but seeing the poor results he had taken an evening class at the university where he used a number of different washes, aware that the chemicals used could either completely obliterate the greyish tones that revealed the ghosts, or, on the contrary, highlight them. He took out of the box a whole series of prints showing whitish stains, like clouds against a grey background, rather difficult to interpret. But it was possible his house was only slightly haunted, the way a piece of metal can be slightly magnetised. He was holding a packet of photos, all taken the same evening, like a fat hand of cards he'd been dealt, stroking the edges with his thumb while he thought, bending the prints and letting them snap back the way he would have done with playing cards. A mechanical gesture that suddenly revealed a distinct shape: the outline of a woman's body. Surprised, he repeated the movement. Yes, an outline he felt he recognised. He flicked through the photographs ten times in a row, his mouth dry, his breath catching in his throat.

He put the handful of prints down and got up to search though a chest. He came back with the nylon shirt that the impossible Mrs Norwick had yellowed, shrunk, ruined. He draped it over the back of a chair and set the chair on the table so he could see the shirt from the same angle as it appeared in the photos. Then he picked up the prints and flipped through them again. He gave a long sigh, ending in a whistle. It was the same shirt, it was Jane. Exactly the same.

Jane Hanley, dressed in the shirt she had given him, reaching down to her thighs. He could even make out the light in her spectral eyes and detected a look of suffering in them. Of course she wanted to be rescued, didn't she? After a few enthusiastic seconds, he felt almost nauseous at the idea that probably no one except him would be able to recognise her and people would think he was mad if he talked about it. Then he told himself she might be dead and that was why she was revealing herself to him. No, he must be dreaming, hallucinating. Someone would have told him if she had died.

He flipped through the photos again and repeated: 'Exactly

the same.' Then again, more slowly. A third time, faster, and he exclaimed: 'Almost.'

From that point on he found he couldn't separate the two expressions 'exactly the same almost!' These were the mocking words he had heard from the lips of Dr Stanley Owen: 'Exactly the same almost!' A jabbing pain shot through his head, a kind of dizziness. He lay down on his bed, huddling beneath the blanket, but he couldn't get rid of the vision of Owen, joking and laughing at him.

Do come and have tea with us.

Two weeks later, again sacrificing his weekend searches, his Darling, the reason for his very existence, Will went back to visit Kate Lawson.

And this time, don't forget your Hasselblad! Pushing his hand into his shoulder-bag, he stroked the little box: this little secret creature soon to emerge into the light. And readied with high-speed black and white film, flash attachment and tripod. There it lay at his feet like a faithful hound while Will, sitting in a flowery chintz armchair, sipped at his tea. And talked.

'Do tell us, Will, tell us how you do it . . .'

Their words were music to his ears. He had just moved on to gin – at the same time they did, in fact – after chit-chatting for nearly an hour. While they waited for the light to fade and the ghosts to come out – just like fishing, the best time to get a bite is at daybreak or nightfall – he drank quite a bit more than the ladies. And as for Kate Lawson's ancestors on the walls, the ones he was expecting to photograph, they were already warming to the cheerful atmosphere, the gentle rosy glow of the opalescent glass lamps in Kate's favourite Art Nouveau style.

'Do tell us, Will, why a photo can show us what the eye can't see.'

This from Liz, the nun thrown out of the convent, as impish

212

as always. And Will, in no way disconcerted, replied: 'Well, my dear Liz, that's because your eye is hiding something from you.'

'My eye!' she exclaimed.

And Will was off, talking about the light that is inseparable from the shadow that makes us who we are. Away he went, about Peter Schlehmil, the man who sold his shadow, poor devil. *Gesundheit.* He raised his glass.

He had just a little trouble standing upright, as if a clock had been chiming in his head. Fishing for spirits . . . I ask you. The dim light swallowed up the portraits in a semi-shadow where they were already beginning to move. The bearded judge with the round nose even seemed to be trying to speak.

' No noise,' Will announced, before climbing onto a stool that put him on the same level. Then; 'I won't use the flash so as not to frighten Rita,' he said.

'My great-grandmother's name wasn't Rita,' Kate protested.

'Your . . . ' He blushed. Why had he thought of Rita Angus?

The old lady in the portrait had hair like a spaniel's ears framing a knife-blade of a face. 'Was she the judge's wife?'

'Yes, of course.'

'And the judge, how many did he send to the gallows?'

'Two or three at most,' Kate replied gaily.

Standing on the stool, Will raised the Hasselblad, shining in the dim lamplight, and positioned it level with the judge's mouth.

Two or three at most, a good man then. I've found him. I've found him guilty all the same. He mustn't tremble too much in spite of his uncomfortable position; it would be a long exposure. Smile, ghosts.

When he pressed the shutter release, a fiery tongue cut through the semi-darkness. The flash, didn't I disable it? But

213

the flame was red, nothing like the white light of magnesium. Liz shouted: 'Look out!' Will, turning his head, lost his balance and fell into the arms of the imposing Liz, who staggered back under the impact and found herself on the couch with Will's whiskery nose in her ample cleavage. Will breathed in the smell of her, her skin, the ocean of her flesh.

'Well, well,' she murmured, 'your camera likes to play tricks.'

'You scared us,' said Kate, who had her hand to her mouth and seemed drained of colour.

'Music,' Will ordered as he got to his feet. 'We need some music.'

Kate obeyed without a word. She put on a Brazilian record – some bossa nova, to set the ghosts a-skipping.

I can dance this, I had classes in Zurich, he thought. Ballroom dancing, never tested in public. But he didn't move from the armchair where he had collapsed.

Liz was hot now and perspiring lightly. 'The living are hungry,' she said, giving Will a strange look.

The record came to an abrupt halt. Will would really have liked another drink, but Kate wasn't serving any more alcohol: she wanted him to keep chasing ghosts. 'No, really, it's just not possible now,' he explained, 'after all that racket they won't show themselves again.' He shrugged, but she seemed disappointed.

As Liz was driving Will home to Bishophill, the rain came crashing against the windscreen and the wipers sliced out a swathe of night that the headlights couldn't penetrate. 'We're speeding into nowhere,' Will said.

'Not really,' Liz replied, driving in a slightly mad way, swerving from time to time, alternating this activity with long pensive moments when she slowed and pitched forward onto the steering wheel as if she was falling asleep. When she stopped the car, Will stammered that no, he couldn't ask her in for a nightcap: there wasn't any room.

No room?

'Anyone home?' Liz asked, grabbing at his crotch.

He was so stunned to see Liz's hand there that it took him a moment to mumble: 'No, no.'

'That's not what it's telling me, down there,' Liz replied. But Will twisted himself away from Liz's grasp and opened the door partway. The cold wind and the rain on his face gave him some relief.

Liz dropped her head onto the steering wheel with an audible thump.

'I ate so many communion wafers that I got fat.'

He had trouble getting out of the car, took a few steps in the rain and then stopped behind it, looking at the red holes of the tail lights, big red holes in a big dark rump. Not for him. The icy wetness wasn't sobering him up.

He went to bed with his clothes on and dreamed about his sister Claire. My sister who was twenty years older than me and came on holiday with us to the beach at Riverton to help Mother take care of the young ones. In the dream she was walking out into a pond. The water was already up to her waist and she was complaining: 'I'm looking for my photos.' The photos of her ancestors, the ones she really did lose on a train, here in England a few years ago. I called out to her, I begged her to come out of there, I showed her the gold sovereign with the head of William IV, the one that belonged to our great-grandfather, with the chain that would link Claire to her entire past. I shouted to her: this is for you, but she didn't want it; she needed her own photos. She raked her fingers through the water, she worked the mud with her feet, all in vain, she brought nothing to the surface.

This dream resonated so strongly that it woke Will in the night. Ten past seven. The house was silent. He went downstairs to the kitchen, put some water on to make tea, and still Claire haunted him. She would be washed away under the shower, maybe. The hardest thing was the shameful thought that this big sister he had always known as an adult and who had died of a heart attack just a month ago, had probably been with him the previous day and seen him playing the drunken imbecile with Liz and Kate. Perhaps it was even worse than that. Perhaps . . .

And he didn't have a single photo of her. In any case no photo could ever do justice to what he saw in her, it would be an illusion at best.

Morning wouldn't come, but Will knew he was not going manuscript hunting today, and that he was never going back to visit Kate Lawson. It was over.

He ate a piece of toast, calmly, with concentration, his moustache collecting crumbs. He closed his eyes, and thought of Liz with a shrug.

Two weeks later he wrote to Winnie that he would never be depressed again because he now understood the mechanism of depression. And, he added, 'I have sold my camera: it was taking up too much space in my life, it was too heavy and dragging me down. I'm not going to take any more photos of ghosts, and that's all for the best. Besides, what shows I'm better is that I've found an extraordinary print, and I believe it has come to me as a sign of fate. It shows the *George III*, a ship that was transporting convicts to Australia in 1835 when it sank off the Tasmanian coast. On board this ship there was a woman who had given birth during the crossing, a few days earlier. One hundred and twenty people drowned, but this woman spent forty-eight hours in the water with her own baby in one arm and another woman's baby in the other, and all three survived! The shipwreck happened in winter as well, in cold seas. It was an absolute miracle, recognised as such by all the witnesses at the time, and I have just written to the Tasmanian Museum in Hobart to find out if they hold the original. Love makes anything possible, all the more so, perhaps, when it is blind.'

216

THE PROPHET

'There was an Anglican orphanage in Motueka,' says Will, 'where children who had wet their beds had to go to school with a sign around their necks that said, in big letters: "I wet my bed."'

'I wet my bed,' he repeats, thoughtfully.

He stops, and even from a distance, even from the back rows of the semi-circular lecture theatre where she is sitting, Sara Tinkerbell has the impression there are tears in his eyes. He is a powerful speaker, her uncle, more passionate than she would have believed.

Almost all the seats are occupied. Will had predicted it: there'll be a full house at the Southland Community Hospital. There may even be one or two members of the police force there. Sara, on the other hand, is there by chance. She has stopped in Invercargill after a short stay at her mother's, on Stewart Island, and happened to be there the day of the lecture.

'What were the results of stigmatising the children this way?' Will thunders. 'They were turned into future arsonists, and alcoholics. Or even politicians completely incapable of grasping the best interests of the community.'

He pauses again, steps away from the lectern to allow his last words to resonate in the minds of his audience. Then he steps back, lifting his head hopefully.

'On the other hand, I knew a Jungian therapist in Zurich who treated an enuretic child by taking him out into the garden, gathering branches to make a fire and asking him to put it out by urinating on it.'

Sara imagines a slightly damp wood fire, leaves going up in smoke, twigs crackling – good times on Stewart Island. Too good to want to put it out. And then she wonders if her uncle's formula works for girls as well, if they have to squat over the flames. She would like to support Will, but is it possible? Half an hour into his speech, you would have to be really slow not to understand that for him, women are responsible for practically everything that can go wrong. If they smoke, it sets off a worldwide disaster. If they work, they neglect their families. He has just referred to the dreadful case of a mother who, for the sake of convenience, sent her little bedwetter, aged only three, to boarding school. How does Will plan to put out this inferno? By pissing on it? Sara looks round: the audience is impassive; hard to know what they are feeling.

Her uncle straightens, throws back his white hair, like a horse's mane, and for a second he looks like a prophet. His eyes glitter, he rages against a world that in its perversity is doomed to self-destruction. A dramatic state of affairs, he explains in great detail, where nature has become the invisible hand of God – Smith's invisible hand of the market having never been, in his opinion, anything but the hand of the devil.

Is he going to make the connection with masturbation? No, she thinks, he wouldn't dare: he'll stick with enuresis.

Now he's on about little causes that have great effects. 'If Henry VIII hadn't hated his father he would never have been disappointed in his wives and England would not have become Protestant.'

Disappointed in his wives? Well that's one way to put it, when you remember he had a couple of them beheaded! Small causes. Changing the course of history with a few drops of pee. Printing, Will announces, brought about the Wars of Religion. (Once people were able to read the Bible translated into their own language they were able to judge the Church of Rome.) Radio made the Second World War possible (he doesn't explain that one very well). And as for television, it was the match that lit the fire of widespread criminality and terrorism.

Sara shakes her head. Does a man so full of good intentions deserve to make such a fool of himself?

Now he is gentle, soothing, lamenting the world's many misfortunes. It's true he can also look like a kindly university professor, completely lost and out of touch with the world. With his Harris tweed jacket, corduroy trousers, moustache and horn-rimmed glasses, you find yourself feeling fond of Will Bodmin, the way people were fond of Captain Cook's goat, wanting to protect him when he gives examples of the commitment he put into treating his patients in England. But now he's gone back to thundering. Once again, his eyes burn and blaze, he throws his head back sharply, probably to get the hair out of his eyes. He tells yet another story about a woman who smoked and fell asleep in front of the TV: the cigarette dropped from her fingers, set fire to an armchair made of polystyrene (never trust modern materials), and her four-year-old son ran away to safety. Sadly, the little boy picked the wrong door, sheltering in the bathroom instead of going outside, and burned to death. She went mad, her husband left her, she was treated in a psychiatric hospital and then a year after she got out she set fire to herself with a can of petrol!

He lowers his voice to conclude that forty years of working with psychopaths, murderers and all kinds of mentally ill people has convinced him the only way to live humanely is through religion.

Saw that one coming, thinks Sara Tinkerbell. At least

on that subject he won't upset anyone. But which beliefs? Maori? Aztec? No, of course not, he needs some variety of Christianity. Or Quaker pacifism.

His Eve is a smoking Eve, tempting Adam with a lit cigar instead of an apple, the way that old witch from Snow White would do. Did he ever find a painting illustrating this scene of iniquity?

In her irritation, Sara Tinkerbell almost feels ashamed for him. Fortunately the audience applauds (but another part of the room has emptied as soon as he finished) and just as she is going up onto the stage to join him, still wondering how she can congratulate him, a woman jostles past her to pounce on the prophet. 'Oh, Dr Bodmin, what a pleasure to finally be able to talk to you!' A woman in her forties, elegantly dressed, her cheeks on fire. And without stopping to catch her breath she tells him about an urgent problem the medical experts haven't been able to solve. It's a living hell: she is unable to rest because as soon as she gets home her feet become so hot she has to put them into cold water! She spends hours sitting with her feet in a basin. And of course she can't get to sleep any more. The hardest thing is that no one takes her seriously. The doctors pretend to believe her when she describes her suffering, but they just listen to her chest unenthusiastically and end up advising her to consult a psychiatrist – which she does, to no avail. One of the doctors, when she saw him again, even had the nerve to ask her if she managed to heat the water in the basin with her feet!

She stares at Will with her big, wounded eyes, and Sara can tell how much he enjoys that kind of look. 'My father,' he starts to say, 'couldn't walk until the age of seven.' Then he stops, looking thoughtful. He gives her his card and suggests she come to see him at the hospital's mental health centre. 'I'll see you for free,' he says.

*

And when she gets back to the house on Stewart Terrace, Sara understands why Winnie didn't want to go to the lecture; she protested that she didn't understand a thing about these learned speeches, all those stories about crazy people. That afternoon in May 1994, Winnie preferred to stay at home where, among other things, she prepared the evening meal as usual. It's true that she does it with flair, setting a very attractive table with a tablecloth and old knives from Rockhaven – Sara recognises them. They aren't at all out of place either, in this doll's house filled with childhood souvenirs.

Winnie has cooked fish with a sauce, blue cod caught in Foveaux Strait – because I know you like it, she tells Sara, and you probably can't get it in Auckland. But it's also to celebrate Will's speech, she adds, and since she has opened a good bottle of Marlborough Sauvignon Blanc they raise their glasses: to Sara! to Will's lecture! Will himself, still glowing with success, drinks a mouthful that leaves its glistening mark on his moustache – it makes him look like a seal, thinks Sara. And as she sticks her fork into the cod, she announces:

'Rawaru.'

'Rawaru,' Winnie echoes. 'You are so lucky to have learned Maori.'

'There was nothing stopping you,' Sara replies.

And as if this slightly aggressive answer has set her free, she says to Will: 'Women who leave their children to go to work don't do it for fun. At least, not the ones I know.'

'Excuse me?' he says, in surprise. 'Oh, yes. No, I'm not blaming them for anything, not at all.'

'You're not blaming them for anything? As soon as you start talking about a problem, there's a woman who didn't look after her kid.'

'But these women are the first victims. It's the system, it's inhuman.'

Sara smiles, keeping her face expressionless. There's no point arguing.

221

For once, Winnie gets involved. Shaking her head as if Will is some kind of precocious child. 'Will grew up surrounded by women who obeyed his every wish. We all spoiled him, and it gave him the idea that women are responsible for everything.'

'Oh, come now,' Will says with a shrug. 'Another one of Father's ideas.'

'Not at all,' Winnie answers, offended.

'If I take my mother's word for it,' Sara says, now wanting to support Winnie, 'your mother wasn't always very easy on Will. Otherwise why would she have sent him off to another family?'

'Sent who?' asks Will.

'You.'

'She sent me off to another family?' He bursts out laughing. 'First I've heard of it!'

Sara can see that Winnie is staring down at her plate, a sign they're on dangerous ground. Too bad. Her mother has given her the start of her autobiography to read – she has a copy here, in her luggage – and it happens to tell the story of Will's birth. 'My mother says you lived with another family for a year.'

Silence. A little smile has affixed itself to Winnie's face, like a ticket window closing. Will raises his eyebrows, with a superior expression. 'Oh really? Is that so? She always did have a good imagination. And why would I have been sent away?'

'I don't quite know, but I think it had something to do with wetting your bed.'

Catastrophe.

'Wetting my bed?' Will repeats, trying to laugh. But suddenly his face reddens, turns purple, a sneer curls his lips, moves up his left cheek and half closes his eye, making the eyelid quiver. Sara suddenly feels guilty, blushes and looks away. Yes, of course it's a tic. That's what Mother had written, a tic. As a boy, he had a tic on the left side of his face and that's why he was sent to a family in the country, not for wetting his bed! And now the tic has come back. I shouldn't have said anything. It was true, my mother didn't make it up! I should have been careful not to upset him, Winnie either. They're old, monarchists, religious . . . I should have . . .

'I'm sorry,' Sara says. 'It's all rubbish.'

Will's face finally relaxes – like a stuck drawer freeing up. Winnie sighs and smiles. Will shakes his head, as if to say: trust my sister Julia to kid around. And for a few seconds everything seems normal again, except that something has been triggered, a kind of tick-tock under the surface that can end only in an explosion. After another mouthful of wine Will asks: 'May I read what your mother wrote? She always did have a good imagination. It was her specialty, you might say.'

Sara hesitates for a second. If that's all it takes to make up for it . . . 'Yes, why not?' Her mother has given out several copies, so it's pretty much public – and there's nothing out of the way in it.

Now Will turns to Winnie, who is on her feet, intending to slip away to the kitchen.

'You were over ten at the time, you must remember.'

She stops, turns. Her eyes are such a pale blue, they look washed out. 'You were away for a while, yes, I think that's right.'

'Oh really? You think that's right? Why?'

'Well, Mother sent you to the country, I don't know where.'

'Oh? What for?'

'I don't know. It's really not important, Will. It was so long ago. What matters is that you came back happy, better than before.'

'So, apparently I was placed with another family, and I don't remember it?'

'Look, I don't know if "placed" is the right word. You should ask Joy, she has a much better memory than I do.'

Joy, in her retirement home, the third surviving sister.

At this point, Winnie seems absolutely distraught. She looks skywards. 'You know, everyone adored you, Will.'

'I don't give a damn about being adored. If I was placed! For heaven's sake . . . And you never told me? You or anyone else?'

'I thought you knew, that you remembered. It's really not important, Will.'

'No, maybe not. Maybe . . .'

He's stuttering. He doesn't want any dessert. He asks Sara again for the manuscript, and as soon as he has the typed pages in his hands – about fifty pages at most – he estimates the weight of them, looks at them suspiciously, and shuts himself away in his bedroom to read them.

One of my earliest memories,' Julia has written, 'goes back to the day my brother was born. We had been promised that if we were good, our mother would give us another baby as a reward. The midwife, an impressively corpulent lady wearing a large white apron, came out of the kitchen and announced that we had 'a marvellous big fat baby brother'! This news was a great disappointment to me. What I wanted was a LITTLE brother.

'Strangely, I have forgotten my reaction on seeing this newborn baby for the first time. But I know he grew into a very brilliant little boy whose brain, according to the doctors, was developing in advance of his body. In fact, the doctor strongly recommended not sending him to school before the age of six, whereas everyone else started when they turned five.

'Will was a very tense boy, and long before he started school he developed a nervous tic below his left eye. There were so many adults and older children in the house that he was the focus of too much attention and suffered from overstimulation. At least that is what our father said, and the family GP was of the same opinion. The doctor therefore advised that he should be sent to live somewhere quiet, and Mother placed him with a small family in the country. If I hadn't known it was for his own good, I should have been sad to see him go. We had two maiden aunts living with us in Invercargill, and they continued to lavish their attention on the rest of the family. Of course nowadays a very different treatment would have been prescribed. But the fact is that when Mother had our little Will brought back, he was remarkably better. He was bigger and stronger, he no longer wet his bed, his face no longer froze into a sneer when he was annoyed; and above all, he was smiling, kind and gentle. Today's drugs could not have achieved better results.'

Will practically skims over these lines and carries on to read, a little further on, the story of Julia's marriage – also narrated in such a romanticised way it is hardly recognisable. But a moment later, he starts to mumble: 'They're all cretins, these doctors, stupefied by multiple-choice questions.' No, he can't ignore the section he skimmed through, and he goes back to it. He will read it very slowly this time, go over it with a fine-tooth comb, and do his calculations. If what his sister says is correct, he wouldn't have been placed until he was four, which is less damaging: the greatest harm is to children separated earlier from their mothers. What's more, Julia mentions the bedwetting only at the end of the story, with the words 'he no longer wet his bed'. It can be deduced then that enuresis was not the reason he was sent away.

On the other hand, Julia has such a tendency to embroider the facts that it's possible she might have skipped something even more unpleasant. Would Joy in her retirement home know something more about it? In any case, Will is certain he won't hear anything else from Winnie's lips – she will definitely have shut everything out of her mind.

But what about him, why can't he remember anything

about it? At four or five you normally remember. Am I a victim of abandonment syndrome? Can I not trust myself? Or has the whole thing been made up? But Winnie confirmed part of what Julia writes. Are the two sisters in cahoots?

The fear he feels, his irritation, the enormous shockwave spreading through him like the massive blows of a battering ram trying to knock down, wall by wall, everything that is still intact inside him, all this shows him he too must have known something. He *knows*, but he *cannot* know.

Something twists inside him, tears at him, something that says: if I was abandoned as a child, then I cannot trust myself. In that case, taking it to its logical conclusion, he must also refuse to trust this affirmation. (If he cannot trust himself, then he cannot declare 'I can't trust myself.') His mouth stiffens, twists to the left; he can feel the spasm moving up towards his eye, the trembling, the pain. Nothing else, nothing more to say. Trapped inside his sneer.

The next morning, Sara reports, I thought the incident would have shrunk to its proper dimensions during the night, that is, that it would have been forgotten. But the Will Bodmin I saw coming to the breakfast table was blinking away as if he hadn't slept at all, and his face was grey and drawn. I admit I felt sorry for him. I would have liked to tell him it was overreacting to torture himself because of something so banal. Who hasn't wet the bed at the age of three or four? What does a childhood tic matter? Even his stay with the family in the country couldn't have been especially difficult, since he came home in better shape. My mother wasn't lying about this, I was sure, just as I was sure that in writing those pages she was convinced she was saying something harmless, an innocent little adventure in the family saga, nothing dramatic about it. For my mother, it was a success story. For Will, it had become a story of failure. He was wrong.

It wasn't until later, after Will died, after I read his

226

notebooks, that I realised he had repressed deep within himself, in some unreachable place, any awareness of this episode in his life. The most astonishing thing was that his psychoanalysis – admittedly very superficial – didn't reveal the strange construction he developed around his forgetting.

But that morning I couldn't say anything. Will gave me a fatherly smile and after slowly eating half a piece of toast, explained where what he called my mother's inventions came from. First, he declared, it was highly likely he had been sent away on holiday to another family – he would check that out. It was even possible he stayed for a month or two. But Julia, probably with the best intentions, had interpreted this absence as a punishment, a placement, and she had exaggerated the length of it too. Yes, he nodded, a punishment for which she had needed to find an explanation, such as the bedwetting or the tic. But the truth was that the little boy was guilty of not being liked by her. And why didn't she like him? Because he was taking her place.

'Just think,' he said, suddenly excited, 'she was the sixth daughter. Just imagine, when she was born, how disappointed old man Bodmin was, when he'd been wanting a boy for years. And her own mother's disappointment. That must have been unbearable for her. So she fought with all her might, swam against the current to try to get a little love from her parents. And just as she's starting to make some headway, boom! there's her mother pregnant again; and worse still, the longed-for little brother arrives. What was left for Julia? To behave as if she was happy, so as not to lose everything. But at heart she wanted the little intruder to go to the devil, to disappear. And she wanted it so much that she concocted a story about a placement and ended up believing it herself. It's so much better if it's true. Your mother has always believed that writing is a way to prettify things. Well, she's still at it. She has altered reality to satisfy her desires, the way children do; it's a lasting trait of her personality because she still loves Peter Pan.'

I think I might have accepted his attacks on my mother if it hadn't been for his mocking, defensive tone, which made me feel he wasn't entirely convinced by what he was saying. If my mother had detested him – which I didn't believe – why wasn't he giving me any other examples, more concrete ones, instead of throwing me a bunch of general statements taken from his readings. Because his tone got my back up, I told him point blank I refused to discuss this whole business. He could check for himself whether he had been placed in a family. And if the subject was taboo, he had only to discuss it directly with my mother. 'I was wrong,' I said, 'to get involved, I was even wrong to read my mother's autobiography and I'm asking you to forgive me for it. But now I have to go and catch my plane.' I was astonished all the same, and saddened, to see their childhood rivalry was still alive, just as if they hadn't grown up. And I couldn't resist the sly pleasure of telling him with a tired smile that my family needed me in Auckland and I would be a very bad mother if I spent another day here.

Of course he agreed with me.

DEBATE

Piecing together the story of my uncle's placement, writes Sara Tinkerbell, I find myself confronted with an unexpected responsibility. I don't know what order to follow in presenting the events of his life, and I'm afraid of giving a false picture of him. It would be easy to say I caught him in his own trap: will it be possible for this man, who has always avoided being in the company of anyone who might have been abandoned by their mother, to put up with *his own company* from now on?

When I assembled the parts of this particular episode, it seemed to cast light on a whole aspect of his existence, and at the same time everything became murky. I think I understand why Will divided his life into two separate parts: his therapy, and his collections. In both cases he was repairing the past: the therapist justified the collector, the collector lent prestige to the therapist, and the two jogged along together, thinking they were invulnerable. But I could also say he built his life around a blind spot; then I would have to ask myself why the blind spot was there, and that would push me towards an even foggier background.

So I remain, as the famous Dr Webster might have said, 'the public's most humble servant'. And that allows me to state that my part in what happened next to Will, in other words his illness, is negligible, trivial. Besides, no one has ever blamed me for anything – especially not Will. I say 'especially not Will' because my mother did make reference to it, as I will show later.

When I think about my role, a story comes to mind, a little adventure that happened to me at Rockhaven when I was six or seven. On the third storey of the house, in a big room where we sometimes played, there were objects from all over the world, in particular an English suit of armour that I liked. I was fascinated by it, and even a bit frightened. One Sunday afternoon, I plucked up my courage and went upstairs by myself. The room was quiet and still, full of mystery, and I tiptoed towards the armour. Reassured because nothing had happened so far, I climbed onto a chest to get a closer look. Through a slit in the helmet, I peeked inside. It was empty, or almost empty. There was darkness and a smell of old leather. I put two fingers on the steel, where the cheeks would be. I barely had time to feel the coldness of it when the armour moved away from my hand. It folded in two, then all the pieces fell one on top of the other with such a hideous racket that I thought the whole house was collapsing. A little cloud of dust rose up into my face and then I fell, in turn, onto the pile of armour. And started to cry.

The adults who came running when they heard the noise comforted me, but no one would believe I had hardly touched the suit. Until someone noticed the leather or cardboard that had been holding it together had been completely eaten away by insects. I had happened to be there at the very moment when a simple draught could have brought it down.

I now became a hero: I was the one who had sounded the alarm. I had revealed the presence of dangerous insects that, after devouring the ties of the armour, would have attacked the wood of the house and perhaps brought it to the ground.

Well, my role in relation to Will was the same. Something

in him had given way, and I put my finger on it without meaning to.

His physical symptoms manifested themselves two or three months after his famous lecture at the hospital, and would probably have appeared even if he hadn't known a thing about his placement. ALS – the name of the sclerosis he had – doesn't develop overnight. It was there, lurking, it was probably written into his genes, and his life had merely given expression to it.

That's what I say, but I'm not entirely in agreement with myself. Sometimes not at all.

The first symptoms were his mood swings. Will was becoming unpredictable: happy in the morning, furious in the afternoon, for no apparent reason. And definitely grouchier. He would start sentences but never finish them, and sometimes he would say really quite harsh things about the Bodmin family – 'a den of liars'. Or about Winnie: 'If you'd told me I'd been placed in a home, I would probably have got married.' Which left her bemused, between laughter and anger. But he didn't do any concrete research into his placement: not a single phone call to people who could have given him information, not a single question to Julia, nothing. Wasn't that essentially a way of admitting the truth of what my mother had written?

The situation between him and Winnie deteriorated so much that he threatened to move into the Kelvin Street building. But he needed to give notice to his downstairs tenants first, and he held back. He decided at that point to give up his work as a therapist, which, in hindsight, seems a sign that he had been more deeply affected than he was admitting. He claimed, however, that he wanted to devote more time to his collection, in particular to his search for the famous pamphlet.

Then he had a fall from his bike that sounded the alarm

with his doctor. The tic seemed to be spreading to the whole of the left side, and instead of 'tic' the term 'spasms' began to be used. These contractions, often painful, alternated with periods of weakness, as if there was no strength left in the muscles once the cramps had eased. The doctor suspected a neurological problem but didn't refer Will to a specialist until after a second, more serious incident, following a visit from a journalist for *The Southland Times*.

The newspaper had decided to publish another article, more in-depth than the previous ones, about Will's collection.

'One day,' Winnie told me, 'Will arrived waving the newspaper, practically in tears as he showed me an article covering a whole inside page.' It was by far the most positive of any the newspaper had published about him. In big black letters the headline summed up what was at stake:

NEW ZEALAND TO LOSE ANOTHER
WORLD-CLASS COLLECTION?

'A world-class collection!' Will repeated.

'To all my sisters,' he accused Winnie, 'I've never been anything but a kid. Your little brother. But to them,' (he thumped his chest, the inside pocket of his jacket where he had just slipped the newspaper to take it to Kelvin Street) 'I'm a man. A real man. A great man.'

This article, over four columns, referred first of all to the deplorable Rex Nan Kivell case and asked if the current government would at last be up to the task.

Mr William R. Bodmin, an exceptional researcher, has devoted his life to preserving the memories of our nation and the South Pacific: will our country make a gesture of recognition in return?

In the middle of the page there was a photo of Will Bodmin with one of his major finds, a broadsheet showing 'The Remarkable, Moving and Fascinating LIFE of the Poor and Unfortunate Elizabeth Watson Including her Dreadful Suffering.' It was the story of the very moral adventures of a poor girl abused by an English merchant, then sentenced as a prostitute to be deported to Botany Bay, where she became more or less a saint and the inspiration for a number of popular ballads. Will had found an original copy of the broadsheet telling the life story of the repentant sinner – published in London in 1815 – and had a thousand copies reprinted. He sent thirty or so to various Australian institutions for the bicentenary in 1988 of the founding of the colony of New South Wales. He sold the remainder. Right at the bottom of the poster, in small print, was the address where it could be purchased: Will Bodmin's address in Invercargill.

It was to this address on Kelvin Street that Samuel Smith, the *Southland Times* journalist, came to interview him. Smith later told me about the strange atmosphere at their meeting. For a start, there was the almost decrepit look of the building and the wooden staircase on the outside leading up to the first floor. At the top was an ordinary door, so thin a burglar could have smashed it in a matter of seconds.

Then when Will opened it, Smith found himself looking at a row of huge potplants, a kind of wall of greenery with unpleasant-looking masks hanging here and there, probably the actual protectors of the premises. Smith raised the question of theft a few minutes later – after all, there were real treasures piled up in here – but Will just shrugged his shoulders. 'I'm not worried about the downstairs tenants,' he stated, as if that were the answer to the question. And he started to explain that the tenants, young people, were very decent, honest and hardworking. But what protected him most was that they had been brought up on television, drinking in the programmes practically with their mothers' milk and spending 'far more time in front of the screen than at school. It's not very likely, but supposing one or the other of them did get in here after an evening's drinking,

233

what would he see? Piles of old books written in an English they might find hard to understand, portraits of ridiculous-looking women, objects they would consider useless: they would think they had fallen into a time-warp and would run away.'

In other words, Will Bodmin considered himself to be relatively outside the world; he too was plunged into the time-warp that protected him. Which might explain the strange impression created by this place stuffed with books, in unsteady piles reaching to the ceiling like the columns of a temple, Samuel Smith said. In fact this strangeness didn't frighten him. As a history teacher – and occasional journalist – he liked that sense of walking into a gallery and going back into the past, even when he stopped near a window, in front of a display case whose shape particularly interested him. It was long and narrow, lying on its side, and had silver handles.

It looked like a coffin.

It was a coffin. 'I had it made to measure,' Will said, 'it's a good fit.'

'It's a good fit?'

'Yes, made from Monterey pine and lined with blue velvet, as you can see.'

He hadn't wanted native New Zealand wood for ecological reasons. Samuel Smith stood there, considering. Even the coffin was overflowing. Will had fitted it with little shelves and filled it with books and items he was especially attached to. Smith took a few steps back: you could clearly see the shape of a man. A man nourished by books.

'The original bookman,' the journalist quipped, with a smile. He moved closer again to see what Will was displaying there. On one side he saw a parchment with Captain Cook's coat of arms, as might have been expected. There were a few prints pinned along the same side. Next, about fifty books with red, black or blue spines and titles in gold lettering. Will showed him a few: a volume in which he had bound together the handwritten notebooks of several Australian convicts; a biography, published in 1828, of Corporal Ledyard who had witnessed Cook's death; various explorers' accounts. Which was his favourite book? It would have been hard to say. Possibly Captain Edward Boys' autobiography with its terrible war scenes and his amazing escape from Napoleon's gaols (plagiarised by Frederick Marryat in 1834 in *Peter Simple*, Will informed him). Or perhaps the life story of Captain Jackson Barry, who landed alone in Australia at the age of ten. 'My father knew him in Dunedin, and we had a portrait of him in our house, Rockhaven. But my father was jealous and poked fun at his adventures, saying he probably came to New Zealand on the back of a whale.'

Smith nodded. 'Tight as a drum,' he said at last. 'No room left for a human body.'

'For me? For my body?' Will asked.

He stood there, a gaunt vulture of a man with piercing eyes, staring at Smith. Suddenly he started pacing up and down, in the very narrow space remaining between his shelves, and Smith wondered if he might crash into a column and bring the whole lot down.

'I've got room,' Will said, stretching out his arms.

Smith refrained from saying he hadn't meant the room, but the coffin. Now he felt he was intruding.

Will shook his head. No, no, Smith had put his finger on something important, and he had noticed himself that his favourite works were almost all stories of escapes and derring-do, but he had never previously suspected he might do something underhand like fill the premises to the brim to avoid moving into the place where he claimed to live. He did an about-face and looked out the window, then came back to Samuel Smith and said sternly: 'So apparently I've always filled up my living space so as not to live there? No, I don't think so.'

235

The reporter shrugged. He had made his comment spontaneously, perhaps because he was impressed. People might be surprised, though, he continued, that a firm pacifist like Will, an anti-nuclear militant, a practising Quaker, had surrounded himself with works written by soldiers, pirates, shipwrecked sailors and adventurers of every kind, full of the sound of boots marching and stories of cannibalism.

Will had to agree, but suggested no explanation.

Smith spent a long time examining the shelves of books, getting Will to explain how they had been grouped. Will had read them all and was able to say what they were about, even the ones that were only 'passing though', to use one of his expressions. These latter were mostly novels. Among the several thousand books in his library, there was very little poetry – although both Will and his sister Julia had written poetry – just three or four works by philosophers, not a single academic study, and the novels were there purely for trading. 'I don't keep a single one, not even my sister's,' Will says. 'And the day I got my hands on an 1849 edition of Melville's novel *Mardi*, I sold it on with no regrets.' There was no sign of any work on psychology either, not even Jung. 'Nature abhors a vacuum, but culture adores it,' Will said simply, justifying his choices. The books he would keep permanently were extraordinary testimonials, the real-life adventures of the few Europeans who had been able to report them. Texts which, contrary to popular literature, in other words novels, survived in only a few rare copies, according to Will. Voices now isolated. And those authors – certainly not the greatest in the eyes of the general public, but the most important for him – were never professional writers: rising up from history's troubled depths, they had been pushed into writing by life's unpredictable shifts and changes. Their pages were dictated by something bigger than they were – the real reason, Will claimed, why Homer and Milton were blind. Seen from another angle, they were often eccentrics with whom he identified, individuals poorly

236

equipped for ordinary life, misfits and marginals who had come into their own when faced with unexpected obstacles, acquiring an unsuspected extra dimension in the challenge. And the universe they had breathed life into for a moment – very briefly, the way our lives are no more than a spark in the darkness – had found a place here, on Kelvin Street, in these paper pillars, in these walls of bound volumes and on the shelves where rays of pale sunlight played.

Will was more and more agitated: he would go to the window where he seemed to gaze out at the garden, then come back to Samuel Smith who, thinking Will was beginning to find his presence annoying, decided to speed up the visit by moving on to the photographs. He suggested taking Will's picture in front of the Elizabeth Watson broadsheet, as this would allow him to tell the readers about one of his flashes of genius. Will agreed, and felt a moment of real pleasure contemplating the poster – an instant that Smith was able to capture with his camera.

The reporter then shoved the Treaty of Utrecht into one of Will's hands and an antique map of the Hawaiian islands into the other, then got him to step back beneath the masks before firing off a number of shots. A little dazzled, Will tried to tell him the map wasn't genuine, it shouldn't be in the photo. The journalist nodded, but without interrupting his series of flashes, and when he had finished he insisted on hearing what Will was looking for now, what he most wanted. The answer came without hesitation: the cornerstone of the collection he had been building for forty years was still missing. The piece that would be its solid foundation; it would guarantee the value of the whole and set the seal on his quest like a superbook compared to which all the rest, everything you could see here, was just so many sheets of paper: the pamphlet against Governor Darling.

'And I shall find it!'

'In New Zealand?' Smith asked, smiling faintly. 'What

makes you think it might be in this country?'

'Because I'm here,' was Will's reply.

Smith nodded slowly. If the pamphlet was where Will was – like his shadow, in fact – what was stopping him from picking it up? A question Will countered with another: 'How can anyone pick up their shadow?' And gave a sly smile. But seriously, in the meantime he would keep on combing the secondhand bookshops and book fairs in the South Island. He would put ads in the paper. 'And if I personally should happen to escape death, there will always be enough room in my coffin for the pamphlet.'

Smith smiled, thinking about his article. They said goodbye, both rather moved by their meeting. Will had just opened the door for him when his left leg gave way suddenly and he fell in the doorway. 'He wasn't down for more than three or four seconds, and I don't think he really hurt himself,' Smith reported. 'But he had been humiliated, and when I helped him up I noticed he was very pale. Probably furious. After he got his breath back and rubbed his thigh, he remarked that you feel really stupid when your body fails you, because it's the kind of thing you can't predict. In any case he assured me he could manage without my help, and off I went.'

JOURNEY

Almost in passing, as we were talking on the phone (about her, of course, she was quickly bored by any other subject), my mother told me Will was terminally ill. 'But you know, Sara, I've forgotten the name of it; Winnie can tell you better than I can.' Maybe she didn't want to know, maybe she was simply afraid of seeing her little brother go. To her, he had always been the admiring little boy she enlisted to act in the plays she was writing already at the age of thirteen. She put them on at Rockhaven at parties that have gone down in family history. She would dress Will in a pageboy costume and entrust him with the task of collecting the grown-ups' entry fees. And if he did a good job of that, he was allowed to appear on stage in a minor role while she played the beautiful captive or the lady of the castle longing for her distant knight. All of this happened well before I was born, and I know it only through stories, but what stories! The family applauded her genius, and a number of outsiders joined in, like the young woman who wrote the arts column for the *Southland Times* under the name of Cousin Betty.

When I imagine this period in my mother's life, I remind myself it wasn't easy for her to leave Rockhaven, and her attachment to the place is probably the source of her infatuation with Peter Pan. Let me say it again, I just loathe Peter Pan and I hate his creator James Matthew Barrie even more, the impotent little dwarf who made up my hideously ridiculous second name, Tinkerbell. And his universe, where children have no right to grow up or they'll have their heads cut off, became an ideal for my mother, and probably also for Winnie and Will – otherwise why would they have remained until their dying day eternal children from old-fashioned fairy tales?

I hadn't given much thought to Will's illness until I went to stay with my mother for the weekend, about two months later, in her house on Stewart Island. My sister and I went there fairly regularly, but not for holidays. No, we were on a mission – to keep an eye on her, because we were worried about her. This wasn't a recent development either: as far as I was concerned, it went back to well before I was a teenager. Yes, we were the ones who had had to become grown-ups while she stayed an irresponsible child, forgiven everything because she was a genius.

Just before this visit, I had learned from my older sister that our mother was taking masses of valium: about four times the dose she had been prescribed. How was she getting hold of it? I was so cross I threatened to go and complain to the chemist. Of course my mother refused to tell me and we had an argument. So on my very first evening there, I went to bed seething with a great sense of injustice that kept me awake most of the night. Why did I have to be my mother's keeper? Could I make this woman, who was seventy-seven years old at the time, take care of herself if she didn't want to?

She must have had a bad night too, because we were tired the next morning and inclined to mend our fences. After feeding grapes to the parrots that came onto the deck to eat out of our hands, we went for a stroll to the Wohlers monument. It's one of our favourite walks, and I like it because it allows me to measure my mother's physical state from year to year. Some parts of the route are difficult, very

240

steep or slippery, especially when the grass is long and the path hasn't been cleared. And we have to climb over a couple of fences, which requires a certain degree of flexibility.

I was happy to see my mother getting through the first part of the walk (the most difficult because of the steep climb) without too much effort, and that she was even looking quite sprightly. The valium and her migraine medication hadn't crippled her yet. That word 'migraine' is a loaded term. Whenever my mother said she had a headache, I would feel the grievances building up in me, going back to the time of Dad's illness. His was serious, as proved by the bacteria that killed him. Whenever he felt sick, she felt sicker. And she left the four of us children alone a lot, to go to the hospital with Dad where she could spend a whole week reading, daydreaming and complaining. Or else, at home, she had such violent headaches that she couldn't deal with anything except her books, and shut herself away in her room for days at a time. Since we, her real kiddies, made her life difficult, she never stopped writing fantastic stories about other, imaginary children, creatures from Nowhereland. Easy to see why I've always hated her migraines.

So we were walking up the hill that morning towards the monument, not talking much, conserving our energy. And then, when we came to the graves of Pastor Johann Wohlers and his wife, my mother stopped to catch her breath. This Wohlers is a local celebrity, the first Lutheran pastor on the island; apparently he was so attached to the place that he reappears periodically as a ghost. They say that for a long time he haunted the bedroom of the female teacher who took over the school after him. Because I liked the story, I asked my mother for any news of the phantom. She shrugged and said hardly anyone believes in ghosts these days, which of course makes them less visible. And setting off again, she added, grumpily: 'Too bad for him!'

'For the pastor?'

'No, for Will.'

Since I didn't understand, she added, shouting because of the wind: 'Too bad for him if he doesn't get treatment.'

We had finally reached the top of the hill: we could see the sea on either side, as clear as a photo in a tourist brochure, very blue, with frothy whitecaps. The wind that had just carried away my mother's words wrapped itself around us, keeping us separate, and I liked the feeling of protection. I moved closer to my mother and shouted that there was no treatment for Will's illness. She shook her head without answering and we went back down the hill. We were walking along Ringaringa Beach beneath the giant eucalyptus trees when she returned to Will's situation, saying sharply: 'When I spoke to him on the phone he was almost pleased to have ALS!'

ALS is amyotrophic lateral sclerosis, which does irreversible damage to the nervous and muscular systems. The body is weakened and the patient eventually dies when the muscles can no longer work the lungs and get rid of the carbon dioxide – a death at once gentle and terrible. As I found out more about the symptoms of ALS I automatically made a connection with my uncle's life – with his daily suffocation, his lack of space and the fact that his activities invariably ended up hemming him in, preventing him more or less from living. And I found the comparison terrifying, dreadful.

I answered my mother: 'Almost pleased! That's a bit much. What can he do about it?'

'He could fight.'

Silence. She continued: 'He never was very brave. Besides, pacifists never do much for other people.'

'But there's no cure for ALS.'

'Of course there is,' she answered sharply. 'And Winnie has been suggesting it for a month.'

She was trying to convert him to Christian Science.

I nearly burst out laughing. My mother had converted

three or four years before – under Winnie's influence already
– and, as far as I know, her migraines and depression hadn't
stopped. And as for her consumption of pain medication,
ergotamine and valium, enough said. Now she was explaining
Will's symptoms as she saw them. His sclerosis, she declared,
was absolutely in line with his life. (But although this
reasoning was just what I would have expected from her, it
wasn't how I saw things.) As a child, my mother said, Will
had suffered from a muscle spasm in his face, and now this
spasm had spread to the whole of his left side. Soon it would
take over his entire body and then, goodnight! The proof that
the disease was spiritual in origin was that it was triggered
when he found out he had been fostered out. Along with
the memory of this placement, the spasm had resurfaced,
probably accompanied by a renewed awareness of the moral
failings that had brought it on in the first place. 'You see,
it's all in his head,' she concluded calmly. 'And that's why
Christian Science can cure it.'

'So he's faking it?'

'Let's not over-simplify. What I think is, he should start
by reading Mary Baker Eddy and saying his prayers.'

Apparently he wasn't about to do so.

'When I talked to him on the phone,' she continued, 'it
was all big words, just as empty as ever.'

'Such as?'

'Oh well, like, during the war there were a few hundred of
us conscientious objectors reviled by hundreds of thousands
of rabid militarists. And who stood up for us? The Quakers.
I'll be a Quaker till my dying day!'

I nodded. It was one of the rare occasions when I was
proud of something Will said. He sold books, but he wouldn't
sell himself.

Two days later I went to visit my uncle in his house on Kelvin
Street. To my surprise, he was in better shape than before

243

the announcement of his sclerosis. Happier, lighter – even a touch ironic. He seemed more at ease, because contrary to all the years I had known him, he had *more space*. His usual confinement had loosened up. He had started the clean-out by gifting part of his collection to the University of Otago. A gesture that also committed him not to give his collection to Australia, something he now said he was very happy about. He had been able to do these things partly because of the interest created around the country by the *Southland Times* article. Other newspapers had taken up Smith's argument, and Will had received some serious offers, which allowed him to decide between what he could let go straight away and what he needed to keep. 'But,' he explained, 'I am keeping the heart of my collection; it won't leave me until I'm dead.'

He had just mentioned his death with a smile. Was this an effect of his illness? It was forcing him to make the decisions he had always put off till later. On the one hand, it weakened him physically and he was beginning to fear the loss of his independence. On the other hand, it freed him from much of his hesitation, and along with this new freedom he had found a new interest. 'A new interest,' he repeated, laughing '. . . at my age!' He felt the urge to paint again and for once he listened to his inner voice. Familiar movements he thought he had forgotten since his time at Art School came back to him from out of the blue, and he had done a painting.

'It's nothing much,' he protested, 'nothing to write home about, just the two sailing ships from Cook's last expedition, copied from some old prints.'

Getting up, he led me past a wall of books to an easel where a canvas around three feet high showed the *Resolution* in a Hawaiian bay and the *Discovery* a little further out, both under full sail and surrounded by small canoes manned by Hawaiians. These images might have seemed very ordinary, especially since the painting wasn't finished, and the lower part in particular was still white with dribbles of paint. But it was very striking. I could almost feel the air moving around the big ships.

Hawaii: wasn't that where Cook died? I began to suspect a performance. It probably was a set up, because Will got to his feet and, with a certain solemnity, placed in my hands two bronze medals on which two ships were embossed, one of them the *Resolution*. Then he explained that these medals, with the effigy of George III on the back, made cheaply and in large numbers during Cook's lifetime, had been distributed in the islands where the navigator landed, creating a good impression on the natives. He was then able to bargain with them, to take on fresh water and food, but most of all – and here again we encounter the double face of things – the medals were kept by the natives and proudly shown to later arrivals. These visitors, other Europeans probably just as power-hungry as the British, would know England had beaten them to these lands. In showing off the gifts they had accepted, the natives would unwittingly reveal that they had already fallen under Crown rule.

And now my uncle was giving them to me. I hesitated.

'Are they very valuable?' I asked, stupidly.

'Very,' he said, laughing.

'Then I can't take them.'

I could feel the weight of them in the hollow of my hand; they made me feel uncomfortable, especially now he had told how they were used. He wouldn't take them back.

'They're for you,' he insisted. 'If you don't like them, sell them. They're for you, really.'

He was staring at me; I lowered my eyes, said thank you and slipped them into my little backpack. Even today, those coins make me feel uncomfortable – maybe because they made victims of my Maori ancestors, like my Hawaiian cousins. But I still have them. I'm not selling them, I hide them but I don't completely forget about them, as if I was afraid that if I showed them I would be pledging allegiance to some unknown power. I promise myself I'll get rid of them and then I don't do it.

In any case, Will then proceeded to tell me in detail how the Hawaiians in the canoes went on board the *Resolution*, how they took Captain Cook for one of their gods, by the name of Lono, and how this misunderstanding eventually caused the captain's death. It was a story he told with passion, with tears in his eyes. At the end of his harangue – that's the term that seemed appropriate to me – I had a quite different view of the splendour of the two ships he had painted, the majestic white sails of the *Resolution*, the red of its flag, the carving on its lofty prow. All this beauty was now revealed to me as the death and destruction the ships brought to Hawaii, only to have them strike back against the expedition.

I was coming to the conclusion that this was all just Will setting the scene for his own death and that it wasn't really to my taste, when he announced he was cured.

Cured?

He believed so. He had made contact with a Filipino healer who was famous for his success with ALS sufferers, and he planned to make the trip at the start of November. His stay was already organised, he would be met at Manila airport, and he was convinced that after a week his condition would be sufficiently improved for him to carry on his treatment by himself. So he would take the plane to Hawaii, landing at Kona, from where a boat would take him to the bay where Cook had perished. Then he would go home to New Zealand.

I was speechless, incredulous.

Winnie, he continued, thought the trip was risky, dangerous, in a word, absurd. You wouldn't expect her to say anything else, really. But he felt he had no choice. The ALS had freed him from certain constraints, but was now becoming the greatest threat. If he allowed it to progress he would soon be unable to do anything much: the spasms affecting his right side could only worsen. He was already finding it very difficult to ride his bike, which he did against medical advice. He might be paralysed sooner than he expected. And he didn't want to die before he found the Darling.

I left not long after, and I remember how good it was to ride again on the bike Winnie had lent me, how much energy I put into pedalling as if I had just escaped from grave danger. I was running away, probably because I had been afraid my uncle might ask me to go with him on his journey – I would have had to refuse, of course. I had another family, didn't I, much more important to me.

And then once I got to Elles Street, I found myself riding past the Rockhaven house and slowed down. I even stopped. Rockhaven had passed into other hands a long time ago and all I had left were some childhood memories that were probably distorted. But the exterior hadn't changed: still the handsome stone façade, the little tower, the grey roof; only the hedge surrounding it had grown so high now it was about to hide it, to engulf it – which was only right, I thought, because Rockhaven belonged to the past. I even wished for a moment that it would disappear: that the earth would open up and swallow it.

More than a house, for me it was a family tomb where our histories were engraved, as in a Victorian novel where all the secrets are family secrets, adultery, hidden connections, stolen legacies.

For my mother, on the other hand, Rockhaven had been a brilliant stage where the play-acting had nothing distasteful about it, where even the Pirates of Penzance – in the operetta where my grandfather played the pirate leader, refusing the comic role of the major-general – are revealed to be sons of good families who can therefore marry the young ladies they have pretended to kidnap! We all adored that house much the same way as the previous century adored Cook's white-sailed ships. My mother had believed in Rockhaven the way people believe in their families, and she had been stunned to see the big house getting away from us, slipping through our fingers as if its stone were only sand.

It was an illusion, a cathedral built on a dream, one that required us to keep our eyes shut to convince ourselves it would survive.

I stood there for quite a while, contemplating the house where I would never again set foot, and the thoughts in my head weren't as clear as the ones I'm writing now. But on that day in February 1998 when I set off again on my bike, slowly this time, as if with regret, I was disappointed to think that Will, who had spent so many years in distant countries seeing and studying things I admired and which ought to have set him free, had come home to live with his sister just as if he had never left his father's grand house, as if he had been incapable of doing so. It was the house that had left him. So I made a wish for him to go and join his old captain in Hawaii or the Philippines.

THE LEGACY

I remember, Sara Tinkerbell writes next, Winnie's little voice on the telephone telling me it was to be expected: 'A heart attack, surrounded by his books. He collapsed right beside the coffin.'

At least he didn't die at sea like their father, or out there in Hawaii, with all that administrative fuss and bother to bring the body home. How considerate of him.

It was to be expected, although Will hadn't always been considerate.

Once she had finished writing this episode, which was to be the last one, Sara added it to the pile of documents she had assembled, to the letters, the diary extracts, the passages she had written based on her own memories. For over a year a mass of papers had circulated between the two of us, and I had become attached to this book in its struggle to be born. But at present it was still a pile of bits and pieces, seething restlessly and pulling in different directions, and Sara was in despair because, even though she had all the elements to hand, she was still quite unable to put them in order, to reach a conclusion. 'Every time I try to tackle it,' she said, 'I'm overcome by a mysterious exhaustion. I don't think I can do it, and I'm not even sure I want to try.'

We saw each other again in Auckland three days before

I was to leave for France. I urged her to finish – she would inherit the collection, it would be the beginning of a new stage in her life. And if she was having trouble getting the book into shape, all she need do was hire a writer and it would all be done and dusted in a month. She didn't agree or disagree. Her husband would really like her to be done with it. And then the following morning – I remember we were walking back up from the beach at Mission Bay along a path bordered with tree ferns and giant palms bursting into rays like green suns – she announced that the reason she wasn't going to finish the book was because she had come to the conclusion it would be betraying her uncle.

'Betraying him? He's the one who wanted a biography!' I exclaimed.

But Sara shook her head. After her long exploration, she saw the family in a different light. 'A lot of the things I sensed have taken on a definite shape, and I'm sure Will wasn't like that.'

'Like what?'

'Well, it wasn't his style to blackmail me with the legacy, to give me money to write a book singing his praises.'

I stressed that it was exactly what he had specified in his will. And Sara was under no obligation to sing the praises of anybody.

No, Sara insisted, the will was a double-edged gift. She was shaking her head more and more vigorously, her hair flying left and right.

'But he's the one who wrote it!' I repeated.

'Yes and no. I'm sure Will wasn't one of those horrible characters in a novel who use their legacy to make their heirs as ugly as they are.'

Of course Will wasn't a character in a novel, and I couldn't see why she should have taken him for one.

'I've come to respect him, more than I did while he was alive, to be honest. He wouldn't have done that. Don't forget, he was a rebel. He disobeyed his father, he was a conscientious objector . . . To be faithful to him, I have to disobey.'

I rolled my eyes. Who could say with any certainty what Will really wanted? Did he know himself? Was it even important, at the stage we were at? No, Sara must have other reasons for reaching such a decision.

'It's degrading,' she went on. 'Writing his biography as though I'm filling an order he's placed, it's degrading for him and for me. That's what's stopping me from finishing. Do you understand?'

If I thought it through, I might very well agree with her. And then I told myself the decision wasn't mine to make. She had every right to believe her uncle was better than he was. Actually, her rebellion didn't upset me: it was the sort of thing that ran in her family. 'I've talked it over with Ron,' she said. 'He'll support my decision if I make it. So I'm making it.'

What was there to say? I didn't speak.

'The collection won't be completely broken up,' she continued, 'it'll be divided between a library and a museum.'

So they were turning down all that money? I found that hard to believe – it wasn't in line, shall we say, with current practice.

We reached the top of the slope between the ferns, and walked a little further up along a tarsealed road. The view over Mission Bay and out to Rangitoto Island was sweeping and stunningly simple, with boats that looked like a child's crayon drawings on an unrippled sea.

'I don't want anything from the collection,' Sara went on. 'Except the few objects he left me specifically and the Darling.'

'The Darling? Are you looking for your Darling too?'

There was a mocking tone in my voice. Sara took my arm.

'I'm not looking for it,' she said. 'I've got it.'

'Really?'

'You don't understand. I've had it for the last ten days. No, well, for four years actually, but I didn't know. I found out ten days ago . . .'

She wasn't joking. The day after her uncle's funeral, Sara had gone to the house on Kelvin Street with her husband and Winnie, who wanted to give her one or two things to remember Will by, in particular his painting supplies. 'We were putting what we were taking into a bag,' Sara said, 'And in between two boxes of acrylic paints, I saw a thick volume of poetry entitled *The Home Book of Verse*. It reminded me of my grandfather the inventor's book – the anthology my mother inherited and that had been a part of my childhood – and I asked Winnie if I might take it. She gave me her blessing, but when I opened it I was disappointed to find it was a fake book. The red cover with its embossed gold lettering was indeed an anthology cover, but the inside had been cut away to hold a flask of whisky. It was probably a book produced in the United States during Prohibition . . . I would have left it there, but Ron put it in the bag anyway.

'Ten days ago I opened it by chance and noticed the pamphlet around the edge of the hollowed-out middle, still marked with the shape of a flask. I pulled it out to look at it because, after studying my uncle's life, I felt I had the instincts of an expert; and beneath the thin paper cover, torn in places, I saw that it was a pamphlet dating from the early nineteenth century: against Darling.

'If I'd found it a year earlier, I think I would probably have thrown it away, out of ignorance.'

I was now walking carefully along the edge of the road.

'So all those years, your uncle had the pamphlet close at hand and didn't know it?'

'He may have had an inkling. Didn't he say he was looking for it wherever he was himself?'

252

He had hidden it too well . . . like the Hawaiian islands in the past. And yet they do exist, the Hawaiian islands, they do exist.

We walked on, exchanging a few words at intervals, buoyed by the beauty of the huge bay. In my mind I played with half-sentences about secrets, the past, blindness.

'Are you planning to keep the pamphlet?'

She shook her head. Then: 'We're going to sell it. Pass it on. It's bad luck. We'll take the dirty money, as always.'

AUTHOR'S NOTE

I would like to express my gratitude first of all to Mervyn and Rosemary Taiaroa for putting me on the collector's trail and giving me generous access to their archives. I am also grateful to Wendy Hallett for our discussions about the collector's family, and to Denis Harold for sharing his insights on the collector.

The idea for this book was born during my time as Randell Cottage writer in residence in Wellington in 2004–2005. My grateful thanks to all who contributed to my stay there, especially Jean-Michel Marlaud, Ambassador of France in Wellington, and the Embassy's Cultural Services. In 2006 a Stendhal writer's grant allowed me to travel to Dunedin where I continued my research in the ideal setting of the Hocken Library, then under the direction of Stuart Strachan. Research for this novel has drawn on documents in the Ernest Godward and Bruce Godward collections, Hocken Library, University of Otago. I was also fortunate enough to stay in the Robert Lord Cottage in Dunedin, where Claire Matthewson was extremely helpful.

My deepest thanks to Jean Anderson for her superb translation.

And I am grateful to my New Zealand writer friends who encouraged me to write about their country, which I came to know and love.